A WYATT BOOK *for* ST. MARTIN'S PRESS

The Virgin Knows

Christine Palamidessi Moore

A Wyatt Book *for* St. Martin's Press
New York

Production Editor: David Stanford Burr

Design: Basha Zapatka

Library of Congress Cataloging-in-Publication Data

Moore, Christine Palamidessi.
     The virgin knows / Christine Palamidessi Moore.
          p. cm.
     ISBN 0-312-13203-4
     I. Title.
     PS3566.A4557V57   1995
     813'.54—dc20   95-15460
                                                              CIP

First edition: July 1995

10 9 8 7 6 5 4 3 2 1

For Ruby and Ruth

Quale allodetta che in aere si spazia
Prima cantando, e poi tace contenta
Dell'ultima dolcezza che la sazia,
Tal mi sembiò l'imago della imprenta
Dell'eterno piacere, al cui disio
Ciascuna cosa, quale ell'è, diventa.

Like to the lark that soaring through the sky
First sings and then is silent, well content
With the last sweetness that doth satisfy,
So seemed the image of that imprint sent
From joy eternal, whereby everything
Desiring it, to its own form is bent.

Dante Alighieri: *The Divine Comedy*
PARADISE XX, 73–8

Part One

One

During the years we were apart, my brother Carlo became a king on Hanover Street in the North End of Boston. He opened his shops at six in the morning and closed them at six in the evening. Twice a day, except on Sundays, he made his rounds, emptying the old cash registers in his four stores, stacking warm ten-, twenty-, and fifty-dollar bills into a black zippered bag. He didn't take checks or credit cards. He wanted only what was real, not what he couldn't pinch between his fingers.

While my brother collected money, the respect of his community, and a secure future, I was a shadow in Italy. He never turned to look for me until the next generation of Barzinis had set their feet down in America. When his children's mothers disappeared, I was the person he called. It was then our own mother's prayers were answered, and mine beside hers. Carlo was trusting no one but his own blood.

He found my phone number in the bottom drawer of his oak desk. The number was written on a torn sheet of paper, scrawled in the ink from the fountain pen our Papa had given to him when he left Subiaco. When I picked up the telephone, I wasn't surprised to hear my brother's soft and humble voice.

"Alicia," he said. *"Ho bisogno di te.* I need you."

I crossed myself and let the line go silent. But echoes of voices were trapped like the dead in the wires between us. I held my breath.

"They've gone," Carlo said more loudly. *"Sono solo.* I'm alone."

I knew the American women who had lived in his house. In my worst moments I cursed them; in other moments I asked God to give the women back the souls I had asked Him to take. To be without a soul is to have no dignity. The women were not my enemies, but I did not have that realization until many years had passed.

"I want you to come to America and stay with me," Carlo said. My brother had built his life inviting hope. I was the one who looked for hairs inside an egg, and I had nothing.

My heart beat under my chin. "You need your sister," I said. "You need someone you can trust."

"Certamente. Of course," Carlo said.

I nodded yes and wiped a tear from my cheek, expecting Carlo to have seen my answer.

"Alicia?" he asked.

"I will certainly come help you take care of the children," I added. I was filled with joy. At the same time I didn't want to give him reason to suspect that during the time we were apart I had wanted to destroy everything he had earned. Since the day we were born, I had been dreaming my dreams alongside Carlo's. I wanted exactly what he had. It took me thirty-six years to accept that this was impossible and to create my own desires.

Carlo and I were twins conceived during World War II in a shack on the flatlands between Rome and Subiaco. Our father was an army officer from the north who wore a black shirt and carried a gun. Once, sometimes twice a month,

Mama rode a horse down from the hills to see him. She wasn't a young girl, but was dark and lovely and widely admired for her beautifully shaped calves. One September, while she was trading kisses for cheese, the Allies bombed Subiaco. Her parents were killed.

In Italy, during the war, female citizens were not permitted to be the property of men but were considered to be the property of the state and of the future. They would bear the children that would make Italy great. Papa didn't want to marry Mama. She was poor. And Mama didn't want Papa because he pretended to be smarter than he really was. Meanwhile, Carlo and I were pressing against each other inside Mama's uterus. His hands tickled my waist, I licked his forehead, and we knew nothing better than each other's presence.

Finally, during our eighth month together, Mama and Papa married, and Papa moved in with us. That very night, Carlo shifted to the bottom of Mama's belly. He became the cradle holding the real fruit of the family, which was me—though no one knew that then. I prayed for nothing to change. But it did. It always did.

"It's time to get going," I mumbled. *"Vai via."*

My brother didn't move.

I kicked him. It started.

Carlo rolled and howled like a spinning top. Mama's insides crushed hard against his waxy bones. I worried he wouldn't get to the end of the pink hallway in time.

With the point of my elbow, I held the back door open, and the other end of Mama's hole opened. She screamed. Her veiny hands grabbed to tug Carlo out of her body. She found him, and I held tight to his heel. But Carlo was gone. I was alone for the first time in my life.

"Mio Dio! My son! *Mio figlio!"* she cried.

Carlo had stretched the passage, so I came rushing out.

No one expected me. I landed face up on the floor, covered with white cream and the same blood that slicked Carlo. I should have known, at that moment, not to ever want what Carlo had. He smelled Mama first.

I saw Carlo mix his soul with hers. She pressed his hunched body into the curve under her chin and whispered, "I'll love you forever."

It was the first time I played second fiddle to my brother, but not the last. "Thank goodness they don't have red hair," Mama said when she noticed me.

Infancy was difficult. Fortunately, I was my father's favorite, but he was often at the war and not at home. It wasn't until Carlo and I were three, and Mussolini died, that Papa spent more time with us.

One day Papa sat in the kitchen. He carefully folded the newspaper printed with the news of the Italian dictator's death and laid the paper under the table on the seat of a rope-back chair.

"*L'Italia potrebbe essere un grande stato,*" Papa started. "Italy could have been great, but the people aren't serious enough. They take the easy way." I watched his toes curl into knots inside his black shoes.

He pounded the table. "Twenty years of sacrifice gone to oblivion. We'll never get it back! The world will laugh at us, call us *buffoni,* clowns! Who will return our glory?"

Clutching my doll, I came out from under the table. The veins in Papa's temples bulged. I thought, If I smile, he will calm down.

"Italians are children. They don't have discipline." He spat when he talked. "It's the southerners' fault. They are the ones who cannot look forward." Papa pointed a finger at the ceiling before storming across the kitchen to the stove. He hit Mama. Once. Twice. His open hand landed on her face. She dropped her spoon.

Mama had been stirring a pot of beans. She covered her shame with the skirt of her apron. Carlo stopped rattling a clothespin in an empty bottle. Papa left the room. None of us called for each other. We listened to the clock.

On the chair next to me, on the folded newspaper, I saw a picture of a man and a woman hanging head down from a tree. The man wore the same kind of clothes as Papa, and the woman's hair was pulled back in a bun.

I rushed to my mother. "Don't worry," I said, clutching her beautiful calves. "You can't die, not yet." Mama had taught me everything I knew about salvation, sin, and eternal life. I feared if she did die, so would her promises.

Mama's face was still covered behind her apron. The side of her lip bled. She hesitated.

"We must hurry to the closet and ask the saints to protect us," I said. On Sundays Mama, Carlo, and I hid in the closet, because Papa didn't like God, and we prayed.

"Papa and Carlo can come, too," I said, shoving my nose between her smooth knees. I wanted her to soothe me.

But Carlo was next to me, crying for Mama to hold him, too. I pushed him away. He came forward, kicked me twice, and ran out the back door.

Mama picked me up. I laid my hand on the damp strands of hair that stuck to the back of her neck.

"Carlo didn't mean to hurt you," she said in a cooing voice. "He saw what Papa did to me. Boys don't know how to use words, that's all." My Mama was sweet and receptive. She taught me more about caring for other people's happiness than believing in my own.

I leaned my head between her breasts. She wasn't going to say anything about Papa hitting her, or Carlo's kicking me, or Mussolini's death. Mama hugged me, and we were quiet together. These moments were the best part of being a child, and the moments didn't last long.

Carlo clumped a trail of mud over the clean kitchen floor. "Come sit," Mama said, grabbing the tail of his shirt, not scolding him.

I slid to one side of her small lap. *"Avete fame, bambini?* You're hungry, aren't you?" For months we hadn't eaten anything but bread, beans, and dry pasta. Every once in a while Mama was lucky enough to catch a bird for us, in a trap in our fig tree, but during the war there were hardly any birds in Italy.

Carlo stuck his thumb in his mouth. He leaned back into Mama's arm, and Mama bent her head over his as if he were an infant again. I was both jealous and hungry and restrained myself from biting Carlo's wrist.

"You both need red meat," Mama said. "Enough sacrifices. Your blood has been thinned for long enough."

"Alessandro!" she called to our Papa, raising her voice. "It's time to kill the horse." She shoved us off her lap, wiping our bony imprints from her apron. The war was over. Mama was making demands.

We followed her through the dining room, which didn't have any furniture because she had sold it to buy flour. Papa was in the front room smoking the last of his cigarettes. His thick brown hair lay flat against his scalp. His skin was sweating.

"There's no reason to wait any longer," Mama said. She stood behind Papa's bare shoulder.

Papa hiked up his pants. His gun was hanging on a pole in the bedroom, next to his bed. He belted the creaky holster through the loops of his pants. Its black leather smelled like an animal.

Since they had married, Mama's gray horse, Geremio, was living in the barn. Papa didn't allow Geremio to roam the field because he was convinced a hungry person from town would see him, come over the hill, and slice off a piece of the horse's hip for his dinner.

We opened the barn door, which was falling off its hinges. Geremio closed his eyes. The horse was so weak he couldn't swish the flies off his back.

Papa propped a ladder against the beam near the horse's stall and looped a rope over a broad board that ran across the loft of the barn. He knotted one end of the rope around Geremio's neck and the other end through a pulley on the beam. Papa wiped his hands on a musty rag before tugging the rope taut and lifting the horse's head.

"Who wants to shoot Geremio?" Papa looked at Mama, who folded her arms over her small breasts. Papa's green eyes flickered like candles at the end of their wicks.

Frightened to see this side of Papa, Carlo and I stuffed the hem of Mama's skirt into our palms. She almost stepped forward to take the gun.

"No, Alessandro. You do it," she said. I had never heard her use that tone of voice. She was taking control, without apologizing. Mama made the sign of the cross—for the horse, she said—and then pinched Carlo's shoulder and mine to direct us out of the barn, but the blast of Papa's gun hollowed our ears before we turned. The bottomless noise ached inside my head long after Papa fired two more shots into Geremio's neck.

Mama picked up Carlo and ran out of the barn, expecting me to follow. But I stayed. I watched blood, the same color as mine and Carlo's and the cut in Mama's lip, pulse out of Geremio's neck and splash my father's bare chest. The horse's dumb eyes met Papa's. Papa bowed his head in respect.

I heard a thump and whine and a sad snort. The horse fell on its side. The small barn smelled from metal and gunpowder and Geremio's excrement. I saw a powdery white light rise out of the horse's body and hover in the stall. The light quivered, confused, not knowing where to go. The rope slid from my Papa's hand. Papa stepped inside the stall and closed Geremio's eyes.

Just then, I puckered my lips, as if I were giving a kiss, and blew a stream of air toward the dead horse's soul, blowing it out of the barn and into the open air, where I was sure it would find its place in the next world above the clouds. Death was noisier and took a shorter time than being born, I thought.

I wondered if Papa had noticed what I had done. He usually did. But not this time. "Carlo!" he called. Papa's excitement had sunk back into his hips, and his eyes were cooler now that Geremio was gone.

Carlo came to him. Papa lifted him onto the ladder and put the gun into his hand. "Your turn," he said.

When Carlo saw the dead horse, he struggled to get out of Papa's arms. "No! Mama! Geremio's already dead," he cried.

"*Lascia che vada.* Let him go," Mama said, raising her arms to take her young son.

Papa didn't let Carlo climb down the ladder.

Carlo's mouth opened as if he were going to scream and never swallow again. He vomited on Papa's shoes.

Mama stationed me squarely in front of her. I wanted to be with my brother, on the ladder, sitting on top of Papa's shoulders. I figured my turn would come next.

Carlo pulled the trigger. There were no more bullets.

"*Andiamo.* Come with me, Alicia," Mama said. And I left because Papa didn't call for me. He was giving Carlo the privilege of tending the dead, while allowing me to witness only the craziness of killing. I was no longer my father's favorite. I followed Mama out of the dry barn.

It was a summer day, noon, and the sun was bright. Crickets, locusts, and flies, hiding between blades of grass and above me on the soft leaves of trees, continued to rub their wings together, making buzzing noises, as if nothing out of the ordinary had just happened. But I was dizzy. I had just lost my position in the family. I tried to find comfort by telling myself I had Mama for an entire afternoon. But Mama was different, too. She even smelled tighter. We straightened up the house and measured our salt. Mama spoke to me as if I were her friend, not her child. She was no longer who I desired to be.

Just as Mama grew stronger, Italy recovered from the war with miraculous speed. Everyone in our town had Brazilian coffee, gasoline, and radios. My mother's brothers reclaimed their hill outside of town and grew Frascati grapes; one uncle became Subiaco's fire chief. My mother worked at home doing piecework for a Roman clothing designer. She was paid well. Papa eventually folded his military uniform and put it in a box on the floor of the closet. He secured a clerical position in a nearby government office, was promoted, and began going to church. The new pope believed in a unified Italy, which was important to Papa. All over the country, churches and museums replaced the artifacts that had been stolen or destroyed by soldiers or bombs with new displays of statues and gilt-edged paintings that had been stored in their underground chambers. Tourists flocked to our country to view the new collections.

In our house, Carlo settled into being both Mama and Papa's favorite child. That might have bothered me if Carlo hadn't possessed a deep streak of kindness. He loved me best. Carlo recognized I was the wisest of our pair. I had no hidden agenda—at least not back then.

Carlo was a very likable boy, and later man, who never threatened those who were close to him. He didn't compete, but was always the winner, someone others called lucky, and they said it with a smile, not envy, on their faces. Our cousins and schoolmates were happy to be counted as Carlo's friend. He was fun, and never whimpered over bruises or toys he didn't have. If his weakness was his determination not to be like everyone else in Subiaco, mine was my sensitivity about being different. I, unlike Carlo, was not an attractive child. Carlo protected me. He guided conversations around my sensitive spots—such as my nose, which was large and odd. He told me to go home when bullies ran after us to play. At night he stayed awake until I fell asleep. But Carlo wasn't perfect.

One day, when we were nine, Mama didn't permit Carlo to ride his bicycle into Subiaco square. "Take my side," he begged. "I want to go play cowboys and Indians."

"Take me with you and I will," I said.

"No. I want to go myself." He twisted my arm. I cried because it hurt and because he said I could never go to the square with him. "You can't fight, and they'll make fun of your nose."

I pointed to a religious picture on the bumpy wall behind Mama's sewing machine. The picture showed Jesus holding his robe and chest open to expose a bleeding heart pricked with more needles than were stuck in Mama's pincushion. "You better be careful. He's watching," I said.

Carlo laughed, but stopped twisting my arm.

Mama put down the collars she was sewing. "Carlo," she said. "Your sister is not a stranger. Get used to being with people who are your family. They're the ones you can depend on. They're the ones you live your life with."

I agreed.

Carlo dropped his long eyelashes. Everyone noticed his eyelashes, and I got furious when people admired them, especially Mama. If I had been born first, the eyelashes would have been mine. "Please, Mama, can I go?" he asked again. "Alicia and I need to be apart for a while—so we don't fight. I don't want to hurt her."

Mama let him go to the square.

Carlo was never knowingly insincere, people responded with affection. He wasn't complex or moody, but agreeable, and was pleasing to look at. Carlo had a broad forehead, golden skin, and wide-set green eyes. His hair, like Papa's, was thick and brown and grew like groomed grass on a head that Mama said was an ideal shape. His chin was neither too pointy nor too square, and he held it high when he walked into the house, through the field, or to school, always looking forward, his arms swinging by his side.

My parents mistook his natural smoothness as brilliance. They were determined to send Carlo to the university to be a doctor or lawyer as soon as he grew up. I knew it would never happen. Carlo was an adventurer who needed to be noticed and who needed to have his fingers in twenty different pots. He couldn't settle his mind on any one thing. And if I knew anything, I knew Carlo's mind. From the time we were eleven, when our bodies began to change into a man's and a woman's, my senses clutched on to Carlo. I dug in my heels, refusing to let go of my brother. When we weren't together, I would press my eyes shut and picture him in my mind. If I was very still, I could listen to his thoughts, and smell what he smelled. It was like being back in the womb with Carlo. On Saturday, if he and his friends stopped on his way home from school at the bakery for chocolate, I could taste the powdery sweetness. At night, while he waited for me to fall asleep, instead of investigating my own desires, I listened to Carlo's thoughts. He fantasized about being a musician, a tightrope walker, a movie star, the president, a pirate, a cowboy, an American. His thoughts made my head spin. I couldn't keep up with him and wasn't sure if my fantasies were less exciting because I was a girl, or because I was born second, or because I was less attractive and therefore less attracting of opportunity and other possible personas.

On our fifteenth birthday, my eyebrows connected like a strip of ink. This mishap didn't flatter to a girl with a narrow forehead and small eyes. But my hair was lovely, black, shiny and sprouted from a well-defined hairline. I tied my hair into braids and wound them around my head like a halo. While everyone else in our family had angles in their faces and fine bones, I was tall, round, clumsy, and wide-hipped. My skin was fair. I tried to ignore my nose, but even on the best of days, it shot out from the center of my face. I got upset whenever anyone in our family touched their own nose, thinking they were sending signals to each other about me. Carlo warned them not to do it. I developed the habit of cupping my nose with my hands.

"*Guarda.* Look," my older cousins teased. "Alicia's *nasone* is sharper than a kitchen knife." They laughed. "She can't hide it!"

It was my sixteenth birthday. I stood there, in the field behind our barn, ashamed, angry, and devastated. I wanted to disappear. I dropped my head and covered my face with my long loosened hair. Carlo stepped in close to me. I smelled him and knew I was safe. I never wanted Carlo to be too far from me and vowed I would go wherever he went.

Our last day of secondary school classes, Carlo and I walked home together. It was windy, and blue flowers danced on the edge of our dirt road. We were seventeen and dressed in outfits my mother had copied from a fashion magazine. Carlo walked slowly so I could keep up with him.

"I have decided to go to America," he announced. "I want to be rich and famous."

"We'll go together," I said.

"No." Carlo was stern. "One of us has to stay with Mama

14

and Papa. You can do that better than me." He was right. There was no use arguing. "But once you are rich?" I asked shyly, not knowing how rich was rich, since we were no longer a poor family.

"Then you will all come to America and be with me." Carlo had more confidence than a grandfather. "While I am away, neither of us should marry," he added. "Marriage is the shell that protects the yolk and egg, and you and I have not split yet."

I persuaded myself to be happy. The money our family had set aside for Carlo's education could be used for mine. I would study English and nursing. Nursing was a profession I could carry with me when I left Italy.

When Mama heard Carlo's news, she put on a black dress. My father tried to bribe Carlo to stay in Italy by arranging a marriage to a friend of his cousin's daughter who lived in Livorno and whose family had agreed to help support the young couple if Carlo studied law. Unlike me, my brother wanted nothing to do with marriage. He refused to make a contract—with a woman, or his future.

"I can't grow a beard yet," he said.

Carlo didn't want to be in Italy. "If I stay, I'll wait in endless lines to collect papers and licenses. I don't want to hate my life. I don't want to walk worn trails. I want America, open spaces, freedom, the future. I want everything to be new."

I understood. Though Papa spoke against Americans, we remembered the soldiers who had saved us in World War II. They had guns, cigarettes, and big clean smiles. Nothing could hold down their spirits. They were going to protect every person in the world. We forgave them for all they took, including our church's statue of St. Benedict, slabs of frescoes from the vestibule of the convent, and a portrait of St. Francis without his stigmata and customary halo.

The summer before Carlo left, our parents sent him to Rome. They hoped the big city would distract him. It was the first time Carlo and I were separated. How awful it was not to hear Carlo's footsteps in the house! Not only that, while he was gone Mama and Papa sent me away, too. I went to a fancy Adriatic resort where I met other chubby teenagers like myself, and together we were supposed to melt off our pounds by eating fresh vegetables and pastas without butter or cheese. But I gained weight and learned how cruel girls from other families could be. At night, without Carlo beside me, I sat awake in my seaside cottage either praying to saints or yearning for my brother. Reaching into the world offstage, I ran through it to find Carlo and stayed there for as long as it took for Carlo's life to take shape in my mind, like firelight shadows on the inside of my eyes. Only then was I not lonely.

One afternoon, while I lay dreaming at the Adriatic resort, I found my brother in Rome. He had borrowed a motorcycle and was winging his way through crowds of Americans. I rode along with him, thrilled by the rumbling sensation of the machine, but also sad. Carlo was so happy. And Mama and Papa hadn't known foreigners would be taking over the city, its squares, and monuments. That summer the Americans were in Rome to film the movie *Ben-Hur*.

Carlo managed to get himself through studio blockades and into the restricted areas. I watched him with the big American men, in blue jeans and with their T-shirt sleeves rolled high up on their biceps. The men put down their huge lights and cameras to hand Carlo money. "Sure, boy," they said. Carpenters and electricians flipped Carlo quarters and half-dollar coins. They smoked cigarettes which Carlo was quick to light. Carlo brought the men jugs of mineral water, or cups of espresso, so they wouldn't have to leave their equipment. The tips got larger. All this made Carlo more determined to go to America. The men encouraged him, telling Carlo he was more American than they were. "You always sell us something, no matter what, kid," they said. Carlo told me later he was most impressed with how the Americans got whatever they wanted. "They are so at ease, pleasing, and entitled," he said. At night he dreamed of being the same way.

At the end of the summer, when we returned to Subiaco, I helped my brother pack his suitcase. We were in our bedroom. I folded a pair of blue jeans, white T-shirts, and a black sweater. I wrapped his one suit between sheets of paper and mended his socks. He watched me. I was the only person in the family who was on his side.

"Alicia," he said. "There's not enough room for both of us in this house." Carlo shrugged his shoulders—it was a recent gesture, one he had assumed since meeting the Americans. "Mama will miss me, but you can take better care of her than I can. Besides, she likes you better. She always has." I wanted to believe him, but I understood how my brother's mind worked. Mama loved him better, so did Papa, and Carlo knew that. He was sweeping his stars behind mine, hoping I would not resent him, or our past. I bent over his suitcase, assured of my brother's love.

He put his hand on my arm. My tongue stuck in my mouth. I couldn't move. I was sad. I knew I'd never feel the warmth of his touch for a long, long time. "And don't forget to study your English. You don't want to know less than me," he said. For a short moment, Carlo was afraid, as I was, not to be together.

I sat down on my bed and imagined that the space between us was the Atlantic Ocean. "I'll think about you every day," I said. Wherever you are, I'll be with you. We've been together since before we were born, and we won't ever lose each other, will we?" I shook my head no, answering my own question. Carlo was silent.

"Our souls are split from the same flame," he said, wiping his lips with the side of his palm, not looking at me. I didn't understand that he was breaking away. There would be more than an ocean between us. "I have to go," he said. "Everything stays the same here. We can count on Giuseppe standing on the corner by the drugstore from yesterday until the day he's gone and then his son, or nephew, will take his place. The buses will never travel faster into Rome."

"You don't have a choice, do you? America is calling you. She will stand by your side." I wanted Carlo to tell me I was wrong. He didn't.

During Carlo's last week in Subiaco, Mama refused to get out of bed, not even to sew. She prayed the rosary whenever he stepped into her room. Papa felt the tuggings, too. "I won't know how thick or how quickly his beard will fill his chin, or what kind of women he'll kiss," Papa said to me. I told Carlo what Papa said.

"When he was my age, Papa was restless," Carlo said. "But he sold his dreams to other people and the corners of his mouth turned down. I won't do that. I want to stand on my own two feet and be my own man."

I hugged his head into my chest and patted his cheek. "You want to be bigger than Papa." Carlo pulled away and put his head down into a cradle he made out of his own arms.

But in our last hours together as children, Carlo never asked me to speak of my dreams. If he did, I would have told him I wanted to be loved. I wanted to be the heart of a family, to serve and nurture a husband and children who would fight with each other to sit close to me. I wanted a magnificent dinner table set with china plates and silver, a home filled with order, and to walk as if I held a warm light inside me. I wanted Carlo to have exactly the same things, and be by my side. I wanted him to protect both our families from outsiders. Looking back on those days, I suspect Carlo didn't ask me about my dreams because his heart told him not to. He hadn't the courage to say he wanted something different.

"America is your woman," I repeated to my brother. "You have to go to her." I said this with both humility and sarcasm. I wanted to be strong enough to withstand our separation, I wanted America to disappoint Carlo, and I wanted to learn how to live without him.

Papa wrote several letters of introduction, on official Italian government stationery, to the few men from the Benevolent Society who had moved to America after the war. I knit Carlo a long green scarf that dragged on the ground if he didn't wrap it around his neck twice. Carlo stayed outside in the barn, clipping stories about America from the newspaper. Hawaii was the fiftieth state, and New York City was wanting to be the fifty-first. He practiced saying President Dwight Eisenhower's name.

The leaves changed color, but it was still warm enough to lean against the fig tree in the front yard with Carlo after dinner on his last night in Italy.

I crushed a blade of grass between my back teeth. "You don't speak English," I reminded him. I was the better second-language student and had helped him with those studies in school. "No one will understand you. You can't remember the verbs."

"I know enough to get started," Carlo said. He closed his eyes and smiled. The radio was playing his favorite American song, "He's Got the Whole World in His Hands." I looked at him, and in my eyes my brother's smile became a smirk. It was the first time, since the incident with the horse, that I disliked Carlo. He stood against the tree, so self-assured. I wanted to blow away his bones, making him crumble, so I could roll what was left of Carlo into a ball that I would put in a box until I was ready to love him again. "It's time to go inside," I said, gruffly, not knowing if the emotion I was feeling was my protection or my sin.

Early the next morning, despite the sudden distance between us, I walked behind Carlo to the wooden gate in the front yard that was beginning to peel its paint. Our neighbor Lena's roosters were waking up. My eyes were bleary. Carlo put his hands on my waist and kissed my cheek. He was shorter than I was. I wondered if he would grow taller in America.

"*Ciao,* Alicia," he said.

"Carlo—" I put my lips near his ear. "Do you think our children will want to be bigger than we are?" I was challenging him.

It had been years since I had seen my brother cry. His eyes were the same color as the green wool scarf that I had knit for him, the scarf that he was wearing.

I couldn't punish him for leaving. "Stop crying," I said. "You have much to look forward to." We held on to each other. But my love for him was probably what Carlo had already been feeling. "I'll knit Mama and Papa scarves like yours and tell them you are watching them," I whispered.

Carlo let go of me, and when he wrapped his arms around me again, I wanted to get down on my knees and beg him to stay. *"Ti voglio bene.* I love you," I said. "We all love you." I didn't want anything to change.

Carlo went to the airport alone. I ran down the road following the hired car. He was taking part of me with him. I called out, "Good luck!" The car sped up.

"Has he gone?" Papa asked. He and Mama were waiting for me at the kitchen table. Their shoulders bowed to gravity, and their heads dropped forward like two sad sacks. They had lost their only son. I turned my back so they couldn't see me cry for them, and Carlo, and for myself. My tears dripped into the coffee I prepared for them.

Mama, Papa, and I dipped our bread into the salty cups of coffee. It was All Saints' Day, November 1, 1960. We listened to the church bells celebrate the everlasting life of the dead.

"I wonder if Carlo hears that." Papa said. "And if he knows he can't take us with him."

"*È solo*. He's all alone," Mama said.

"God goes with him," I said.

Papa shook his head no. "There is more God in Italy than anywhere else. Never forget that, Alicia. The world tried to steal God from us. Now America has taken our son."

After helping Mama get dressed, I went to mass with her. On the walk home, she confessed that she had asked the saints to follow her son to America and make him come back to her.

"Mama," I said. "Nothing costs so much as what is bought by prayers."

T w o

Carlo wrote two times a year. His letters were as short as these few notes I saved.

11 February 1961

Dear Mama and Papa,
I am not working for the American movies. I am sharpening scissors for barbers and hair stylists in New York. Next week I go to Boston.

With affection,
Carlo

4 November 1962

Dear Mama and Papa,
I moved to Boston to live in a neighborhood of Italians—they come from both the north and the south. Boston is more comfortable and less expensive than New York. If I stay on the North End side of the city, I don't have to speak English. I hope you are well.

With affection,
Your son Carlo

4 June 1964

Dear Mama and Papa,
I own my own store! Tourists from all over the world come to do business with me on Hanover Street. I sell them aspirins, bumper stickers, and sunglasses, and I sell scissors and combs to other drugstores and barbershops. I named my store Freedom Drugs to honor the red bricks outside my door, on the sidewalk. In 1776 Paul Revere rode his horse on the Freedom Trail to announce the American Revolution. Paul Revere was an Italian-American. There is a statue of him two streets up from my store.

Greetings,
Carlo

1 March 1968

Dear Mama and Papa,
I bought two more stores on the same block—a cookware shop that I call Carlo's, and a music store, which already had a name, the Blue Note. I think about you every day. I am sitting here now, writing to you from my office. How is Alicia? There is a lot of money in America.

Greetings,
Carlo

My parents crumpled the flimsy blue notes from Carlo. He always included a fifty-dollar bill, which they gave to me, and I never spent. In our house Carlo became bigger from far away. His letters reminded us he wasn't dead.

"Sooner or later he'll find a wife and belong to someone

else," I assured my parents. "Then you won't have to worry." Though my brother was an arm of my own body cut off and I wanted him to succeed, I could not cheer for him without upsetting my family. Carlo lived too far away for Mama and Papa to keep an eye on him. But since he was their child, he was also their responsibility. They felt like failures. Perhaps that is why Mama and Papa became sickly before their time. I was the only person whom they allowed to take care of them. In other families, this early reversal of duty would be considered unusual, but I was a nurse, and a good one.

I was trained and worked at the St. Scholastica Clinic in Subiaco, less than a kilometer from my house. If I walked through the back field and over several rocky paths that passed St. Benedict's monastery and the steps to the Sacred Cave, I could be there, at the clinic, in fifteen minutes.

St. Scholastica was a private institution specializing in heart, lung, and kidney ailments—performing eye lifts and chin tucks on the side. It was cleaner and less crowded than most other Italian hospitals and was also quite expensive. Subiaco was a small, elevated town with good air, not too far from Rome, and patients came to our clinic from all over the country to fix their hearts and/or faces.

After three years at the nursing school, I had not only learned my vocation but had also been required to empty strangers' bedpans, clean floors, and scrub toilets. I elected to be a surgical nurse, preferring to care for unconscious patients rather than tidying bandages and making conversation with men and women, whom I always seemed to make uncomfortable no matter how hard I tried, especially the ones who had come to our clinic for cosmetic reasons. I supposed my nose frightened them. The hospital administrators agreed it was better for me to be stationed in the operating theater. I took one more year's training. After a while I didn't care anymore if the town people whispered, "Alicia Barzini has made nursing her profession because she is too awkward and ugly to catch a husband and needs something sharp in her hand to fall back on in case she never loses her virginity." Their whispers caused me much unhappiness. As we all matured, I had hoped to be included in their circle. But they treated me the same as when we were children. I didn't have a brother to defend me—or to help me around the house.

I worked long hours at the clinic—from four in the morning until noon. When I got home, I injected Mama's thigh with insulin. She was diabetic. Then I made the midday meal. No matter how much I fed Papa, he continued to melt like wax. In the evening, I stayed in the house, mending dishtowels, studying English, or sitting with Mama to sew costumes for saints.

In the summer of 1969, the letter that came from Carlo informed us he had bought a five-story building in the North End of Boston. Carlo said he was proud to own a piece of America. He lived on the top floor of the building and rented the other apartments to pay the mortgage. I stashed away the fifty-dollar bill he sent with the letter and wondered how much money he would pay to American banks.

"No possession is joyous without a companion," I said to my parents.

Papa patted my cheek. "We will never leave Italy, no matter what, even if Carlo has made a place for us to live," he said.

"*L'Italia è la nostra patria.* Italy is our home," Mama added.

Realizing my fate, I was filled with terror. I was stuck. We wouldn't be going to America, and Carlo was gone from my life forever. Mama, Papa, and I had only each other, and they reminded me of this every day. I convinced myself to be desperately good, serving my parents and the holy saints in heaven. I accepted my position and vowed not to be jealous of Carlo. God would reward me later by giving me something everlasting.

One cold winter afternoon, Papa called me into his room to tell me he had transferred the house to my name. "Take good care of your mother," he said in a shrinking voice.

A small ball of sun dropped outside the window, and I switched on the bedside lamp. Papa closed his eyes. His hand became hard and limp. His soul lifted from his flesh and hovered for only a minute, disappearing like a scent. I pulled the sheet over his face.

"At least Papa wasn't alone," Carlo said to me over the telephone. "Did he say anything about me?"

I cleared my throat to make a disturbing noise. My brother hadn't asked how I was feeling, or about Mama. I waited. I wanted to tell Carlo I was relieved Papa was no longer suffering, but now that he was gone Mama would be dependent on only me. I was tired and wanted Carlo to come home. I never considered what he might have given up to be in America, or the sadness he might have concealed to hide his guilt. I put Mama on the line.

Mama told me Carlo said, "I'm so sorry. Oh, Mama! Please forgive me." He couldn't travel to Subiaco to comfort her, or bury Papa, but begged Mama to understand how painful it was to be away from her during this sad time. "My passport and papers aren't up to date," he said. "If I leave the country, they won't allow me back into America." But Carlo promised to come to Subiaco soon. "Then we'll sit in the kitchen and remember Papa together," he told Mama.

I put a shawl over Mama's shoulders.

My brother sent us a roomful of flowers that made me sneeze, and, a few weeks later, a black trunk. Mama pounded her chest with her fist for an hour after she opened

26

the front door and saw the trunk on our stoop.

"I swear my son is inside it," she said. "His father's soul went to America to get him."

But the trunk was filled with gifts—a tape player, music cassettes and records from his music store; green T-shirts from the Boston Celtics for the cousins' children—whom we never saw; shiny tins of oyster crackers; bottles of whiskey and maple syrup that Mama mistook for varnish; scissors we didn't need; cosmetics; bleach for my mustache.

The note said, *Buon Natale from Carlo.* I told Mama, "Let's forgive him. It's the best he can do."

His next letter was written on thicker paper, and before I read the letter to Mama, I noticed Carlo's handwriting had become less tight. The loops of his *p*'s and *y*'s dripped into the lines below them, and he often forgot to cross his *t*'s.

3 April 1970

Dear Mama and Alicia,
I am falling in love with a woman who is teaching me to speak better English. She also sings and has taught me America's national hymn, "Oh beautiful for spacious skies." Her name is the same as the ex-President John F. Kennedy's wife—Jacqueline. I call her Jassy.

Love,
Carlo

Instead of money, he included her picture. I picked it up off the worn wood floor. "Jassy," I snipped. "What saint looks over the shoulder of a woman called Jassy? It sounds like an American joke—like jazz music, or ass. How can Carlo kiss someone named Jassy?"

But there was something more disturbing about Jassy than

27

her name. Jassy had red hair, which in the picture was smoothed into bangs and cheek curls. Mama believed red-heads brought families bad luck.

"Don't worry, Mama," I said. "This woman dyes her hair with products Carlo sells in his drugstore. She's not a real redhead."

I assured her Carlo's girlfriend had thick brown hair like ours. "All Americans have either brown or blond hair. Jassy's not a redhead."

I held the photo close to Mama's face so she could get a good look. "Maybe you're right," she said. Mama was going blind.

We examined the photo for an hour and agreed Carlo's girlfriend was a beauty. What I envied most about her was her perfect nose. She had the nose of a patrician, elegant and fine-nostriled. Without it, her eyes might have looked less intelligent and her large mouth more vulgar. Though she was my age, her generous forehead was as smooth as a teen-ager's. I imagined a woman as beautiful as Jassy moved like an angel. She must be full of grace, like a bird. No wonder Carlo was falling for her.

I tacked the picture to the cupboard above the kitchen sink. When I washed dishes, I reminded myself not to envy her good looks, or her relationship with my brother. For a week or two I deliberated about dying my hair red, but I didn't. Mama would have considered me no better than the devil. Instead, I took to wearing big earrings like the ones Jacqueline wore in the picture. I thought I, too, might be able to find someone who loved me, someone whom I could spend afternoons with, talking and listening.

No men looked my way. But had a man wanted to talk to me, I wouldn't have known what to do. Back then I was shy and tormented. In the operating room, where I was most competent, if a surgeon glanced at me as I handed him the plastic hose that goes inside the aorta, I quickly covered my nose, which was already covered by a mask, with my hand.

We waited to hear of a marriage. The news never came. Every several months Carlo sent us music cassettes, usually Verdi for Mama and either Tammy Wynette or Beatle songs for me. He wrote that Jassy had selected the music. She worked in his store, The Blue Note, and that is how he had come to know her better.

After supper, I gave Mama her shot, and we listened to Jassy's music while I stitched red capes for the miniature statues of saints that the Benevolent Society of our church sold at summer festivals. It was a side job which earned me extra money, but I did it mostly for Mama. She had sewed costumes for the organization since the war had ended, when Papa joined the Benevolents.

When the capes were finished, I began knitting baby sweaters for the child we were sure would arrive, Carlo's child. Mama fingered the skeins of soft wool and said she had stopped praying for Carlo to fail in America. Instead she was asking the Virgin to forgive her son for leaving Italy and to bless the woman with the falsely painted red hair.

I prayed, too, to St. Monica, the patron of marriage. If Carlo married Jassy, the curse of my being single and childless would be broken. Carlo and I had promised one another not to marry, and I wondered if he remembered. I didn't want to hold Carlo to it. Since he was the firstborn, he had the right, and duty, to marry first. I told St. Monica that until he did, the path would not clear for me. And if Carlo married Jassy, Mama and I would move to the North End of Boston. There I would be able to find someone to whom I could tell all my thoughts.

When Carlo's card came at Christmas, in 1970, Mama and I waited until after dinner to open it. We sat by the stove in the kitchen and were sure the note would include information about their wedding. It didn't. Inside the envelope were photographs of the Old North Church—not even a Catholic church; an old cemetery on Cobb's Hill; a statue of Paul Revere; a picture of men in red capes giving a tea party in Boston Harbor; and this letter:

Dear Mama and Alicia,
I have passed the citizenship exam. Jassy tutored me in English and history—I studied speeches by George Washington and Abraham Lincoln. I vote. I am an American, and I'm adding a fourth store to my collection. Next week I get the keys to Spediamo, an import and exporting business. I am healthy and happy and hope you are, too. I rented my downstairs apartment to Jassy and her girlfriend Virginia. I will not be so lonely anymore. Best wishes for the New Year.

Love,
Carlo

Mama could no longer stand up straight, her eyes were completely clouded with cataracts, and her hearing was bad. "What did you say?" she asked. *"Non ti ho sentito!* I didn't hear you!" She was not only my mother, but also my daughter, and my friend. I never lost patience with Mama.

I reread Carlo's letter, letting her figure out herself what Carlo might have meant by writing "I will not be so lonely anymore."

A few days later, a new decade arrived. We stayed up late, wrapped in our blue robes, praying to St. Lucy to restore Mama's vision and to St. Jude, the patron of lost causes. I spoke to Mama as if she were the girlfriend I didn't have. I told her that if I had to sacrifice falling in love with a man during my youth, I could content myself with the dream of finding a husband later in life, when I reached forty, when most women lose their faces anyway.

"You better save your money," Mama instructed. "That's what men like more than faces."

"Do you think Jassy is rich?" I asked.

"For Carlo it doesn't matter," Mama answered. "He's handsome and has money."

After she fell asleep, I went back to the kitchen and prayed a second time to St. Lucy. Since Carlo had left Subiaco, I had respected his decision to begin a new life, apart from mine. All along I trusted he would one day send for me; I needed to dust the dirt off my certainty. That New Year's Eve I asked St. Lucy to help my eyes leap across the Atlantic to see Carlo in Boston and check up on how he lived, and what promises he was making for the next ten years.

I opened a window and looked up at the stars. It was a cold, windy night that smelled of singed wood. Wherever he was, I hoped Carlo was looking at the sky and noticing the brightest star. I lifted the collar of my robe and continued staring at the sky, allowing my thoughts to disappear. I felt the vision click on. The sensation was like a vacuum hose tugging the top of my head. For a second everything went black. I didn't exist. My senses leaped across the ocean to the shore of the new world.

Floating far above it, I saw Boston and the North End peninsula, a thumb, separated from the rest of the city by six lanes of highway. Moving in closer I found Carlo. He was on the balcony outside his building, with Jassy. They were wrapped together inside a blanket. It was colder in Boston than in Subiaco. When they laughed, steam blew out of their mouths. The air cracked. They were watching fireworks explode over the harbor.

Like Carlo, I turned away from the noise and watched the

pupils of Jassy's eyes shrink and expand. She had brown eyes flecked with amber. Her face was kind, she was tall, proud-shouldered, and not at all primped or perfumed. Jassy was bigger than Carlo. The top of his head met her nose. When I saw she wasn't a delicate woman, I was satisfied I wouldn't be an ox next to her. Jassy's hair hung loose. Colored lights from the fireworks raked through it. I could see through the blanket that Carlo's girlfriend didn't wear a brassiere. I should have turned away then, after seeing Carlo fill his palms with her breasts. But I continued to watch. If the woman didn't support her own breasts, did she expect Carlo to do it for her?

They laughed. Her breasts, large but buoyant, jiggled under the blanket. She laughed big, like Carlo. I wanted her to stop and spare my brother's hands.

"Let's get married," Carlo said, saluting her. "Our marriage will be like the shell that protects an egg. You can be the yolk."

"What?" she said. Her breasts began jiggling again, with laughter.

"No, really," he said, holding her close to him.

"Carlo! I don't want someone wrapped around me, breathing down my neck!" Jassy teased.

"Someone? I would be a husband!" Carlo said. "Our thoughts would coin inside."

Jassy laughed. "You're funny, Carlo. Did you say 'coin inside' on purpose or did you mean 'coincide,' which means to happen at the same time?"

"Yes, that's what I meant."

"Which?"

"What I said." Carlo was enjoying himself completely. "We'll be more complete together than apart," he said. In one way I didn't blame him for wanting Jassy. She gave her spirit away freely, as if the source was inexhaustible. But she

32

was too free to be good—I decided that about her right away.

Jassy stopped smiling. "Oh, Carlo, I'm honored you ask me to be your wife, but I believe marriage is an oppressive institution that dooms women to insanity and makes men cruel. Why shouldn't we create something better? Why do we need to involve governments and churches in our adventure with each other? Who are we going to disappoint if we don't get married, other than those who lived before us? Think about the next generation. The world has to change. People have to stand beside one another, no matter who they are, and not just because they are married and in a family. That's what I want to do. We must reinvent our relationships. They should never stay the same."

"And you want to do it with me?" Carlo asked. What Jassy said made sense, but he wasn't sure what he had to do.

Jassy nodded. "With you. But no one belongs to anyone. Marriage is about more than being in love—it's about property and children. I don't want the baggage. I want to travel light."

Jassy had said the same things about marriage before, but Carlo was testing her, making sure she was serious and not wanting to be pushed and pursued. He decided he would not ask her again.

"You let me know if you ever change your mind," he said, wanting to connect his life to hers. Carlo wanted to watch her grow old.

If I had been him, feeling what he felt, I would have screamed louder than the fireworks, demanding she be mine. Jassy's ideas would interfere with having what we both wanted.

"It's bone cold out here," she said, gathering the blanket around her long neck. "And it feels as if someone's watching us. Let's go inside."

I followed them.

Inside, unwrapped from the blanket, Jassy stood in front of Carlo. She was wearing a long burgundy-colored robe that tied in the front. I couldn't help comparing her body to mine. Her hips were rather slim for such a big woman. She held most of her weight in her chest. I was the opposite. My hips were as big as a factory. I was weighted to the earth; she was ready to fly.

Carlo propped his feet on the purple ottoman and folded his hands in his lap. He refilled their champagne glasses.

"Tonight I'm going to sing to you from 'Vedrai, carino.' It's a soprano tune, but a mezzo can do it. If I mispronounce a word, you let me know." Jassy shook her arms and stretched her fingers backward, before clearing her throat, preparing her body to sing.

"Mozart!" Carlo said. *"Don Giovanni."*

Turning, Jassy dropped the needle of the record player onto the thick black disc. "Ready," she said.

Even lowered to a whisper, her voice was magnetic. The room vibrated. Every molecule of air twisted like a whirlwind, eddying against her strong body. A sour sound, or word, never slipped from her tongue. Along with Carlo, I knew one day she would perform for a larger audience.

"Vedrai, carino, se sei buonino," she sang. *"Che bel rimedio ti voglio dar! . . . Saper vorresti dovè mi sta? Sentilo battere, toccami qua!"*

She slid her hand over her heart and motioned to Carlo with her eyes. "I have a cure for what ails you—come here," she said, capsuling in English the seductive words of the Italian song.

Carlo brushed his forehead between her breasts. To him, she smelled like lilies and oranges. He unbuttoned her robe, feeling her skin, smooth and cool and naked against his own. He kissed a circle around her flushed face.

Jassy didn't resist. With her hand, she brushed the bulge in my brother's trousers and ran out of the room, down the hall, to Carlo's bedroom.

Carlo followed, not bothering to turn off the lights in the front room. I turned away in shame. I knew what they were going to do. Carlo was going to go against what Mama and Papa had taught us was good.

Shaking, I pulled my senses back to Subiaco. I assured myself Carlo had indeed forgotten me and our deal. But it wasn't his fault. His American woman was leading him astray.

But something in my mind, soul, or fibers of my flesh urged me to reconsider. Carlo had not forgotten me. While Jassy was singing, Carlo had thought about me, Mama, Papa, the bay laurel wreath in our kitchen, and the field behind the house. I don't know if it was because Jassy sang to him in Italian, or if it was because her voice was beautiful and persistent, and lifted a curtain into his past. Perhaps Jassy wasn't as evil as I had first wanted her to be.

Mama's condition got worse.

I needed to take time off to care for her, so I took a pregnancy leave from the hospital. At the time I was twenty-nine and convinced I would never be a mother myself. Since every other nurse I had trained with had taken theirs, I wanted to collect the same socialized benefits. The administrators didn't ask me questions, but I suspected they gossiped behind my back. I didn't care. I had to be with Mama.

I wrote to Carlo telling him she was very sick.

He telephoned in the middle of the night. The moon was waning and no stars were out. The clocks had been silenced. Mama had just died.

"Are you really my brother?" I asked, feeling cut away from all the living.

"Our connection is bad," he said, tapping the receiver on

the other end with his fingertips. "Are you all right, Alicia?"

I was painfully frightened, alone, and cold. The windows had been opened so Mama's soul could escape, and except for a slit of light on the side of the refrigerator, the house was dark.

The next day, Mama's body was carried feet first out of the house. I insisted she be buried in the field behind our house, not in the church cemetery. I couldn't bear Mama lying in the same earth as strangers. For a large fee, the priest from St. Benedict blessed the ground out back and also moved Papa's corpse to be near hers. Mama's cousins threatened to sever me from the family. If I ate so close to corpses, they said, I would smell of the dead. But I never saw the cousins anyway and couldn't understand what difference a few corpses in the backyard would make in my life.

Fifteen hours later, when the sun was at its peak in the late May sky, Carlo knocked on the door. His sideburns were as long as his collar, and his skin was thinner than I remembered.

"*Dov'è Mamma?* Where's Mama?" he asked. He hadn't grown any taller in America.

"In her grave," I said. "We buried her yesterday. It's been hot."

He dropped his shoulders, sighed, and set down his leather traveling bag. His forehead wrinkled. "I'm not a good son," he said. "I didn't say goodbye to Papa either. Why didn't you call me sooner?" He looked as if he hadn't slept in three days.

Though he wept when he held me in his arms, when Carlo pushed his hair back from his forehead, I saw that his green eyes had gotten jollier in America.

At the kitchen table, my brother and I sat on opposite sides of the bouquet of sage and rosemary that I had set on the table to protect the living. I poured him coffee.

"Did she suffer?" he asked. His thick brown hair curled over his ears.

"Less than when you left," I answered.

We examined each other, unfamiliar with the lines and shadows in the other's face.

Carlo tugged the cuffs of his sleeves over his wrist bones. "So how are you?" he asked. I was all he had left.

I had spent the past twelve years bending over sick people. In the hospital, I had scrubbed and shaved chests, handed over hemostats and saws, and pushed breathing tubes into lungs. At home I injected Mama's thigh four times a day, and swabbed Papa's spittle. I hardly knew how a healthy human being smelled. Carlo sat across from me, unwounded and whole. He was someone I no longer understood. I was ashamed of myself for not having as much as he had. "I'm fine," I said, setting my jaw.

"Now you must come back to America with me," Carlo said.

"No." I didn't want my departing to be too easy for Carlo. If he wanted me, he would have to fight for me.

Carlo put his thumbs under the waistband of his gray pants and leaned back in his chair as a huge man might do. "Did Mama and Papa leave you money?" he asked.

I hated him. I picked up our cups and saucers and took them to the sink. Their money was my money, not his. I had earned it. I wouldn't give any to Carlo, and my parents had not instructed me to do otherwise. As I spoke, I kept my back turned against Carlo. "You always managed to do exactly what you wanted to do," I said. "You never wrote especially to me to ask how my life was going." I wiped the imprint of my brother's lips from the rim of his cup.

"You could have written to me!" Carlo didn't know I had stayed home every night with Mama and Papa.

Sono una infermiera. I am a nurse," I continued. "Since

37

the day I put on my white uniform and emptied a bedpan, I was guaranteed a salary for as long as I live. I don't have to go to America for my money, and I don't have to depend on Mama or Papa's money. I work as hard as you."

"I don't want money from you, Alicia. I wanted to know if they had taken care of you—repaid you for all you did. Why not sell everything and come to America with me? You don't have a family to protect you. Am I right or wrong?"

I turned to face my brother. "In America you don't have a family either. Only we two are left. We promised never to stray from one another. Now we are strangers!"

"*Sono un uomo*. I am a man," he said. "And I have Jassy."

I shook my finger at Carlo. "Don't you remember what Mama taught us?" I shouted. " 'Marry a virgin so you can teach her careful ways!' "

He paused a moment. Carlo wasn't upset with my criticism. He was a person too satisfied being who he was. "Do you think Mama was a virgin for Papa?" he asked. I didn't answer. "Mama turned to God after the war. When she was a young woman, she turned to men." I glared at Carlo. "You have no companions—not even a dog or a cat. Alicia," he said softly, touching my cheek, "tell me. Are you still a virgin?"

I was as naked as a worm. "*Fuori!* You don't belong here anymore. Get out!" I said. He had uncovered the source of my frustration, or at least he thought he had, and his righteousness infuriated me. "*Fuori!*" I couldn't say I was the right one for having saved myself, nor that he was wrong for having thrown both our futures away to that foreign woman with red hair.

"Don't ever come back here," I said. "I have washed my hands of you, Carlo. I am the only person left in this family.

We share only the clouds of childhood drifting in the same sky."

I was blind with my anger, ashamed, and I didn't want Carlo to leave me. I wanted him to grab me and hug me and tell me he was sorry for having made me wait so many years. I would have walked out of Subiaco with him.

But Carlo picked up his hat and lowered his head. He wasn't accustomed to arguing with women. "If that's what you want," he said.

I watched my brother walk down the path to the front gate. This time our parting seemed much more final. I cursed myself for sending him away, and for having insisted that Carlo agree I was right.

Three

I couldn't let him go. I followed Carlo, not in my flesh, but with my vision, like an angel or ghost, hoping to find a reason to soften my heart. I sat on my bed, closed my eyes, and concentrated, not caring if what I saw was hallucination or truth.

In Subiaco square, he got on a bus to Rome. During the ninety-minute ride, while he slumped in the backseat, Carlo remembered a conversation he had had with Papa the summer he had been sent to Rome, over a dozen years ago.

Papa had told Carlo there was so much beauty in Rome that a hole twisted through the sky connecting it to heaven. The center of the hole was the dome of the Vatican. Papa suggested Carlo go there and pray for success in a career as an Italian lawyer. "You'll have a direct line to God," he said. But the first time Carlo had been in Rome, he hadn't gone to St. Peter's, having found the Americans filming *Ben-Hur* instead. But this time, Carlo decided, St. Peter's was where he would go. He might find a thread of Mama's soul, or Papa's, and he wanted to say goodbye. Carlo wasn't convinced heaven existed, but he was open-minded.

Inside the cool basilica, hundreds of saints huddled above Carlo, painted on the dome of the ceiling. "The chosen," he mumbled. "Thank God I never believed I could be one of them."

He crumpled the twenty-dollar bill he had planned to put into the copper alms box and passed a wall of candles flickering in red cups. "God wouldn't end up with my money anyway," he said to himself. "The pope will buy a case of spaghetti for the cardinals, or the janitor will sweep it into his own wallet."

Carlo followed a group of tourists into the adjoining vestibule. They paused in front of a statue that was exhibited on a raised platform roped off from an altar area.

"This is the *Pietà*," the thin tour director announced. "Michelangelo's only signed sculpture."

At first, Carlo stood still, allowing the presence of the statue to sweep over him. He thought about how heavy it must be and how hardness penetrated through it from surface to surface. The image of two people, one grieving, the other dead had been carved from one huge chunk of stone. The artist must have lived inside the stone, feeling its grain and knowing its weak spots, making what was imperfect perfect. He shook his head. A dead son draped across the lap of a virgin was an image of complete suffering, and a curse Carlo refused to carry. Life wasn't as bad as the *Pietà*, he told himself. Mothers and sons were co-creators. Sons die. Mothers die. It was natural. Carlo decided Michelangelo must have been commissioned to show death and denial, otherwise he would have carved something less painful from the beautiful rock.

Carlo glanced to his right and left. The men and women standing next to him were as serious as the statue, seeming to believe in its suffering. Their breathing compressed to a hiss. Carlo wished he had chocolates or chewing gum to hand out to them. Better yet, he wanted to stand on the platform himself, to topple it down and say, "Hey, I'm Carlo. In

41

America, In God We Trust—we don't fear Him. When you visit Boston, find me on the Freedom Trail."

But Carlo didn't move. He had come to St. Peter's for a revelation. He waited for a beam of light, or a song, to relieve the explosion in his brain. Too many voices screamed behind his forehead. His Mama had died, he hadn't seen her to her grave—or Papa—and his sister Alicia hated him. Carlo could hear them arguing inside him, taking away the peace of his own thoughts. It all would have been okay if his sister had embraced him, and asked to depend on him now that she had no one else. He had come as soon as he could. He was a generous man. She had pushed him away from herself, their own mother, and the soil he had first stood on. Carlo looked up at the *Pietà* again and felt as if he were the Virgin holding on to his dying self. It wasn't the revelation he wanted.

Just then, a skinny man with stringy red hair scaled the balustrade to the right of the statue. His eyes frightened Carlo. He might have a gun. No one moved.

The man didn't pull a gun from his baggy trousers, but a huge iron hammer, and he began pounding the Virgin's face.

"I am Jesus Christ," he shouted, pausing to whack his own chest before continuing to hammer away at the statue.

The crowd screamed and held their hands over their hearts, but not Carlo. It was an opportunity, perhaps the revelation he was waiting for. He pushed to the front of the crowd and knelt on one knee, lifted a flash camera, which he had hidden under his gray jacket, and snapped pictures of the man destroying the Virgin's head. Carlo advanced the film and pressed the shutter as quickly as his short fingers could move.

A guard blew a whistle. "Quick!" he shouted. "Somebody get him!"

The red-headed man stood on the platform, at Christ's bare feet.

Chunks of marble fell to the floor, and tour groups from other rooms pushed into the vestibule where they could hear the pitch of metal hitting stone. The crowd pressed shoulder to shoulder, a mass of uplifted heads mimicking the faces painted on the dome above them. They watched the man with clenched teeth hammer the Virgin's face.

A piece of marble landed near Carlo's foot. He picked it up.

A young guard scaled the statue's balustrade and seized the criminal's arm. The hammer dropped.

"No one leaves this room!" the guard commanded.

Another guard blasted three short screams on his whistle.

Carlo hid his camera under his clothes.

The crowd hovered under the damaged *Pietà*. "It's ruined. She's ruined," one person wailed. "It will never be the same," someone else said. Strangers held on to one another. "God help us! *Mamma mia.*"

In the rage of the event, Carlo slipped out of the Basilica into the spilling Rome sun.

In his hotel room, he turned on the television. Laszlo Toth's act was already news.

The Hungarian had cleaved the nose off the Virgin, gouged her left eyelid, her forehead, and veil. His hammer strokes had broken her left arm at the elbow, and when her hand hit the floor, the fingers snapped off.

"This has been the world's first act of violence against a work of art," the TV journalist reported.

The station ran a dramatic reenactment of the event.

"Why didn't the madman hit Christ?" the journalist asked. She pointed out that Christ's face had been an easier target than the Virgin's.

43

The pope and his entourage appeared on the television screen.

"This has been a terrible act," the pope said. He pinched the crucifix around his neck. He asked that all pieces of the Virgin be returned to the Vatican. "Her fragments are not to be considered souvenirs," he said. The camera zoomed in on the pope's well-scrubbed face. "Please. Return her to us, to your church, to Italy. Don't let her leave this country. We have already lost too many of our precious possessions."

The pope blessed the TV audience before reciting the twenty-four-hour telephone number set up by the Vatican to receive calls regarding the Virgin's missing pieces. Eight-one-seven six-two-two-oh.

The journalist continued her report: "Already the Vatican is receiving bids from artists who want to repair Michelangelo's statue. Some say it will take years, others say only a few weeks. If all the bits of marble are returned, one woman, the daughter of artist Domenica Sica, guarantees she can fix the Virgin in three days by using a tough glue containing an Italian cheese."

Next, Giovanni Urbani, president of Rome's Restoration Institute, appeared on the screen. He spoke from his wood-paneled office. "Let's leave the statue as it is," he said. "Think of Venus de Milo. Why not let the *Pietà* be fragmentary? Why hide damage? One must, at a certain point, accept an accomplished fact of this sort. If not, there is a risk of falsification, an offense to the work of art."

Another group, academics, began to discuss whether or not works of art had lives of their own.

Carlo switched off the television. He lay belly down on the yellow bedspread. He had the Virgin's nose. Though he had been holding it for more than forty minutes, the marble was still cool in his hand.

He slid the top of his little finger around the delicate wings

44

of a nostril. Touching the marble, Carlo enjoyed its sheer slickness and the energy within the rock. The pulse of Michelangelo's hands still vibrated a pressure on its surface, making it perfect. He rolled onto his back, pressed the cracked tip of the Virgin's nose against his own nose and imagined looking into Michelangelo's eyes.

Carlo saw the face of his creator, the person who had turned the dark center of the universe inside out for him. Michelangelo's eyes would be green, he decided, and as humble and invincible as his own. But his eyebrows would be bushy, his forehead more deeply lined, his mouth smaller, and Michelangelo would say "so long" when he was finished and simply walk away. Then Carlo closed his own eyes and imagined what it might be like to be the statue, and be admired by hundreds of millions of people.

With his stone nose, Carlo sniffed what had already passed. A vapor of joy, so unlike the sensation of being carved from a chunk of marble, filled his heart. If he were a statue, he would never die, he said to himself. Then, a fragile but persistent floral odor, which faded as quickly as he consumed the smell, drifted into his nostrils. It came from the fragmented side of the nose, not the nose's smooth finished surface. As he inhaled the scent, Carlo desperately wanted to have something that he could hold on to. He thought of Jassy. He wanted her forever. Was that possible?

He kept the Virgin overnight, placing her nose on the pillow next to his own, and he pulled the covers up to where her chin would be. He skipped dinner and sat in the stuffed green chair next to the nose, thinking about his own children who weren't born yet and who would never know his mother—or his sister. There was nothing in Italy that he belonged to anymore. He was like the nose, cut off from the rest of the statue.

I turned my head when Carlo wept. I was ashamed that I had told my brother to drop dead and disappear. What did I expect to gain by sending him away, besides an inheritance, the land, and my own stubbornness? I thought I should give him a second chance. Carlo had grown to be a sensitive man. It had been a mistake to send him away.

At midnight, Carlo crawled into bed with the nose. I watched how careful he was. He didn't dare to touch the Virgin's waist or face. She was a grown woman, not a child, and she was his sister, he told himself. I was ashamed when I realized it was me he was farewelling. Carlo heard my mean voice: "We share only clouds of childhood. *Fuori!*"

Carlo fell asleep, dreaming about my cloud moving away from his and how he wanted his cloud to become thinner so it could stretch across the sky. But it got too thin, and disappeared like a scent.

I wanted to change my words and his dream. I hadn't yet realized that getting involved in other people's dreams got you nowhere.

The next day, after he had showered, Carlo called the Vatican. He wanted to return the nose. When he peered out of his hotel window, to check for the official black car that was to pick him up at ten, he saw me instead. He didn't know what to think, since he had already made peace with my decision to cut him from my life.

I stood on the sidewalk and lifted my black grieving veil, blew him a kiss, pointed to my valise, and lifted my thumb into the sky. I had decided to go to America with him.

Carlo nodded and indicated for me to wait on the sidewalk until he came down. I feared he would send me back home. I was pushing and pulling on him. "So what?" I said out loud to myself. "My mother has just died." I knew Carlo was thinking I was a woman who couldn't make up her mind and that I wasn't as determined, or clearheaded, as Jassy. But I was his sister and had certain rights.

Carlo rushed out of the hotel to me. "I have a meeting with the pope," he said, as if the meeting were not anything unusual. Then I remembered Carlo had always assumed he was as important as anyone else. He was freshly shaved, his golden skin glistened, and he had doused his cheeks with pine-scented aftershave.

"Oh?" I said, expecting Carlo would tell me to wait in his room.

"Come with me," he said.

A black car pulled under the hotel canopy. At the moment, I suspected he was inviting me because there was no time to do anything else. But later he explained my face had looked so frightened and unsure, he was certain if he left me alone I would change my mind and go back to Subiaco.

A man in a red cassock motioned us into the car. A black-frocked priest—whom I would know more intimately in the future—took my suitcase and put it in the trunk of the car. I sat in the middle of the backseat, between the holy man and my brother. The priest drove.

"*È sua moglie?* Your wife?" the cardinal asked Carlo, eyeing me somewhat critically. I admit I was very unattractive.

"*Mia sorella,*" Carlo answered. "Our mother died two days ago," he said, explaining my black dress.

"I will say a prayer for your mother," the cardinal said. Then Cardinal Ulbaldini rolled back his sleeves and introduced himself. He was Direct Counsel to the Holy See, Ultimate Venerator Supreme of the Vatican Museum Collection, Head of the Limbo Society, and the Official Terra-Firma Father of the International Benevolent Society. I squirmed, wanting to tell the cardinal I worked for the Benevolents in Subiaco, but I said nothing.

"Where is the nose?" the cardinal asked.

Carlo gave it to him, passing the marble piece over my lap.

The cardinal wiped the marble nose with a cloth handkerchief before dropping it into a gold box. He was a fiery-looking older man, with black curly hair and pulsing gray eyes.

"Now, do you want to make a confession?" he asked, leaning forward to bless Carlo, behaving as if his holy grace dared not land on me. It was uncomfortable to be treated as if I were impure—compared to Carlo I was a saint.

"Confession? Me? Never," Carlo laughed. "I don't need it."

"Do you have the camera?" The cardinal became businesslike.

So did my brother. He patted under his arm. "Sure do." Carlo had strapped the camera to his body as if it were a gun.

"We'll be wanting that, too." Ulbaldini held open a leather sack into which Carlo was supposed to drop the camera.

"Wait a minute." Carlo put up his hands. "I speak Italian like a native, but I'm an American. I have individual rights. Here's my passport." He pushed the cardinal's sack aside. "I want you to know I also called the television station. They're going to meet us at the Vatican. They know I have the nose and pictures of Laszlo Toth. Your people said they didn't want pictures."

"It's against rules to take pictures inside St. Peter's. Flash bulbs ruin the frescoes. Didn't you read the signs?" The cardinal rubbed his cleft chin. "I'll give you five thousand dollars for the camera."

Carlo laughed. The cardinal was offering him money. I nudged my brother's knee, urging him to take it. Carlo had planned on giving the pictures away for nothing.

"Not enough? How about ten then?" The cardinal shifted his legs.

"Don't joke." Carlo reached under his tweed sport coat. He had no way of knowing if the pictures were any good. It was a cheap camera—$7.50 off the rack in his drugstore. "I wonder how much the press would pay for the film," he wondered out loud.

The limousine sped through the bright morning, over the bridge, and past ancient townhouses along the Tiber.

"We don't want the pictures to go to the press. Fifteen, then." The cardinal removed a checkbook from the rear glove compartment. "Look," he said. "It's already signed. By the pope himself." The cardinal touched his lips.

If I had wanted to speak, I couldn't. My mouth and throat had frozen. Fifteen thousand dollars from the pope! The money was blessed.

The signature was fancy. Carlo held the blue check between his fingers. The paper was soft as a wave. Carlo shook his head no. "Sorry, I only deal in cash," he said. "Checks have to clear through banks. There's taxes. Half the money will go out the window." Carlo waved his wide hands. I stepped on his foot.

"You're a businessman, aren't you?" The cardinal leaned over my lap to get closer to Carlo. "Don't you have a Swiss bank account?" he whispered.

"That's for the big players, not me. Fifteen thousand is small change. They'd laugh at me." Carlo scratched his sideburns, which I noticed had a few sprouts of gray.

"Thirty, then," the cardinal said.

For a moment neither of the men said anything. Carlo was dizzy; so was I. The limousine stopped at a red light near a garden rimmed with palm trees and a lush blossoming orange tree.

"Listen, Mr. Barzini, let's make a deal. How about I open an account for you and send you the number? Write down your name and address." The cardinal handed Carlo a sheet of white Vatican paper and a fountain pen. "Go on, write."

Carlo hesitated.

"Forty-five," the cardinal said.

Carlo laughed. He was sweating. "How can I trust you? Just because you wear a robe, should I pretend we are like bread and cheese?"

We never made it to the Vatican. The cardinal didn't want to run into representatives from the television stations. "Let's stop at this cafe," he said. The young priest slid the limousine into a parking spot.

The men got out. I stayed behind them. They sat at a table for two. I sat at a table for one. The driver—the priest in black—stood by the car, watching. Without more words from Carlo, other than his ordering a double espresso, the cardinal's offer went up to fifty thousand.

Carlo grabbed Cardinal Ulbaldini's hand. "Stop there, please," he said, laughing. "And if my pictures aren't good, forget the deal."

The cardinal relaxed. "It's been a pleasure," he said.

They continued to shake hands, and they embraced. Both men enjoyed finding their own kind, other men who appreciated the intoxication of deal making. It was that simple. It didn't matter that Carlo got what he didn't expect, and Ulbaldini gave more than he had allotted. Carlo and the cardinal had made something happen.

I was crazy with fury. Why wasn't I born lucky? Why not

me? Carlo had no heartaches and earned rewards without bending his back. I struggled and prayed. He saw only the polished side of life. I saw the suffering.

Carlo talked like a rocket, telling Ulbaldini about the North End of Boston, Hanover Street, and his stores. "Cardinal Ulbaldini, you must visit us," he said. "Being there is just like not leaving Italy but better. You can leave," he laughed. "Look at me! I am here."

Ulbaldini was most curious about Carlo's shipping business. "I have family members to relocate—not ordinary people." He winked. "Holy ones whom we lost during the war. I've been looking for someone like you. Will you help me out?"

"Anything, anything." Carlo was smiling so much his green eyes were slits. "We're friends, you and I. We made a deal. Profit smells good wherever it comes from—even from the Church. Money and blessings can move both ways. Sure."

Carlo signed the papers Ulbaldini placed in front of him.

"Non lo rimpiangerà. You won't regret this," the cardinal said.

But Carlo would regret it. "Bring us *grappa!"* he called to the waiter.

He signed the stack of papers the cardinal whisked under his hand. He believed all would work out in his favor and if he himself didn't know what to do, he would hire someone to work out the details—or God would help him.

I too didn't pay attention to what Carlo signed, being busy reproaching myself and being jealous of Carlo to examine what was an arm's length from my own table. I could have noted the red scroll design across the top of the white paper, the name BENEVOLENT printed within the scroll, and the em-

51

bossed seal of the Virgin's figure at the bottom of the page. Then I might have recognized the same papers when they reappeared a few days later in the North End, at Spediamo, on Virginia March's desk.

F o u r

Virginia March and Carlo's girlfriend, Jassy, were best friends. When I met them, Jassy and Virginia were both twenty-nine. They told me they had met each other ten years earlier, at Boston University, in the late 1960s. After graduating from the university, they had hitchhiked to Woodstock, gotten sick, and shortly afterward moved to the North End together. They hoped an Italian neighborhood would be safe because it was old-fashioned. Neither Jassy nor Virginia was old-fashioned.

They shared an apartment, which they rented from Carlo, on the fourth floor of his building on Atlantic Avenue. The moment I arrived in the North End, I could hear the women moving about and laughing below Carlo's blue kitchen. At eight o'clock, they quieted down. It was Jassy's hour to practice singing, and her voice came shooting through the floorboards into my feet. I didn't allow her essence to penetrate farther. "She's studying opera," Carlo proudly said.

It was my first night in America. That evening I expected Carlo and me to talk about Mama, whom I was missing so much, and to make plans. I wanted him to write down his schedule and to tell me what I might expect for myself in America. I also planned on asking him if he minded if I rearranged his furniture. Instead Carlo talked about the girls downstairs. He told me the three of them often shared meals.

"Neither woman cooks," he said, letting me know they were a different breed from myself. From the beginning, I resented their intrusion. "We've joked about cutting a hole in the pantry and installing a spiral staircase so we could have two floors," Carlo continued. "I see them every day. Jassy works at the Blue Note—but she's really a singer. And Virginia manages Spediamo, my favorite business. It's international! When our people here tire of America, Spediamo ships them back to Italy."

I didn't understand. *"Come?"* I said. "How?"

Carlo explained. "Italians move to America to raise their children. The men find work as tailors, barbers, and bricklayers. They're good workers and save money. Then one day, when their sons and daughters are old enough to fall in love, the families get scared about outsiders and move back to Italy. In Boston, these people come to Carlo for help." Carlo got up from his chair to pace.

"Now let me tell you about the girl who runs the business—Virginia. She's smart." He paused, shaking his head. "And she knows all sides of the shipping business. When only one person is moving, for example, she sells them a big trunk for packing their linens and clothes. To a family she rents a huge metal container as big as their driveway. The family has four days to fill it up with furniture and dishes, and they can drive their car into the container, too." Carlo swept his palms together. "Virginia makes letters of credit and buys bonding. Everybody's happy, including Carlo. I don't do anything and can charge my customers a little more." Carlo pinched his fingers together. "The people trust me because I am like their brother."

When he saw the disapproval in my eyes, he announced he

was tired and went off to his bedroom. Below me, Jassy continued to sing from Rossini.

I cleaned up the kitchen, growing more furious as I washed the plates and forks. Carlo intended for me to cook and take care of his women downstairs. Never! They were strangers and foreigners, women who I was sure shunned housework, brassieres, and sexual responsibility. Carlo might love to prepare soups and roasts for them, but not me!

I scrubbed the pots, half listening to my temper and half listening to Jassy sing "Una voce poco fa," a showpiece song about how a girl is going to get her way with the man she loves. I didn't suspect that the gentleness Carlo had felt toward me in childhood might have been transferred to the girls downstairs.

Despite my denial, Carlo loved Jassy. He loved Virginia, too, but he treated her more like he treated me, being generous and also stingy.

He had hired Virginia to run Spediamo a year before I came to America, when she lost her position at a waterfront customs broker's office. Carlo said he was attracted to Virginia's sweet, self-sacrificing style. He didn't understand what darkness could emerge from the underside of a woman's brain.

Though Virginia appeared to be agreeable—and most of the time she was—her velvet veneer provoked an unexpected inside itch that would explode after everyone had forgotten about what might have made her angry. I couldn't speak up for myself either and sympathized with Virginia for that weakness. I also admired her.

She was efficient and clever with numbers. Carlo needed someone like her because he couldn't keep track of details. My brother was happy knowing nothing, thinking Virginia had little ambition other than being a woman who was at peace helping men attain their dreams. He was wrong. Once she became familiar with policies in the North End, Virginia did what everyone else did. With good intention, she took something for herself.

North End Italians transacted their business in cash. Nobody kept records of anything. Dollars were supposed to disappear like smoke. Salaries were taken out of cash registers. Receipts were folded and eventually lost. Customers who used Spediamo services to ship their daughter's wedding clothes to Palermo, convertibles to Naples, or furniture to Montepulciano forgot how much they paid, believing whatever it had been was fair, and that Carlo would take care of them. When the Benevolent shipments began, they paid Spediamo twice the rate for priority service, secrecy, and custom packaging. From their payments, Virginia took what she believed she deserved because she thought Carlo wasn't paying her enough. Everyone involved juggled money, not wanting to know or reveal what or how much the other one had.

I met Virginia the second day I was in America. Her confidence impressed me, but I soon saw it was thin. She was as unsure of her position as I was of mine. Neither of us knew where we belonged. And we were alike in more than one way: no one paid attention to us. We worked hard, often excelling, but were treated as if our accomplishments had nothing to do with our actions or decisions. Other people reaped the respect and praise we wanted for ourselves. But Virginia was different from me in the way she hung on to people; for me, people slipped away. Virginia had Jassy, a best friend. At the end of a day, the women shared their thoughts and complaints, accepting contradictions, and they protected each other.

The first day I was together with them, I was embarrassed for myself. I'd never had a close friend who was a woman, besides my mother, so I couldn't see the connection between the women without longing for the same for myself. I didn't understand how whispering shame, failure, fear, or dreams to a friend could create a history separate from being part of a family. Now, having known Virginia and Jassy, I am sometimes moved to tears when I see two women, who would be their age, sitting together in a cafe.

I met Jassy first. She knocked on Carlo's door late on my first afternoon in America.

"It's Jassy," she said. I recognized the voice calling to me from the outer hallway. "Don't get up. I have a key." Jassy's movements were quick, certain, and unmistakable. "Alicia," she said, "you've got to get out of the house." Jassy had a square body. She propped her hands on her long, straight hips. "Why waste time staring out a window?" I had been sitting in Carlo's front room since morning, thinking about Mama and hoping Carlo would come home and sit with me.

"*Buon giorno,*" I answered slowly. Sooner or later I knew I would have to say something to her, but I wasn't ready. I hadn't yet decided how to treat Jassy. I also didn't know she wore glasses.

"Here, put this on," she said, switching from English to Italian. Jassy wasn't shy. "Pretty, isn't it?" she said, handing me a full-skirted cotton dress, which was hers and smelled of incense.

I eyed the dress. "I'm in mourning for my mother. We wear black," I said, pulling away. "Didn't Carlo tell you our Mama died?"

She was struck by my suggestion that Carlo might keep his own mother's death a secret from her. "Yes, of course." She hesitated a moment. "Sure. I understand." She tossed the dress on the sofa before moving across the room to open the lace curtains and the window I had shut an hour earlier.

Over her shoulder, I could see that the sky was still sapphire blue, bluer than I'd ever seen a sky in Italy; across the expressway, the edges of the tall gray skyscrapers were turning purple; and the orange face of the Custom House Tower clock had been switched on.

"Maybe I have something cool and black downstairs," she said. "We might be the same size." She examined my squat body. I covered my nose. "It's a beautiful summer evening. We'll go out together."

"I'm fine here." I switched our conversation back to English. My English was much better than her Italian.

"I want to be your friend," Jassy said. Her eyes were not false.

No one had ever been quite so forward with me. Jassy had the quality of going after what she wanted, enveloping me with a warm firmness, which I curiously welcomed but doubted. I had noticed the same trait only in men.

"Carlo told me you might stay with us in the North End." Her voice was deep and unwavering. She looked straight at me.

Hmmphh! I said to myself, defying her. "When were you talking to Carlo?" I shivered. Might he have shared his bed with this tall American woman while I was asleep in the same apartment? Wasn't he grieving for our Mama?

"Today," she said. "Earlier this afternoon. Why?"

I wondered why my brother hadn't called to warn me about her.

"Ready? Let's go." When Jassy smiled, her cheekbones rose up into beautiful, smooth pink mounds. "I know you'll feel better if you get out," she insisted. "A little walking and coffee will kick the jet lag out of your system."

"I'm content," I said, insisting she leave. If we breathed

the same air, I feared her principles might penetrate me. I wanted to remain holy in America.

"I won't let you sit here alone," she added, sliding next to me. I felt her thigh against mine. She patted my arm.

"Where's Carlo?" I finally asked. Jassy was making me uncomfortable.

"Working. Carlo's always working. Sooner or later, you'll find out about that!" She rolled her eyes. Her nose was lovelier than in the picture Carlo had sent us.

We sat silent for a few minutes. Her timing was impeccable. "Ready?" she asked. "Virginia's waiting for us." She handed me my pocketbook. "It'll be fun."

I followed her down the five flights of steps. "Fun," I mumbled, mimicking the twang of vowels in her deep voice and the spring in her heels. I thought I knew more about Jassy than she did of me, and that she must be a contagious disease. Already she had overtaken my brother, but I refused to accept that she was interested in me, or that her unrestricted ideas were good ones.

Outside, the screeches of sea gulls were louder than the rush-hour traffic backed up on the ramp at the end of Atlantic Avenue. Dusk was beginning to stretch over the sky. Jassy took my hand in her strong palm and led me through the side streets to Hanover. When she heard me sniff, she explained that an offshore ocean breeze scented the air with salt.

We crossed short blocks and passed clean cement stoops. I had seen the same streets before, from Subiaco, when I had closed my eyes and gone searching for my brother. But my eyes were open now, and I was aware of something besides the affirmation of my vision: no one had held my hand since I was a child. Jassy held my hand the whole way to Spediamo. I was flying with an eagle.

Spediamo was on the third block of Hanover Street—the

block inhabited by merchants who had moved from near Rome to Boston, Jassy explained. "Each block of the North End belongs to someone," she said. "The first block belongs to the people who relocated to Boston from Avellino; the second block, to people from Abruzzi; the fourth, to those from Pescara; the fifth and beyond, to the Northern Italians." She squeezed my hand. "No men cross out of their territory to buy cigarettes or coffee, or to do business, except to go to the third block. Rome belongs to all Italians. Carlo's lucky to have a store there."

When we arrived at Spediamo, Virginia was sitting at her metal desk, surrounded by five men wearing white shirts and brown trousers belted high above their waistlines. Their black shoes were newly polished, their hair was neatly parted, and they held hats in their hands. The overhead lights had been switched off. Virginia's face was shadowed by the softer bulb of a desk lamp. Her hair was blond, nearly white, and she had black eyebrows which arched smoothly over her brown eyes. She was reading a document. Had I paid more attention to the papers Carlo had signed two days ago in Rome, I would have recognized them.

"Hey, what's the mystery?" Jassy asked. "It feels like someone died in here." She switched on the overhead fluorescents.

I didn't know if it was the sudden lights, the interruption, or the sight of wild-haired Jassy and myself, a wide woman in black framed in the open doorway, that caused the men to jump.

"Thanks for the lights, Jassy," Virginia said, brushing her hair over her shoulder. A straight fringe of bangs ran across her forehead. She stopped reading to wave to me. "Hi!" she added. "I heard you were here. Welcome!" And then Virginia went back to attending the men's papers.

I glanced around Carlo's favorite store. It was nothing special—just a hodgepodge, like Carlo. The walls were covered with beige paper thinly striped with green. Behind Virginia's desk, a row of gray file cabinets and shelving exhaled reams of paper. To the right of the entry was a glass display case filled with onyx and agate knickknacks, and behind the case a rack of soccer shirts. An iron grate protected the plate glass that faced Hanover. The room was carpeted with a green- and gold-flecked rug. Maps were tacked to the walls. The cash register sat next to the adding machine near Virginia's desk.

She looked up from the papers. "Alicia, maybe you can help me out. My Italian's not the best. I can read, but talk?" She lifted her shoulders. "These men are representatives of the Benevolent Society of Boston," she said. "Maybe you can keep them busy while I finish going over these papers."

I was surprised. "They're everywhere," I whispered to Jassy. "I met one, a cardinal, in Rome two days ago." In all the years my mother and I had stitched for the Benevolents, we never suspected the group existed beyond the hills of Subiaco.

Out of habit, I covered my nose for a moment before greeting the men. I wasn't sure if they were priests or monks. In America holy men could wear street clothes. I blessed myself. "I sewed costumes for the Benevolent Society in Subiaco, a town two hours south of Rome," I said. "My name is Alicia Barzini. I'm Carlo's sister."

One man said he didn't know anyone in Subiaco. Another, who wore an eye patch, said he thought he knew about the monastery there. "Was it bombed during the war?" he asked. Another man explained to Virginia that they had nothing to ship now but would have something soon. "We'll come back another day," he said. "Where's Carlo?"

"Wait! I have an idea," Jassy said. She took off her glasses to speak to the men. "Since Alicia sewed for your brothers in Italy, perhaps you can give her a job here. We have to find something to keep her busy, or she'll spend hours looking out windows." Jassy must have had the mistaken idea that sewing for saints would be like constructing costumes for theater and opera productions, that I would be doing the stitching in a lively room full of camaraderie. It was the kind of environment she was accustomed to creating around herself.

The men were charmed. They began speaking to Jassy in English, which they had known how to speak all along. "Good idea. Many of our Madonnas need new capes, or repairs to be made to their headdresses," they said.

There I stood. I had been on American soil for less than forty-eight hours and was already employed! This surely was the land of opportunity, I remember saying to myself, though I didn't consider sewing a great job. But I saw that both Virginia and Jassy were encouraging me to be independent by earning my own money. I was sure I could earn more money nursing, but would be first required to register and most likely supplement my training. I didn't know how difficult it would be to get a work permit in America.

The men handed me their card. It was white with red letters: BENEVOLENTS: 776-8425.

"Until I adjust to the North End, I'll needle and suture for God, instead of man," I said, referring to my surgical background. No one understood my joke. I was awful at making people laugh.

The men tapped their heels and smiled at me. Most of them were older than Carlo, and I noticed a few weren't wearing wedding bands. Maybe sewing was a good idea after all, I thought, convincing myself I needed a break from nursing. I remembered that during the last two heart surgeries I had attended in Subiaco, I had seen spirits floating about the operating room. The luminous lights might have resulted from my being tired, but at the time I was sure the lights had been patients' souls.

"You'll need fabric and sewing tools," Jassy said to me. "Tomorrow we'll take you to the Teatro. Renato has an extra machine."

The men left. Virginia recorded the day's receipts in pencil on lined paper. Carlo didn't loop paper through any of his cash registers. "Done," she said.

The bell tied to the bar behind the glass door rang as we closed it. Virginia checked that the chain and bolt lock were secure, and tucked the key into the back pocket of her jeans. Unlike Jassy, Virginia was small and delicate. Her clothing was much tighter than Jassy's, whose skirt billowed as we walked less than half a block, past men loitering in doorwells and against parked cars. The three of us were all about to turn thirty, but Jassy and Virginia seemed much younger. Between them I looked ancient in my black dress.

We arrived at the Paradiso Caffè and sat outside, at a sidewalk table. Jassy ordered *tre cappuccini*. We sipped our frothy coffees and watched the colored lightbulbs strung across the intersections of Hanover Street turn on.

Suddenly, the neighborhood became noisier, and the succulent smells of sweet sausages and roasting green peppers, meatballs in bubbly red sauce, and cheese, astonished my nostrils. I was hungry. Men pushing carts of food appeared along the street, and a small crowd of tourists sifted through the smells, under strings of triangular flags and lights. A circle of moon scraped the roofs of the North End buildings.

I heard a loud drumroll and a few bugle blasts. "What's going on?" I asked.

"Festival," Jassy answered. "Don't you have them in Italy? They always start on Fridays."

"Yes," I said, though for the past ten years I had been too busy caring for Papa and Mama and my nursing career to have attended a festival. I never left my house, except to go to work.

"This is the first one of the season," Virginia said, rummaging through her white handbag for a schedule. "Let's see. This weekend they honor Madonna delle Grazie." She put her finger over her lips, indicating silence.

The Madonna, on a platform, was being carried down Hanover Street by a battalion of black-shoed men. The men wore yellow sashes. I noticed that several of them had been in the Spediamo office.

I shifted my cup on the tiny cafe table, remarking how the statues in American were bigger than the statues in Italy. "Everything's bigger in America," I said, remembering the doll-sized costumes I had stitched for statues and looking forward to handling bigger and fancier pieces of fabric. Here, the Blessed Virgin wore a gold embroidered satin cloak with a stand-up collar. Pinned to the back of the cloak were ribbons of ten-, twenty-, and fifty-dollar bills. I figured, in America, instead of selling statues to raise money, the Benevolents collected outright donations. "What do they do with the money?" I asked. In Subiaco, I had always assumed Benevolent money was distributed to the poor.

"Who knows!" Jassy and Virginia both shrugged. "But I can tell you what they should do with it," Jassy added. "They ought to abolish virginity. Women are the same everywhere. None of us should be more chosen, or chaste, or holy. Just the idea of virginity causes trouble, between us, and with them," she said. "There's more to God's mother than purity." Jassy pointed to the parade of men carrying the Madonna. "But that's all they care about."

Virginia looked around the cafe before whispering in my ear. "Alicia, do you trust men who worship virgins?" she asked.

Jassy interrupted. "Never trust a man who thinks you can't be as good as God's mother," she said. "They're old-world types and will do anything—cross oceans, die, and kill—to own and possess the Queen of the Night. They want to own and possess the Madonna, but they never touch her. Don't they understand she needs to be touched to feel alive? Life is a sensation, not a sin. That's why I said they should abolish virginity—cut it out at birth. No one could claim to own anything."

I disagreed. "Virginity is an honor," I said. "It's about freedom. When a woman is a virgin, she is free and full of honor. She can share that freedom with a man when she marries. Maybe these men are worshiping the gift we women give to them."

Virginia nodded, stunned. "That's heavy," she said. "I never thought of it that way. Too bad for me. I got rid of mine a long time ago—the first opportunity I had. No regrets." She paused to finish her coffee. "I'm glad Renato isn't into this ridiculousness." She pointed to the slow-moving parade. Renato was her boyfriend, an Italian from Florence who had been in America ten years.

"Ha! I'll bet he's down on the next corner holding his hat in his hand, thinking of his mother and not of what you two are going to do tonight," Jassy teased. The two women sat close together. I was sure they could smell each other.

"I know him better than you." Virginia giggled.

Both women looked at me.

"How about you, Alicia? Do you have a sweetheart in Subiaco?"

"Oh, yes," I said, lying. I wanted them to accept me, maybe for the same reason Carlo was enamored by them. Jassy and Virginia were modern American women, and they were kind. Being close to them made me feel special. They wanted to know what I thought.

Jassy motioned to the waiter for more coffees. "We lose before we begin, Alicia."

"I don't want to be good," Virginia said. Her voice was small next to Jassy's. "There's so much to do, and we've been denied too much pleasure by waiting for men to lead the way. Right?"

"How can we win? Love's not competition. It's respect."

"Being equal."

"And taking our places in the world," Jassy added. "Depending on each other to succeed. We have to help each other, not stand in the way."

I listened. I was the outsider. I allowed they might know something better than what I myself believed in, which was God. I saw they had built few walls, and they were comfortable with each other, and themselves, in a way I could never be. Jassy and Virginia were writing their own set of rules and not living by the ones I embraced, which honored virginity, piousness, cleanliness, obedience, and humility. Still, that night I wanted to sit between them and link my arms through theirs and absorb their beliefs. They spoke to me as if I, too, were their sister. But I wasn't. I couldn't forget who I was. I was an Italian girl born in a small town during the war, not an American who had known only progress, wealth, and comfort. I wasn't prepared to catch up to their way of thinking.

Eventually I would allow Jassy and Virginia help me to unknot my brain, but I couldn't open the curtain completely, not in one swoop. In fact, the next day I closed it shut. I closed it tighter than it had ever been shut before.

$\mathcal{F}$ *i v e*

The women collected me at noon, at the beginning of their lunch hour, to take me to the Teatro for sewing supplies. "He keeps them under the bleachers," they said. It was a special event for them, and for me, too. Virginia and Jassy were going to introduce me to Renato. "He's not an ordinary man," they said. I appreciated their enthusiasm and the gift of his friendship. "He'll help you."

"Renato knows absolutely everything about creating," Jassy added, not telling me Renato knew nothing else. She handed me my pocketbook. *"Andiamo,"* she said. "Let's go."

Renato's Teatro, a former banana warehouse, was on Fleet, a one-way street that connected Hanover to North. Virginia and Jassy explained Renato had partitioned the concrete room into a performing space banked on two sides by bleachers, a lobby, and a narrow hallway for storing sets. "It's magnificent," they said. "Magic."

As we walked toward Fleet Street, Jassy and Virginia filled me in on Renato's odd habits. Jassy spoke first. "Even though he and Virginia are girlfriend and boyfriend, he refuses to be seen on a North End street with a woman. If he were with us now, he'd either be a block behind or a block ahead of us."

"I don't mind," Virginia smiled. "Renato insists on being known as a man with one passion—theater. His reputation is important. He wants the men on the streets to think he has one goal. That way they won't gossip or whisper nasty words. And if everyone says one thing about Renato—that he is an artist—Renato believes their words will give him power."

"You must be jealous of his theater," I said.

"No."

"I guess it's what you want to believe in," I said, hoping to understand. I thought it strange the women accepted Renato's single-mindedness, considering that the night before they had criticized the men who worshiped virgins. They had said those men needed to expand their minds, but not Renato. American women must expect all or nothing, I remember thinking. "What do the North End people say about Carlo and his businesses?" I asked.

"He's an entrepreneur—a king to them. Plus Carlo gets a lot of respect for not showing off his money," Jassy said, lauding what I considered a tic of my brother's character.

"And for having you, Jassy," Virginia added. "Maybe for me, too, I suppose." We walked. "If Renato is the North End's Doctor of Theater, Carlo is the Doctor of the American Girl. We work for him, and we're different from what the men who live here know. They might think we bring him business—and money—from outside the neighborhood." She whispered, "And now Carlo has you, too."

"You're right." Jassy nodded. She must have seen the questions in my eyes. I wanted to know if she was planning to marry my brother. Jassy hugged me closer to her. "Alicia's on our side," she said. I thought Jassy was taking advantage of my brother, the way men usually take advantage of women, and she wanted me to help her.

On North Street, we passed Paul Revere's house, and a line of tourists waiting to enter. "Saturday's Carlo's busiest day, too," Virginia said. "We can't be late getting back."

"Are you cold?" Jassy asked, feeling my caution under her arm. The sky was overcast.

"Tell me," I said, "are you making your men more American, or are they making you more Italian?"

"American," Jassy said. "Carlo's a progressive man. He wants everything to be new, nothing old."

Virginia put her arm on top of Jassy's. I was in the middle, feeling the bones of the two women press against my own flesh. "Jassy's right about Carlo," she said. "But not Renato. He wants to do everything over and over again the same way, the old way, but always better than the last time."

We turned the corner and stopped in front of the Teatro door. "Remember," Virginia reminded me, "until Renato Ricci gets used to you being with us, he'll act as if I'm not his girlfriend, and he'll flatter you with his attention so you won't have time to notice he's shy, or time to think anything about him other than he's wonderful."

I was uncomfortable. I didn't want attention from Renato. I didn't know how to flirt. I knew nothing about men. I was sure I'd be as clumsy as a bad joke.

Virginia let us into the small, neat Teatro lobby. It smelled like moist paper, paint, and dust. Renato had a shiny reputation. Certificates hung in a row on the wall, framed in silver: 1970, 1971, 1972. For the past three seasons, his Teatro had won "Best of Boston" awards.

"He must not be here yet," Virginia said, peering into the performing space. "Renato," she called out in her delicate voice. In addition to working for Carlo, Virginia worked in the Teatro, sweeping floors, managing the box office, and

70

sometimes appearing in plays. "There are no small roles in the theater," she said as she pointed out her own picture on a poster which was tacked on the lobby wall.

While we waited, Jassy and I flipped through a collection of newspaper clips collected in a three-ring notebook. I scanned the headlines: GOLDONI HITS NORTH END. IBSEN EXPERIMENT WINS. O'NEILL AS COMEDY BY RICCI. A MUST-SEE SHEPARD. BOSTON LOVES RICCI. His audience came from all over the state. As I read on, I grew more shy. Renato seemed larger than life.

"The only thing the audience complains about is the parking," Jassy pointed out, reading over my shoulder. "In the North End, there's no space to put a car."

"And Renato complains about their credit cards," Virginia added. "He wants cash—like Carlo."

"Too bad he doesn't earn enough money," they said, shaking their heads. "He depends on us to take care of him." Both women had sad eyes.

Finally Renato emerged from what I believed was the basement. I wondered if he had slept down there. "You're here!" Virginia said, kissing his cheek. He resisted her, smoothing a strand of his brown hair behind his ear. Renato looked at me as if I might be his Beatrice, the woman he had been long waiting for, the woman who would rescue his life. I blushed.

He was a big-faced emotional man with a ponytail, soft brown eyes, and firm lips. He shook my hand warmly, standing close enough for me to inhale his musky scent. In Subiaco, at the hospital, I had noticed that men who smelled like Renato were the easiest patients to take care of. Their sweat sweetened rather than soured on their skin. They didn't complain and I always did extra for them.

"This is Carlo's sister, Alicia," Jassy said. In the new world, just as in the old, I was known as Carlo's sister.

Renato slid his hands into the pockets of his velvety brown pants. He was handsome, broad shouldered, and his arms were very muscular below the sleeves of his black T-shirt. Behind my black veil I blushed again, reminding myself he was Virginia's boyfriend. Besides I was sure Renato was not surveying me with the same zeal as I was admiring him. "You lost your mother," he said softly, tugging the sleeve of my black dress.

In America everyone touched me. In Italy, I had touched others only when they were sick or dead. I looked through my veil at Renato. He took my hand in his own, feeling my melancholy. My heart thumped, and I wondered if he knew it was thumping for him. In his sleepy eyes I saw dreaminess and ambition, a good combination for an artist. He smiled at me as if I were the only woman in the room. "Are you an artist?" he asked in a quiet voice.

I fumbled. The urge to create art, or children, had passed me by. I knew nothing about the feeling Jassy and Virginia claimed to be the highest of highs—Virginia acted and Jassy sang. But I had secretly compared the feeling they described both to the sensation of praying directly to God and to how I felt when I was in a trance, spying on Carlo.

"I'm here to sew," I answered, shaking my hand away from Renato's. At that moment I decided to be practical, not indulge dreams. "I'm not an artist," I boldly said. "Virginia and Jassy said you might help me." No one in America recognized my true profession. I was a nurse, a healer. Why didn't that show in my face?

Virginia draped her sweater over her shoulders. "I'm going out," she said. "I'll be right back. Renato needs coffee." She slipped out the door.

Jassy followed Renato and me into the performing space. He said it was set for a Gozzi farce, with wooden walkways, cardboard bridges, and fringed gondolas in a backdrop of pink Venetian buildings. The women had been correct. Magic lived in the Teatro air.

Renato held my hand and walked me across the stage and over a wooden bridge, pointing out the yards of sea blue satin fabric spread on the floor below us. "If you enjoy working with cloth, perhaps you can create something for the Teatro," he said. "We don't pay, but rewards come to you from the inside."

Jassy interrupted my awkward silence by tapping out a scale on the upright piano, which was in the corner of the stage.

The music distracted Renato's attention. "Did you sing today?" he asked Jassy.

She cleared her throat. "Not since Thursday." She lifted her shoulders. Renato let go of my hand and crossed the stage to sit at the piano. "I'm surprised, Renato. I didn't know you played the piano!" Jassy said.

"Theater is my first love, always, above everything." He played a simple chord. "But I know more. My mother was a minor opera star in Italy, and my father was a violinist," he said. "Let's hear what you can do."

To warm up, Jassy shook her arms and then stretched her fingers backward. She vocalized vowels and popped conso-nant sounds, loosening the hinge of her jaw. "Breathe," Renato said. "Air is wind and life." He tapped the top of the piano. "Let's begin at C and follow through to G." It was a simple exercise. Jassy didn't hold back anything, and Renato didn't push her.

"You're good," Renato said, switching on a working light above the keyboard. I moved offstage and sat on a corner seat in the bleacher, not far from the piano. I was used to no one paying attention to me.

"If I'm going to train a singer"—Renato bowed his head to Jassy—"I want her to be a champion. Let's try a bit more."

Both Jassy and Renato were ambitious people. Jassy's ambition was deposited in her throat. I could see she had an excess of it. It was like a red beacon, and I figured her ambition would either kill her, or the people who stood in her way. Renato's ambition was in his eyes, and when he looked at Jassy, it weakened.

He scratched his temple. "Your voice is big," he said to Jassy. "Huge. But it lacks fine-tuning. I can help you with style, but not technique. You need discipline." He tucked an edge of T-shirt under his belt. "You won't go anywhere without discipline." He pressed his palms over his rib cage. "This time think of your voice as a bellows that blows all thoughts out of the mind of your audience." He extended his arms. "For a singer, gaining a superior presence is as important an exercise as going through the scales." He touched a black piano key. "Ready?"

To my ears, Jassy's voice was loud and clear—a speeding train headed to the top. I couldn't pick up the technique problems—such as the tense tongue, which Renato spoke to her about.

Her cheeks were flushed. Her puzzled expression told me Jassy hadn't expected Renato to coach her. She was a bit nervous. Much later Renato would tell me that on that day he had seen something in Jassy that needed to be given more confidence.

"Do you know 'Die Forelle,' the Schubert ballad?" he asked.

Jassy nodded.

"Excuse me," I interrupted. I couldn't sit through a song. "I need to go to the bathroom," I whispered to Jassy.

The Teatro's tiny toilet was behind the stage. There was

no door, just a plastic curtain strung on a wire. Cans of turpentine and paint littered the floor. And it was dark. Jassy led me with a flashlight.

"Is there any toilet paper?" I asked from behind the curtain.

"No. Never. Renato says people come to the Teatro to see theater, not to piss," Jassy quietly answered.

"Oh, no!"

Back on stage, Jassy sang "Die Forelle," and then she left. "It's past one!" I heard her say. She rushed back to work, most likely figuring Virginia would take care of me. I waited in the bathroom, too embarrassed to stumble out with only Renato there to greet me.

Soon Virginia let herself back into the Teatro, returning with a cup of coffee and bread for Renato. She must have assumed I had left with Jassy. Renato never knew I had gone to the toilet. My flashlight went dead. I sat in the dark, waiting for my eyes to adjust, hoping the Teatro didn't have mice.

Virginia and Renato talked. Then the theater became very quiet. Aha, I said to myself, it's time to go out. But Renato turned on the stage lights. I peered out to the stage through a crack behind the toilet bowl, making sure Virginia was there. But it was too late to grab her attention.

Like children playing, Virginia chased Renato over the wooden bridges, past gondolas and around the edges of the pretend Venice, laughing. Then Renato pursued Virginia, her long hair trailing behind her like a veil. He stopped to take off his T-shirt. He must be overheated, I thought. But then Virginia unzipped her jeans, jumped over the rail of the bridge into the satin blue sea, and Renato jumped after her, grabbing her small breasts.

Virginia pulled down Renato's trousers. His penis shot out of his pants at the angle a flagpole rises from the side of a public building. It was huge—as big as the gondola at his feet. I was flabbergasted. Never in my life had I imagined the soft sausage between a man's balls could have such prominence. Oh, I had seen a penis before—I was a nurse—and in my curiosity I had even stroked a few in the Subiaco hospital. But the men were unconscious, and their flesh shrank from my touch.

Renato's large eyes glistened under the stage lighting. I turned my head sideways and crushed my nose against the toilet partition to get a better look, thinking I might see more with two eyes than one. Renato strutted, his hands on his hips, his chin lifted like I've seen Italian men do when they pretend to be peacocks. Then, *Mio Dio!* Virginia went to her knees and put her mouth over his penis.

Renato kept his hands on his hips and a smile on his big face. The roots of my hair itched. Virginia can't be smiling, I said to myself. I worried about her teeth, her tongue, her neck.

When she stopped, Renato dropped his hand between her legs. I saw a breath of light emerge from under his hand. I wondered if it was her ambition glowing—or her lust?

My head ached. Real people don't do such things to each other, I told myself. Now they were both naked.

"Let's release feelings of every possible color," Renato said. He carried Virginia to the piano, setting her *culo* in the middle of the keyboard. If anyone besides myself was listening, Renato might have pleased their ears. While she wiggled, Renato played high and low notes, lifting his fingertips from the keyboard the instant the song was over. He was sweating.

"Let's sing it again," Virginia said. Her appearance was deceptive: she was not a delicate woman, but a woman of great stamina.

Renato slowly uncurled his palm as if his hands were

flowers and carried Virginia to center stage. Then he turned her over. They did it backward, sideways, and frontward. "You are my challenge," he said. "I don't want it to be over, not yet." From the bathroom, I could see his penis go in and out of her body. I was horrified, but they were enjoying themselves.

She was under him. I blessed myself, feeling sorry for Virginia. They both screamed and whimpered, confusing me. And then, quickly, Virginia got on top of him. Her back was to me. "I love you," she said. I saw Renato's balls shrink from tomatoes to plums.

I blessed myself again. I was sweating, too. "This is wrong." I bowed my head and prayed to the Blessed Virgin Mother. I asked her to intervene. "Holy Mary, Mother of God," I said. "This act is for creating children. Help them have sense."

I peeked out. Renato and Virginia lay tangled together on the wooden bridge. I heard keys drop on the floor. They started over again. The second time they didn't groan as much, and a halo of light seemed to rock their caresses.

"Marry me," I heard Virginia ask Renato.

"I don't have money," he said. "I can't marry you. We don't need to be married to have this. We are perfect together."

"Marry me."

"I've worked ten years. Who will take care of my theater?"

I cried, and there was no toilet paper to wipe my tears. I used the sleeve of my black dress. They had no families to help them be honest; I felt sorry for them.

"My sweet, let me hold you," Renato said. "Can I get you anything? A glass of water?" He smoothed her long blond hair over her forehead and down her back. Virginia lay still and quiet. "Are you all right?" he asked.

In a few minutes they both dressed and left the Teatro. I felt my way out of the toilet, across the dark stage, and into the dimly lit lobby. I let myself out, not bothering to lock the door behind me.

I never did go back to rummage under the bleachers for boxes of fabric and lace, or for the extra sewing machine they had promised I would find there. I forfeited my job with the Benevolents. I found nothing in the Teatro that I could use to dress saints. Instead I had witnessed my own fear. As I walked back to Carlo's building, I told myself if I stayed in Boston, America would bite out my soul.

I didn't want Jassy and Virginia to be my friends. I didn't want to be liberated, go braless, drink coffee in cafes, and criticize pious men. I would not give my milk away for free. I believed that my brother, his friends, and America were monsters. I went flying back to Subiaco where I hunched inside the icy darkness of my heart.

I left a note on Carlo's bed.

Carlo,
I forgave you once, but I will not forgive you twice. Instead I will curse you. I don't want to be like you, or your friends. I am afraid if I stay in America I will have no choice but to blend in to the mess surrounding you and allow my soul to be swallowed. You should have been stronger and sought out your own kind, or stayed in Subiaco. You are a heathen. You have not even taken time to grieve your own Mama. Don't contact me ever again, unless you come back to Italy to live. I mean it.

Alicia

S i x

Along with my virginity, I kept my dignity. If Carlo was living in sin, and not remembering Mama, I would be twice as good a person and a daughter.

I closed off the rooms in my wooden house and moved a cot into the kitchen. For the next three years, I lived like a squirrel, stashing everything I earned away in old cans, inside mattresses, or under the kitchen sink. At first I didn't understand exactly what I was saving for. No one could possibly be interested in marrying me, I said to myself. My own brother Carlo didn't care.

I became painfully aware of my unattractiveness. If I was a shadow to my brother, I was less than that to the doctors and janitors I passed in the halls of St. Scholastica Clinic where I worked. Men turned their heads. They thought I was ugly and were sparing me their pity, I thought. But during those hardship years, I did harbor a seed of hope. I believed God was saving me. I was sure one day he would send me a man who would love my sharp nose, thick shoulders, and inability to carry on a conversation. This fantasy allowed me to feel chosen and also allowed me to become too comfortable being alone. Having lived through those years, I realized loneliness is suffering that no human being deserves to know. There are so few of us here on earth, for so long a time, and we need each other.

To reinvigorate myself, I turned to the sick and dying—my patients—tending their bodies and souls, lavishing them with care. They were unaware of who I was, but I loved them nonetheless. I assured myself God was watching. He would help them and one day would reward me. If I didn't get an earthly man, I was ready to be satisfied with a partner in heaven. When my time came, I would swirl out of my flesh like a fragrant scent.

They promoted me to the position of advanced surgical nurse. That year the cardiologists ceased entering the thoracic chamber through the patients' sides, spreading ribs to remove lung tumors or to relieve pressure in pericardia. Instead, doctors began going directly to the heart, cracking open the front of the chest with air-driven saws. I handed over scissors, sponges, and clamps. And when patients were put on bypass, while their valves, veins, and arteries were being repaired, I operated the machine. After a sternum was fused, the surgical team handed over the needle and thread to me.

Having sewed for the Benevolents for so many years, my fingers were more skilled than the surgeon's. I stitched shut the final layer of the patients' skins. The medical doctors watched, but they didn't see all that I did: I lured the luminous material, which had leaked from the patients' incisions during surgery, and returned it to their chests. I used my nose, inhaling and exhaling with the patients' spirits, to accomplish this task. Thus my most unattractive feature became a valuable asset.

My ability to spiritually refurbish patients, along with my reputation for leaving less than a hair-thin scar on patients' chests, influenced the clinic's top surgeons to request my assistance at every open-heart procedure. The doctors whispered I brought them good luck. They were right. During the three years I was attending, Subiaco's St. Scholastica Clinic suffered only two deaths. One patient had a brittle soul, which I cannot explain. He died. The other's soul was so playful, it vanished from the operating room. The administration honored my mysterious skills with several gold badges, which I never wore. I stored them inside an old coffee can under my kitchen sink.

Each day I walked back and forth to the clinic through the field behind my house and over the rocky path that wound behind St. Benedict Monastery. I rarely passed another person along the way. If I did, my chest pounded, and I struggled to breathe. I developed many fears about unfamiliar faces. Other than go to the clinic and be at home, on Sundays I went to early mass, sitting in the front row so no one could turn around and stare at me. Just the thought of going into Subiaco square caused me to be hot. But one day, hungry for a fresh orange, I forced myself to the square, where I fainted in the fruit store. A stranger touched my forehead.

After that incident, I collected everything I needed from the hospital supply rooms. If there was no fruit, I went without it. Occasionally, when I wanted something wild to eat and was feeling braver than usual, I set wire traps in the fig tree, catching birds, which I roasted in my oven.

The hospital provided me with a uniform, clean linens, and two meals a day. I never wasted a thing. I ran the radio Carlo had given me on batteries taken from the hospital storage room. I never bought a television. Nothing about my life was frivolous. I rarely turned on lights but used an old oil lamp when I read at night or sewed. Although each day a bucket of lire bought fewer things, each week I saved three lire more. I spent money only for gas to boil water and heat the stove. The house was mine, and through some benevolent accident of Italian bureaucracy—of my father's doing—I didn't pay taxes.

In the evening, I continued to sew tiny outfits for the patron saints of Subiaco—St. Benedict, the hermit, and his sister, St. Scholastica—as well as for the Madonna and her son Jesus. Monks left oil and candles, wool scraps, smooth pieces of moire, and spools of thread at my front door.

One cold December evening I fell asleep with a sewing needle pinched between my fingers. In the back of my mind, I must have been longing for Carlo. I felt a tugging sensation on the top of my head. Outside the kitchen window, the inky wind howled. My senses were transported across the ocean. In Boston, the sky was calm, quiet, and as sapphire-blue as I remembered it to be.

I saw the North End peninsula, the familiar thumb separated from the rest of the city by a line of highway. Getting closer, I saw Jassy's red hair, her fur-collared coat, and red cowboy boots. She stepped over a snowdrift. Carlo reached for her hand. I heard the squeak of their boots. They were on their way home. But first, that day like most every other day, Carlo paraded Jassy down Hanover Street.

They greeted several old women in black who were walking their short-haired dogs. Carlo tipped his hat to a few North End men, huddled in doorways. They waved back to Carlo but said nothing to Jassy. They lowered their voices, raised their chests, and roved their dark eyes from her mouth to her hips as she passed. I followed my brother and his mistress to his building on Atlantic Avenue.

"You should be in fur from your head to your knees, not just around your neck," my brother said to Jassy as he held open the hall door for her. There was a Christmas tree set up in their front room.

In the back of the apartment, Virginia and Renato were

setting the table for dinner. I jumped, since the last time I had seen them they were naked. But on this December day they were wearing clothes. Renato's ponytail was longer, and Virginia seemed to have gained weight.

I saw that Carlo had gone ahead and cut a hole in the pantry, joining the two floors with a spiral staircase. They were all together now, and cozy. I wondered who wore the pants. When I saw what they were eating, my suspicion was confirmed: Virginia and Jassy made the rules.

On each blue-rimmed plate there was a pork chop, a pile of mashed potatoes, and a gathering of green beans. Nothing was sauced or overlapped. The arrangement was so very American, practical and handy. No garlic was used to season.

I saw Virginia watch Carlo enter the kitchen. Her bangs exaggerated the pout on her lips. "Sit down," she said. Carlo kissed her cheek.

"Did everybody have a good day today?" Jassy asked. She seemed determined that everyone feel as if they belonged. They sat around the circular wooden table. Jassy was the first to spread a cloth napkin on her lap.

"*Buon appetito,*" Carlo said. My brother wasn't as easy with the arrangement as I had expected he would be. He later assured me the hole in the floor had been his idea and that he never regretted opening his home to the others. He wanted Jassy near him, and if having her meant also having Virginia and Renato, that was all right. Besides, "It just takes a while to get used to," he later explained. "Living together is like adoption, choosing to make a family rather than creating one from blood. This is America, and here we build bridges, not walls, between our differences. The whole world is watching us."

Carlo raised his wineglass. "We must practice. I want to propose a toast," he said. "Since we are together like a family, we will be spending Christmas like a family. We have become varicose."

"What?" Virginia laughed.

"Carlo, do you mean 'very close'?" Jassy laughed.

Renato smiled, but he may have been dragged into the joke by the women. Though he had less of an accent than Carlo, English was his second language, too.

Carlo pressed his index fingers together and lifted his shoulders. "So I got the words mixed up," he said. "We'll be very close, then. Maybe too close." He lifted his drink. The others followed. Under the table, Jassy touched Carlo's calf with her foot.

Carlo wiped his mouth and poured a second glass of wine. He was remembering what Jassy had said to him the night before, when they were in bed: "What's so great about blood? We all have it," she had whispered.

After finishing the pork chops, the men sat at the table while the women cleared the plates and set out a bowl of salad. They ate their salad last, as Italians do, but instead of tossing it with olive oil, they each poured dressing onto the greens from glass bottles.

Carlo pulled the napkin out from under his collar. "What play will it be tonight?" he asked Renato.

"I am continuing with Pirandello," Renato said. He wiped his hands before opening a book. He flattened the pages and his lips at the same time. "The second act of *Six Characters.*" He had a gentle face.

In the kitchen, under the amber of the overhead light, Jassy, Carlo, and Virginia sat to listen to Renato read about the six strange characters who had lost their author:

> *The stage call-bells ring to warn the company that the play is about to begin again.*
> *The* STEPDAUGHTER *comes out of the* MAN-

AGER'S *office along with the* CHILD *and the* BOY. *As she comes out of the office she cries:*
Nonsense! nonsense! Do it yourselves! I'm not going to mix myself up in this mess. Come on, Rosetta, let's run.

[*The* BOY *follows them slowly, remaining a little behind and seeming perplexed.*]

The STEPDAUGHTER [*stops, bends over the* CHILD *and takes the latter's face between her hands*]. My little darling! You're frightened, aren't you? You don't know where we are, do you? We're on the stage. It's a place, baby, where people play at being serious, a place where they act comedies.

Renato continued for four pages, changing his voice for each character. When a Mrs. Pace, a new character, appeared in the drama, he stopped reading, marking the spot with a faint pencil dash. "We will begin here tomorrow," he said. Renato's reading after meals had been Jassy's idea; it made Renato feel important and taught Carlo about the theater.

Renato shut the book. Carlo asked what was so remarkable about the people in the play Renato was reading to them. "*Spiegiami.* Tell me," he said.

Renato scratched the corner of his eyebrow. "They come to life without a writer, and that's what the writer wanted his audience to understand." He said this kindly, inviting questions.

"All actors do that, don't they?" Virginia said, brushing crumbs from the table into her open hand.

"It's not so simple," Renato snapped. Virginia had interrupted him. "Pirandello made it clear that every creature of fantasy needs his own drama to exist."

"Fantasy is a place where it rains," Jassy said. "It doesn't rain every day." She was at the sink, rinsing off plates.

Renato held up his finger. "But in the theater it does. And my life is the theater."

Virginia stopped wiping the table and put her hands on her hips. "What about me—and your baby?" She tightened the hem of her blouse around her swollen belly.

A baby! I counted back the months on my fingers. The child would be born in February, nine months after I had been trapped in the Teatro. It was a miracle! The Blessed Mother had heard my prayers.

Renato shook his head and looked away. "My responsibility is to artists who have written plays and to the audience who come to my theater. You decided to have a baby. Not me."

"I did this alone?" Virginia's face was red.

Carlo wanted to understand Renato. "You're speaking as if you belong to a special race. Is it true, or are you insulting Virginia, and us?" Carlo sat sideways on his chair and looked over his shoulder at Renato, who remained silent. "I look at you now, and I think of an inflated balloon. If I were you I would marry her," he said. I applauded Carlo. Perhaps I had judged him too quickly. My brother was a person with principles not far from my own.

"Renato keeps a lot in his mind," Jassy interrupted, protecting Renato. "When you have a theater, you are responsible for creating an entire world, a universe within the universe we live in."

"What? You don't think Carlo—and I—carry as much responsibility?" Virginia asked.

"Yes," Jassy said. "Carlo makes money. Renato makes art. Both are important. Let's stop talking."

It was clear that Jassy's goal, besides becoming an opera singer, was to maintain the family arrangement. "This is a

86

comfortable situation," she repeated. "We have each other's support. Let's not rattle it up and destroy what we have before it has a chance to benefit us."

"I compete with no one," Renato continued. He lowered his eyes, sadly. "It comes from inside here." He tapped his broad chest.

"Everyone in America has to compete. If you're good, you rise to the top. Business is the same as art." Carlo spoke loudly.

Renato didn't say anything.

"Maybe you should listen to Carlo," Virginia echoed. "Maybe he could teach you something. He's taught me to understand money. How about charging more for tickets? Or getting a bigger theater? You don't have to suffer to be an artist. If you stopped brooding and wishing for a simpler life, we could have one. We wouldn't have to depend on other people. We could get married and have something more normal—instead of this." She sat down and crossed her arms over her big waist. "Did you ever think of that?"

Renato lifted his eyes. "I'm sorry," he said. "I don't want to disappoint anyone. If I start thinking about money, I won't do anything at all."

Jassy interrupted. "Renato is right. He has to feed his soul, not his stomach. And he needs good food." She put a big wooden bowl of pears and apples on the table, along with several knives, and a carafe of coffee. "We've worked out a system that allows each of us to fly. Why make our lives small? We're big people. Renato has his theater. Virginia will have her baby. Right?" She smiled at her friends. "Carlo has his business. We have each other at the end of a day. No one is bored." She rubbed Virginia's shoulders and spoke directly to her. "Why do you want to be alone in a house, waiting for him to come home and never knowing when? You have us," she said.

Virginia picked a green apple from the fruit bowl. With a long sharp knife, she began peeling a swirl of skin. "You haven't mentioned what you get out of this arrangement, Jassy." The silence was as slippery as the tick of the clock.

"Making it work." Jassy brushed a strand of blond hair from Virginia's cheek. Then she pulled her chair closer to Virginia. "Would anyone like me to peel them a pear?" she asked. "Virginia? We know Italian men don't peel their own fruit, don't we?" She winked at Virginia.

Virginia glared at Jassy. "We're moving away from each other, you and I. I don't like it," she said. "I used to be able to depend on you. Now you're taking their side and leaving me out." She cut her apple in half. "You think you know what's best for everyone. Tell me, Jassy, why doesn't Renato marry me?"

"I'm sorry you feel this way," Jassy said. "I hardly know everything."

"Please! Don't start on marriage again." Renato dropped his wide face into his hands. "Can't you control yourself?" he said to Virginia. He splayed his hands flat on the table. "Let me explain something. We live in the North End, and it is a small community. I don't want people to connect me to a woman, or a family. I am an artist. It's like being a priest—I don't know how else to explain it." He fiddled with his onyx ring and then spoke to all of them. "You all do more than I do for this household. Sometimes I feel guilty about that, and more often I feel guilty about having to think about it."

Virginia interrupted the silence. "You don't have money, that's the problem," she said. "It's not because you're an artist." Virginia sliced the apple in half again, so viciously that the plates on the table rattled. "If our daughter takes after you, I'm afraid I won't want her."

"Virginia! You're becoming unreasonable. Calm down." Jassy reached for her hand, but Virginia moved her arm. "Too bad we don't have a piano. I would sing now," Jassy said. "That might relieve the tension."

"Maybe Renato could move the piano from the theater up here, then you wouldn't have to continue going there for your lessons. Is that what you want—twenty-four-hour-a-day singing lessons?" Virginia was about to explode. She had been left out much too often. She cut her apple into smaller and smaller pieces.

"No, that wouldn't work. Not having a piano would interfere with my productions," Renato said, shaking his wide face. "And if you are insinuating I do anything other than teach Jassy to sing, you don't understand my soul. We've gone through this a hundred times. Why do you insist on bringing it back? The piano stays at the Teatro."

"The piano. Always the piano. No problem. I'll buy a piano," Carlo said, forcing a smile.

"We don't need a piano," Jassy said. "Next week I'm going to start private lessons in Cambridge—at the Longy School. They accepted me. I admit, I'm a little overwhelmed. But I'm determined to perfect my technique there."

"Bravo!"

"Why don't we talk about what I need?" Virginia narrowed her pale eyes and dug her fingernail into a thin slice of apple.

"Virginia, now is not the time for an argument. Have some self-respect." Renato took several peeled pieces of fruit from Virginia's plate. "Tell me more," he said to Jassy.

"I guess we're supposed to be one happy family." Virginia stood up. "If we are, I'm at the bottom. No one asks me what I want. No one ever asks me what's good for me." As was her custom, Virginia spoke up for herself too late.

"You're going to have a baby. You said that was all you wanted, that you'd be happy." Renato turned his attention back to Jassy.

Carlo pushed his chair away from the table. "Let's be sensible." He didn't finish his speech. He was going to tell Virginia she was welcome in his house, but if they needed more privacy, Carlo would offer her the second-floor apartment. It was vacant. He didn't want her and Renato to leave.

Virginia grasped the handle of the knife. She raised the blade over her head. The steel glinted against the white ceiling before it slashed down, barely missing Renato's hand. Jassy screamed and covered her face.

"There." Virginia rubbed her palms together. "If anyone is interested in what I can do, I could have hit his hand dead center." She turned on her heel to leave.

"How can you do this?" Jassy followed her. "Violence solves nothing."

"I don't care." She glared at Jassy, and then at Renato. "I'm sick of you. Sick of you all. I'm leaving."

"Don't go," Carlo said.

"I'm sorry," Jassy said. "Stay. We'll talk. Don't leave."

Virginia snatched her pocketbook off the wall hook in the kitchen. "Deposit me as a memory in your collective imaginations." She walked down the long hall, swinging her hips, and slammed the front door.

They looked at Renato. His face was white, his mouth open, and he was rubbing the back of his hand. "She'll come back," he said. "She always does. But I swear—that girl is crazy. She'll ruin me. She'll ruin us all. We better be careful. She doesn't see the light of reason." He tightened the elastic band that held his ponytail smooth against the back of his neck. "I don't understand why she behaves this way!"

Jassy wiped her lips with a napkin. "Carlo, can't we do something? I don't understand why we couldn't talk this out. I never saw Virginia so upset. It's getting worse."

"Virginia lets go of her hinges," he said. "She does it to me, too, at Spediamo. She explodes after many days of silence." Carlo gritted his teeth. "How long do you think she'll be gone this time?"

Jassy brushed her lips across Renato's forehead. "When Virginia cools down, she'll come back to us," she said to him.

Carlo put his arm around Renato's big shoulders. "I'll walk with you to the theater," he said.

"Where do you think Virginia goes when she leaves?" Jassy asked, following the men down the long hallway. "She won't tell me."

The blue sky had darkened and a new crop of clouds hung low in the sky, sagging like blankets of feathers. "It's going to snow some more," Carlo said, taking Renato's arm. "It's only December and already I've used my shovel twice."

"I'm losing my honor in your house. I can't come back," Renato said as they walked through the dusk.

Unlike the women who considered Renato a confident and gifted man, Carlo saw him as sober and severe, a man who was devoted to his passion and who was also trapped by it. "Virginia needs you more now than ever," Carlo said. "I don't judge you, or her, but I say you can be good to Virginia. The baby will be better if it knows love before it is born. Then we talk again—you and me." The men weren't accustomed to being alone with each other without the women being around, too.

"I can't marry her," Renato said. "I have nothing. Virginia says it doesn't matter. It does. I don't know what a wife or child will demand of me, or when they will make a request I cannot satisfy."

The men quickened their steps. A new salting of snow was beginning to fall. Carlo slipped, and Renato kept him from losing his balance. *"Grazie,"* Carlo said. The men kept their arms linked.

"Another thing . . ." Renato spoke to Carlo as if he were speaking to himself. "I don't want to crowd my mind with your life, and Jassy's singing. She could very well become a star. Opera is not an art for young girls. Jassy is thirty—the perfect age. I've taught her all I know, and now she is going ahead of me." Renato looked at Carlo and steadied his hazel eyes. "Sometimes I am very jealous of her."

"These women—our women—are Americans. They're tied to the future and full of hope," Carlo said. "They want to run ahead, not serve us. We must let them go, and then we'll learn something."

"All women are tied to the future," Renato answered. "It's why God created them—to torture us and to keep us going."

They didn't speak for half a block. "You and I aren't so different," Carlo said. "Virginia would be good for you."

"I need a patron, not a wife." Renato unlocked the Teatro door. The men stepped inside. "And not a baby." Renato shook the snow from his shoulders. "The young become hungry for our time and our lives. They want what we have, and they demand it immediately. Don't you remember your own impatience?" Renato unzipped his jacket. "I can't give my time away to a child. Not now. I don't have anything else."

"I have Jassy," Carlo said, looking around the Teatro lobby. "I wanted to share my life with a woman who had fire in her veins. You, and this place, gave her to me. I met her here." Carlo sat down behind the receptionist's desk. "And Jassy has me. We are important to each other. Both of us have lost our parents." He put his hat on his lap.

"Do you want me to stay and sell tickets tonight?" Carlo asked.

Renato nodded.

"When we cut a hole in the floor and joined two apartments," Carlo said, "I was more concerned about you being in my house than I was about living with two women. When you get close to another person, you sit on the same toilet, and you begin to know how often the other one shits. I didn't want you breathing down my neck. But now, after we've all been living together for three months, I think Jassy was right. Why should people hide in small families? I'm a good person. So are you. We're both men. You don't have to do this mixing up with only the people you were born to live with. You can be like a brother to me. Someone I never had."

Renato hesitated. "Everything can change like that." He snapped his fingers.

"Listen to me . . . Neither of us are going to be able to walk from the bathroom to our bedroom without hiding our balls behind a towel." Carlo held out his hand.

Renato shook it. Carlo smiled.

"When the baby comes we should hire a babysitter, someone who is sturdy and slow, and who sings the same songs our mothers used to sing to us. An Italian woman who isn't in such a hurry to get in front of us." Carlo was generous, but he also wanted Virginia and Renato to be content with each other, and for Virginia to continue working for him. Most importantly, he hoped Jassy would change her mind about having a baby. "If Jassy sees children aren't as demanding as she believes they are, maybe I can be a father, too. You can help me Renato."

The men shook hands again.

When Carlo returned to Atlantic Avenue, Jassy was sitting on the floor next to the Christmas tree, drinking tea and flipping through the newspaper. "Was Virginia at the Teatro?" she asked. "What? You didn't find her?" She followed

Carlo into the kitchen. "Pregnant women are so unreasonable! I'll go out to look for her myself." Jassy buttoned the top notch of her fur-collared coat. "She needs to talk."

"I'll go with you," Carlo said.

They didn't find her. "Maybe she checked into a hotel on the other side of Boston and is sleeping," Carlo said.

Virginia stayed away three days.

S e v e n

A month later, I received a letter from Virginia.

January 6, 1973

Ciao Alicia!
How are you? Carlo told us you missed Italy, your job, friends, and house, and that you insisted you belonged on the other side of the ocean. Too bad we didn't get to say goodbye. Jassy and I hope you will come to visit us. When you do, we'll take you shopping at Filene's Basement.

I hope it isn't an imposition, but I need to ask you a favor. As you know, I manage Carlo's shipping business. We have a large shipment coming up. In it we are consolidating ten or more people's goods into one large container. The container is being transported to Italy by boat. If I list one address on the container, it will save me time and paperwork. I was hoping I could use your address. Please don't worry. The shipment will never come to you. Our agent will receive the container in Livorno and break it down there. This would be a big help to me and, to save time, if you don't say no, I'll just go ahead and do it.

But before I sign off, I want to share some news with you. I'm pregnant—the baby's due in March. I've been very moody during the pregnancy, so we're all sure it'll be a girl. That's okay because Jassy and I want to raise more women for America. Why don't you come visit as soon as she is born?

Your friend,
Virginia

While I read Virginia's letter, lightning cracked across Subiaco's sky. I should have taken God's warning and told Virginia no. Instead I was passive. She went ahead with her plan.

Along with Virginia's letter, Jassy included a music cassette. I held it in my palm, remembering earlier times, when Carlo had written to Mama and me, and we had hoped his letters contained announcements of marriage and fatherhood. I opened the cassette's plastic case, finding a note on a small square of folded paper: "Hi Alicia! Listen to this and enjoy. I'm studying opera at the Longy School. I practice every day. Renato says if I want to be a true artist, I need tough skin—no one will hand me bread from their mouths. I'm determined not to give up! Love to you. Jassy. P.S. I'm a mezzo-soprano."

I listened. Jassy sang in Italian, a beautiful song by Rossini, about the mystery of love. In half my mind I thanked her for having taken my brother into her heart and keeping Carlo's culture alive. The other half of my brain fumed. How dare she pretend to be who she wasn't! Jassy was not an Italian, nor was she an honest women. She had no right to be sleeping in my brother's bed, eating his food, or earning her money in his shop. It was her fault I was not in America. Jassy was corrupting Carlo, using him to buy time, perfecting her art while imitating his accent.

That day I prayed Jassy would leave Carlo, and the next morning, as I ran through the damp field behind my house to the path that led me to St. Scholastica Clinic, I reproached myself for being so disgruntled about my own life, and Jassy's supposed interference. I said a prayer to Virginia's unborn child. Children in a womb are pure grace, as holy as sanctified saints, and powerful messengers. I asked that the child transport them all safely through the passage that left no one responsible for just themselves. And I prayed that when she was born, my brother might realized how important I was to him, and that I had taken a step longer than my leg when I had sworn to never lay eyes on him again. I trusted the child would help me.

The months previous to the child's birth, I often transported my senses across the Atlantic to the North End of Boston. I didn't want to miss anything, and I felt guilty about spying on Carlo and his friends but blamed a flaw of science. I told myself it wasn't my own power and curiosity that brought the visions to me; the Early Bird satellite orbiting the earth was leaking the messages. It wasn't until six years later, when I myself moved to America, that I appreciated how much these visions had taught me about the people whom I would live with in the land of the free.

For example, the first of March, when I looked over to Boston from my cot in Subiaco, I heard a butcher's wife moan. *"Mamma mia!"* she said. Carlo was parading not only Jassy, but also a very pregnant Virginia, on his arms down Hanover Street. "Who does the child belong to? Who is the father?" the wife asked, clicking her tongue. "It could be the man from the Teatro who hides his balls in his baggy pants," a customer answered. My Mama was right. She always used to say, "Italians enjoy gossiping as much as they enjoy pasta." It was as true in America as it was in Italy. She also said, "Italians make revenge as good as they make pasta."

I might have had more respect for my brother and the others' privacy. Watching, I learned that Carlo often woke Jassy up in the middle of the night just to hear her voice. After dinner, while Carlo washed the dishes, Jassy massaged Virginia's back and legs and read her poems by female poets. Late at night, I sometimes saw Renato scrounging around the trash in the alley behind Carlo's apartment building. He looked for chairs, lamp shades, or small round tables that could be used in his theater productions. Just seeing him, with his ponytail and strong-boned Italian face, stirred me to bite the moon.

The second week of March was a busy week for me—I attended twelve open-heart operations. On Friday afternoon, exhausted, I lay on my cot, letting my mind drift across the ocean to my brother Carlo's house. It was morning in Boston. Carlo was in the kitchen with Jassy who was preparing the breakfast. While their eggs boiled, Jassy sang him a lullaby. She stood in the yellow kitchen beside the two-oven stove. Sun fingered through the venetian blinds, laying stripes across her slippers and the black and white floor. Her hair was wild and curly. When she looked at Carlo, her eyes widened. So did his, and I didn't doubt they were in love.

Carlo sipped his coffee. She keeps getting better, he thought to himself. Her voice was richer. He was sure that one day Jassy would leave them to perform. But he was also sure she would come back. Jassy would only belong to a man who let her have freedom. Carlo gave her that.

The egg timer chimed. Virginia, heavy bellied, wobbled up

the spiral staircase, followed by Renato, who held her hips to stabilize her balance. "The smell of coffee and sound of singing woke us up," he said. Virginia and Renato held each other's hands.

I felt so cold. At that moment I hated the two sets of lovers for being happy. I screamed at the spring sky outside my window. None of them had made promises to each other. They had no rules. No family. No religion. I had made many promises, lived by God's commandments, yet I was alone. I knelt on the floor, imploring St. Joseph, the Child Jesus's own father, to curse Renato and Carlo. They were not worthy to be fathers, I said. And then I quickly tried to capture my words, hoping they had not bled into the world, penetrating the divine parts of the sky where prayers are received.

I saw them again—Carlo, Jassy, Renato, and Virginia— content and crowded in the big yellow Boston kitchen. The stove made the room hot. The coffee smelled delicious, deep and dark. Carlo made more toast for everyone, buttering it for the Americans and leaving it dry for himself and Renato. Renato stirred sugar into Virginia's tea and spread honey on her bread. Jassy looked up from the morning newspaper and smiled at them over the wire frames of her glasses.

Then Carlo took his hat from the rack near the hall door and descended the five flights of steps to the street. Outside, he hailed the sun shining on the harbor. It was a bright day, as lovely as the previous day had been in Subiaco. He turned onto Richmond Street, feeling like a teenager, filled with the desire to make his life perfect.

He passed delivery trucks parked close to the curb. They were noisy. Their drivers unloaded boxes of meat, flour, and vegetables, and shifted the goods onto carts and wheeled them into the restaurants and shops just opening their metal-grate doors.

The old man, who cleaned Carlo's shops, was waiting for

him. *"È una bella giornata,"* he said. "Today do you have a 'giobbe' for me, boss?"

Carlo lifted Freedom Drugs' metal grating. The red *Herald* truck had just dropped off the morning papers. "Sure. Bring in the newspapers and stack them near the cash register. Then sweep the aisles," Carlo said, handing Tommaso a ten-dollar bill.

"Grazie." Tommaso quickly pocketed the cash. Most days Carlo gave him five.

In his cookware shop, Carlo passed the copper polenta pots and pasta machines and entered the back office. His desk was stacked with bills and purchase orders. He shoved them aside and uncapped his black fountain pen. On a piece of scrap paper, Carlo added, divided, and multiplied. In the past year his businesses, except the Blue Note, had doubled their receipts. Spediamo had done especially well. America had been good to him.

With the tip of his foot, Carlo pushed open the office door. The cookware shop floors were splintered, the tin ceiling stained. The lighting wasn't good either. Still, he figured, if he remodeled, the store might lose charm and, perhaps, customers. In the North End, it was best not to show money. Remodeling was a stagnating prospect. Carlo believed the secret to staying ahead was to move dollars as if they were blood. He told himself he had to push money away to keep more coming back.

I listened to my brother's thoughts, not agreeing with them. You could buy blood with money, I said to myself, but I was too naive to realize money, too, could be bought with blood. Still Carlo and I were alike in one way. We both hid the money we had, and we had more than any of our neighbors imagined.

Saturday, I watched Carlo again. I sensed Virginia would deliver soon. Her belly had dropped and her chin had doubled. I found them in the Spediamo office.

"Carlo, I can't believe so many people want to go backward," she said when he handed her a dozen names and telephone numbers. "What's so great about Italy? Why do they all want to move back?"

Carlo raised his shoulders. "I guess the Italian people feel at home in Italy. They come to America to make money—that's all. After they get it, they leave. Not me. I can be myself better here. Everybody knows me."

"I guess the others don't stay long enough to realize this is the best country in the world," Virginia said. "And there's Renato—he's hopeless with money. He couldn't go backward if he wanted to. He has to depend on me."

Carlo was careful of Virginia's revolving-door temperament. Sometimes she was so sweet Carlo could taste her; other times Virginia was nasty. Once, in a huff, not too long after she had nearly spiked a knife through Renato's hand, Virginia had confessed to him that her nastiness surfaced when no one paid attention to her. Carlo thought that this might be one of those days.

"You're right," he said. "How are you feeling?"

"Good," she answered, satisfied.

But Virginia was doing something right, Carlo said to himself. Customers never walked away from Spediamo. They enjoyed talking to Virginia. She asked them about the houses they had left in Italy and their families. If they were sending a daughter back to get married, Virginia wanted to know about the prospective husband. But what surprised Carlo the most was that the men who loitered on Hanover Street would often stop by Spediamo to say hello to Virginia. They never spoke to Jassy. He didn't know they were the Benevolents, and that Virginia was shipping something special for them.

101

The telephone rang. Carlo and Virginia reached for it at the same time. *"Pronto,"* Carlo said.

It was Spediamo's agent in Rome. "We have a problem," he said. "Your last shipment came into the port of Livorno." He spoke slowly. "As usual, they opened one trunk labeled HOUSEHOLD GOODS. There were five guns in it."

"Guns? In whose trunk?" Carlo decided to blame Virginia. Customers might be fond of her, but she didn't understand psychology. Her customers would lie rather than ask questions and appear to be stupid.

The agent continued. "Now the *carabinieri* are involved. They are breaking locks on every Spediamo trunk. Fortunately, they stopped insisting on returning the goods to Boston. There's going to be a delay." The agent cleared his throat.

"That can't happen. I'll send money." Carlo found a paper cup on the file cabinet and drained its cold bitter coffee.

"What? Are you asking me to bribe government officials?"

"One trunk is full of wedding clothes," Carlo said. "I promised the family that their daughter's white dress wouldn't be unfolded." Carlo couldn't afford to have Hanover Street find out he had disappointed a bride.

"I don't know what I can do." The agent paused, and Carlo knew he was contemplating the proposal, guessing how much Carlo might offer him.

Carlo didn't name a number. "None of us wants the other to know what we have under our hats, right? It's as true in the old country as in America," Carlo said. "Italians hate authority, and we hate other people knowing the details of our business."

Both men waited.

"It's okay. I'll get in touch with my friend in Rome," Virginia whispered to Carlo. "He can straighten it out. The guns aren't the problem. Let me take the call."

Carlo realized Virginia was pulling something from her sleeve, and it might solve the problem without costing Spediamo money. "Here's Virginia," he said to the agent, handing over the phone, scratching his thick hair. Carlo didn't hear the agent's voice crackle on the other end.

The agent said he didn't know Ulbaldini personally but he knew who he was.

"I'll telex him today." Virginia scribbled on a pad near the telephone. "Don't worry, he knows the pope," she said.

"Ah—there's one more thing," the agent said.

"What?" Virginia answered.

"Yesterday, when they went through your shipment, they unwrapped a five-foot statue of St. Lucy. The *carabinieri* stepped back when they saw the statue and her eyeballs on the golden plate. But in a few minutes, a new shift of government officials arrived and rushed the statue through paperwork."

"I guess the saint had her documents in order," Virginia said smartly.

"I don't know. They pulled the papers from my hands before I had a look at where the saint was going."

"Was there damage?"

Carlo spilled a tablespoon of Brioschi into a glass. The water fizzed up like fur as he downed the foamy drink, waiting for a burp to untangle his stomach. He'd have to talk to Virginia and ask her how soon after the baby was born she would be able to come back to work. He knew nothing about operating Spediamo.

I shut off my vision. It was nine in the evening in Subiaco. I looked out my kitchen window. If I stood on tiptoe, I could see the illuminated billboard for Fiat cars at the entrance to the expressway, less than half a kilometer away. I hoped no

103

one would come down the ramp to get me. I was sure the container Virginia had written to me about, the one detained in Livorno, had been addressed to me. I scratched the glass with my fingertips. If strangers knocked on my door, they would ask questions. Why hadn't I told her no? I clutched the collar of my nurse's uniform and opened the front buttons to free my neck. It felt as if someone was choking me. I was terrified. No one had stepped into my house since the day Carlo had come to see Mama, and she had already been buried.

I didn't sleep that night, or the next, and I called the clinic to report in sick. If I stayed home and prayed, I believed the saints would protect me from misfortune.

Six days later I returned to work and began eating my lunch in the hospital supply room. The small room was more protective than the cafeteria, where no one spoke to me anyway. I sat on a rubber-topped stool sipping cans of tomato juice and orange juice and eating cookies from packages and ham sandwiches slated for patients. There were no windows in the supply room, only shelves of adhesive tape, oxygen tanks, and alcohol.

At night I whispered late-night cries against Virginia, Carlo, Jassy—even Renato—but they did not die. I waited and waited and no one from the shipping docks came to Subiaco to arrest me.

Eight

"Today is really it!" I heard Jassy say to Carlo over the phone. Virginia had begun her labor. Apparently during the past few weeks, she had had several false alarms.

Birthing the baby at home was Jassy and Virginia's idea. Carlo later told me both women were adamant about doing it the "natural way," without the interference of drugs. Coming into the world within a loving environment was best for child and mother, they had explained to him. Carlo and Renato had had little reason to argue. Both the men had been born during the war, in Italy, as Carlo said—"when there were no hospitals to house mothers. And we turned out all right."

As far as I was concerned, having a baby at home was a foolish decision. When I found out what was about to happen, had I been able to transport more than my senses across the Atlantic, I would have sent them my hands and common sense. The household needed a nurse, someone exactly like myself, who was qualified to manage the pain and the joy of what was to come.

From my cot in Subiaco, I watched Jassy fill two huge pots with water. It was Sunday and eleven o'clock in Italy; five o'clock in Boston. Jassy put the pots on the stove to boil.

105

Carlo, Virginia, and Renato were in the kitchen with her, leaning on their elbows, losing themselves in her movements. At home, Jassy had always told them what to do.

She stapled shut two paper bags. Inside each bag were several towels and a sheet. "Three hundred twenty-five degrees will do it," she said, adjusting the oven thermometer. "An hour in the oven will sterilize everything."

Virginia sucked in her lips and dropped her fist on the table. Renato's big face whitened. He seemed to be as uncomfortable as Virginia.

"Oh, no. Hurting already?" Jassy asked, guiding Virginia down the hall to her bedroom. At that moment, the women walked alike. Their rhythm was rooted in an old friendship, and from having lived together, doing dishes, scrubbing the same bathtubs, and eating the same food for the past four years. Rather than move like a bird, Jassy adjusted herself, sinking into her feet to help Virginia.

"I'm afraid," Virginia said, clutching her belly. "If this is the beginning, I won't make it to the end."

"Maybe you'll be lucky, maybe your baby will just slip out." Jassy tapped Virginia's bedside copy of *Spiritual Midwifery*. "The book said it can happen during a rush, if you think of pain as a wave you ride." Jassy smoothed Virginia's forehead. "You crash, and it's over. You'll do fine," Jassy assured her. "We're prepared for everything."

Virginia's bangs exaggerated her pouty lips. Jassy stroked her small hand. "Tomorrow, when I hold my daughter in my arms, these fears will be forgotten," she said, adding, "I'll just have new fears."

Jassy handed Virginia a glass of chipped ice. "To suck on," she explained. "I'm going to check on how the guys are getting along with the lobsters." One of the pots of water was for lobsters. "It's the best food for a woman in labor—high in protein, low in fat, easy to digest."

106

The men, in the kitchen, were arguing about what to do with the rubber bands clamping shut the lobster claws.

"Leave the bands on," Renato said.

"No. They must have one last chance to grab something before they die," Carlo insisted.

"Why tease them?" Renato scoffed. "What if they hurt each other?"

"I say, let them think they are free. They will die happy, and their meat will be sweeter."

Renato shook his head. "I want mine with the bands on. Jassy, how about you?" She had just entered the kitchen.

"Without the rubber band," she said, pushing her wire-rim glasses up to the bridge of her nose. "Wouldn't you rather die doing what you like to do best—theater—than be thrown into a pot of hot water wearing handcuffs and a blindfold?"

"You're suggesting lobsters have brains."

"Feelings, maybe, or souls—something. Don't we all?" Jassy said.

"Only humans." Renato tugged his ponytail. "We're the superior species."

"What about the characters in your plays?" Carlo pointed to Renato. "Didn't you once explain that all art has soul—paintings and sculpture, and sometimes buildings, and even theaters?"

They cooked the lobsters without the rubber bands on their claws, except one.

At dinner, Virginia sat at the head of the table. Her pale hair glimmered in the candlelight. But, when a contraction squeezed her insides, her face lost its delicacy, and her mouth tightened into a frightening sneer. Everyone stared at the transformation. Carlo longed to ease her pain, and at the same time knew he couldn't.

"Mia cara," he said, reaching for her hand. "We under-

stand." He noticed her skin was thinner than Jassy's but warmer.

"I'm sorry," Virginia said, "I don't know what I'm doing. I don't know who any of you are." She put her head in her arms.

"It's like the theater," Renato said. "We all pay to be born."

Jassy stood to brush a strand of hair off Virginia's forehead. "We're here with you."

"But none of you know what I'm going through." Virginia dug her fingernails into her forearm. "The way you're all looking at me makes me feel I'm a freak."

"No, no, no."

"You're safe."

"It's imagination talking."

Virginia rested her head in her hands. "What have I been doing all these years? I'm not ready for this," she moaned. "I don't know who I am. How can I be someone's mother?"

"You'll be a fine mother," Renato said. He knelt on the floor beside her, bowing his head to her belly.

Virginia touched his head. "I'm sorry," she said. "We're connected in a way that can never be pulled apart. You're inside me now."

They called the doctor at ten o'clock that evening. None of them had expected the process would take so long. The hour before the doctor arrived, Renato paced the long hallway outside her room. Virginia was screaming. "What! Are we all idiots?" he said. "I can't believe I once suggested she have her baby in the theater! This is not the Middle Ages. This is America. Everyone is born in a hospital!" He threw up his hands. "How will I ever take care of them?"

Carlo paced with him. "I'll call an ambulance. We'll go to the hospital. Right away."

Jassy stayed in the room with Virginia, logging the length

of each contraction. "Everything's progressing according to the charts," she said.

But even from as far away as Subiaco, I could see Jassy, too, was terrified. Labor was destructive and violent, seeming to destroy and create, asking both child and mother: do you really want to be born again?

Jassy stepped outside the room. "I'll agree with whatever Virginia wants," she said to the men. "Drugs could help her."

Virginia shouted from the bedroom. "I don't want to go to a hospital and be pumped with Novocain, or have my crotch slit open with a razor blade. I want to stay here. And close the door," she demanded. "This experience is mine!"

The doctor arrived. She had had trouble finding a parking space in the North End. "Let me take your coat," Carlo said to her. She had gray hair, strong arms, and a small black bag.

"Is the water ready and sheets sterilized?" she asked, before checking Virginia.

In the kitchen, Carlo tied a striped apron around his waist, dumped lobster shells in the trash, and loaded the dishwasher. He thought this night would be the first of many nights when there would be crying in his house.

Renato locked himself in the bathroom. Jassy sat in her bedroom reading an opera book.

When the doctor came out of Virginia's bedroom, she sat at the big round table, drinking the tea sweetened with honey that Carlo had set out for her.

"How much longer?" Carlo asked.

"It could be ten minutes or ten hours," the doctor said, patting the bun at the back of her head. "She's doing fine."

Two hours later, Virginia opened her bedroom door and calmly called out, "It's time." Her eyes shone from the inside.

Jassy took her place on a cushioned chair to the right of Virginia's head. Carlo sat behind the bed in the rocking chair, near the window. He folded his hands in his lap and placed his feet firmly on the floor so the rocker wouldn't creak. When Virginia screamed, he patted his temples.

"Exhale," Jassy whispered to Virginia.

Virginia pulled her lips tight over her teeth, squeezed her eyes shut, and let out a long moan.

"Push again," the doctor said.

Renato stood behind the doctor, at the foot of the bed, leaning forward each time the doctor examined Virginia's progress.

The muffled sound of a car horn drifted through the curtained window.

Virginia bit her bottom lip.

"Okay. Push!"

"I can't," Virginia murmured. "I've changed my mind. I don't want a baby." She pulled her arms together and made a fist. Howling, she jerked forward and pushed the baby back inside her body. The doctor grabbed Virginia's hands. "I don't want a baby!" Virginia shouted. "Not now!"

Jassy patted her friend's sweaty forehead with a cool washcloth. "Don't hold it in. Let go."

Virginia rolled her head back.

Carlo wished he weren't there. This was women's business, he told himself. No man should be here, not even Renato. He tried to disappear into the shadows of the corner of the room.

"Push!"

No one moved. The room froze in silence as the baby's head crowned between Virginia's white thighs. The doctor slipped its shoulders and feet loose from the mother.

"Ringraziamo la Madonna." Renato knelt at the foot of the bed, burying his head in the palms of his hands. "Praise

the Madonna," he said. "This is amazing! I do not believe it. *Questo è un miracolo!*"

The doctor held the child up in the air like a prize. The baby stared down at them with fisted hands and eyes as fierce as the rim of the universe.

"Mamma mia." Carlo blessed himself. A draft from the window caused the long curtains to dance.

"It's a girl," the doctor said.

Jassy stood up. "One of us," she said. "Good work, Virginia!"

The doctor opened the paper bags and wrapped the baby in a sterile sheet, and then placed her on Virginia's belly.

"My daughter. My sweet, sweet daughter," Virginia said, touching her child's creamy flesh. "You're wonderful." She clutched the baby against her bare breast, choking on her own gentle words.

The others turned their backs and left the room.

I had watched the birth from my ringside seat in Subiaco. I told myself the child and I had a special connection. Not only had I seen her soul drop from the sky and enter her mother's womb, I had also witnessed her birth. She might as well be mine, I said.

Less than an hour later, Renato held his infant daughter. Virginia opened the window. "Let's show her the stars," she said, "and show the stars our baby." It was a clear March night, though still somewhat chilly. I hoped the air would not affect the baby's liver.

I reached out into the morning sky to hold the child as if she were curled and swaddled in my own arms, and I asked the saints to bless her.

Virginia closed the window.

Renato uncorked a bottle of champagne, which splashed to the ceiling.

111

The doctor left.

Carlo was not in the same celebratory mood as the others. He put on his hat and said, "I have to go out for a while."

Of course, I followed my brother, walking happily beside him, breathing the same sea-scented air, welcoming the new baby, and introducing her to the saints I was familiar with. But when I realized Carlo was on the way to the cookware store to call me, I stiffened. The birth had reminded him of his own beginning, and of me, his twin. I wasn't prepared to forgive my brother, not that day. That day belonged to the child.

On Hanover Street, Carlo fumbled through his heavy load of keys. His eyes were blurry and his fingers numb. He couldn't stop seeing himself wrapped in his sister's blackness. I don't have a mother or father, he thought. I want Alicia to love me.

In the back room of the cookware shop, he turned on a light and tore through the scraps of paper in the bottom drawer of his desk. My brother hadn't memorized our telephone number. It was four in the morning in Boston, because at ten o'clock in Subiaco my telephone rang.

I didn't answer it. I was unable, at that time, to incorporate forgiveness with my joy and envy, my embarrassment, and my love. It was good I was not able to do so. My hesitation saved Carlo's life.

The moment he hung up, a gang of North End men rushed through the open door of the cookware shop and into the back room. I screamed to warn Carlo. "They have guns," I said. But Carlo couldn't hear me. He was wondering why I might not have answered his call. I grabbed my rosary beads.

As I lifted my right hand to my forehead to make the sign of the cross, Carlo ducked to the floor to pick up a pencil. A gun's bullet blasted a hole the size of a cabbage in the center of the calendar tacked on the wall behind his desk.

"*Aspetta! Aspetta!*" Carlo crouched on his hands and knees. His head dropped, and his heart pressed behind his hears. He struggled to speak. "*Sono io.* I'm Carlo," he said, licking the taste of gunpowder off the back of his teeth.

"Carlo?" someone said stupidly. "Carlo Barzini? *Sei tu?* Is that you?"

"Hey. We almost killed Carlo." The men were surprised.

The blast still echoed on the roof of Carlo's mouth. He wasn't sure if he was dead or dreaming, or who the men standing in his office might be.

"One of you guys, go back there and look under the desk. Find out if it's him," the boss ordered. "*Mannaggia la Madonna!* Carlo wouldn't rob his own store, would he?"

"Not me," one said. "I'm not doing it. You do it."

"Go on. You." One man kicked another. They were bunglers.

Under his desk, Carlo counted the toes of five pairs of black shoes on the floor in front of him.

"What if it isn't Carlo? What if he has a gun?"

"Whoever's under there sounds like Carlo."

"Carlo? Tell us something no one else would know."

"Like what?" he answered. Carlo's arms were shaking. "This is my store. I own it and the drugstore, the music store . . ."

". . . and the tall red-haired woman?"

"Yes."

"Okay. Put your hands on the desk."

"Only if you don't shoot," Carlo said. "I live in the North End and pay extra not to be terrorized." The brim of his cap was wet with his sweat. Carlo crawled out from under the desk.

"Hey! Look at that! He's who he said he was." The oldest man smiled at Carlo as he helped my brother to his feet.

Carlo brushed the dust from his knees. "You almost killed

me." He turned to look at the hole in the wall. "That was almost my head." Carlo's lips trembled. "Why are you here?"

I kissed the rosary in my hand. My brother was safe.

"The door was open," the short middle-aged man said. "We thought someone was robbing you. It's our job to protect you, eh?" He tucked a handgun into the sagging pocket of his leather coat.

"We better get out before the police come," warned another man, who wore an eye patch.

"Who would report a gun shot in the North End?" They shoved the man with the eye patch. *Stupido.* The Boston police don't make their rounds till five-thirty. We've got twenty minutes."

"Let's help Carlo lock up."

Carlo didn't recognize the men who had ambushed him. "Who are you?" he asked, following along in the pack of their footsteps.

None answered.

Years later I understood the men who shot at Carlo that night were Benevolents. Most of the Benevolents were strictly religious men who took no money other than an honorarium for summer parades. But a dozen or more were also members of the North End Patrol, immigrant men who were paid to keep an eye on who was coming and going in the neighborhood. They collected extra wages from merchants, like Carlo, who wanted round-the-clock protection.

None of the Benevolents knew exactly how involved the others were. Not wanting to appear to be stupid, or less important than the other, the men didn't ask questions. And when they weren't in the North End, parading or patrolling, many of the Benevolents worked underground. They were members of the Local Tunnel Union, and, during the 1970s, dug the Boston subway extension. The day Virginia's baby was born, none of us suspected our lives would someday rest in these men's clumsy hands.

After the men helped Carlo cover the hole in his wall, they accompanied him to his building on Atlantic Avenue. As soon as Carlo unlocked the front door, they disappeared.

Carlo crept up the steps. Virginia and the baby were sleeping. Jassy was asleep, too. Renato must have gone to the Teatro, he thought. Carlo spent the morning alone in his kitchen.

I sat on my cot in my kitchen in Subiaco. My brother and I were an ocean apart, but a blanket as warm as the blood that once joined us covered us both. I listened to my brother's thoughts and made them my own. We lifted the lid on the trunk where Mama used to store her extra fabric, smelling the bay leaves and lavender flakes. Together we saw the hills and rocks behind our house, the roosters next door, and we listened to the caresses, whines, and bellows of our Italian tongue. Neither of us went to work that day.

Carlo thought about all he had left behind to come to America, to live in Boston next to the Freedom Trail, which was inches away from where he had nearly lost his life. He had cut his heart, and mine, in half, he told himself. He was ready to sell everything and return to Italy. And I was willing to forfeit my righteousness. But Jassy entered the kitchen, interrupting us. She always did. I cursed her. Carlo had almost been mine.

"Carlo, my dear," she said softly. Her red hair was ruffled and uncombed. "What's wrong? You're sad." She had just gotten out of bed.

He hunched over his lap. "Everything could have disappeared. Forever. You. Me. The past and time that hasn't gotten here yet."

Jassy stood close to him. She patted his thick hair. "You have me."

115

Carlo didn't take her hand. "What do you do when some-one hurts you?" he asked. "Do you forgive them right away and wipe them from your memory, or do you decide not to let their memory reach you? Do you stop carrying them and just go on?"

Jassy stooped to force him to look into her eyes. "You're thinking about Alicia, aren't you?"

He nodded his head. "I shouldn't worry about my sister," he said. "I just hope she is safe and clean and has found someone kind to love her."

Jassy patted Carlo's chest. "Call her," she said. "But now follow me." She led him out of the kitchen, down the long hallway to their bedroom, undressed him, and lifted his feet onto their bed.

I respected Carlo's privacy. I rolled off my cot onto the cold kitchen floor. No one was there to catch me when I fell.

That evening my phone rang several times. I was sure it was Carlo. I was no longer interested in forgiving him. It had been too easy for Jassy to wipe me from his cries. I decided to begin living my own life.

I was brave. The next afternoon, after work, I ventured into Subiaco square to buy yarn for Virginia's baby.

I pulled the brim of a straw hat over my eyes. The sky was big; if I had seen how much was above me, I would not have been able to move my feet. Despite the shield, as soon as I stepped beyond the monastery, my breathing tightened, and I stumbled. A group of people standing at the top of the hill saw me fall. I quickly stood up on my own.

At the first corner, I was able to see it hadn't changed much. The square was still paved with light brown bricks, there was a row of shops on the south side, and Gina Lollo-brigida's statue stood on the west side. Miss Lollobrigida had been born in Subiaco, two years after my mother.

I inhaled the scent of coffee, which wafted from a nearby

cafe. But the delicious aroma did not stir me to enjoy more of the pleasure that I had for so long been denying myself. My feet sank into the sidewalk. I remember thinking, How dare the people sitting, talking, spitting, laughing stop what they were doing to say I was a stranger when I was one of them?

I ran. On the trails behind the monastery I lied to myself, saying I'd go out again another day. But I knew I had no choice but to knit a cap for Virginia's child from the old, unraveled yarn given to me by the Subiaco Benevolents. I had so much wanted my gift to be new and pink.

Once home, I scurried through the barricades that separated my kitchen from the rest of the house. In my old bedroom, I unhinged the locks hammered shut on the trunk to find the dozen soft sweaters and booties Mama and I had knitted for Carlo's baby—the one we were sure would arrive, but had never been born. They were perfumed with bay leaves and lavender flakes. I sent the newborn clothing to Virginia's child.

N i n e

May 3, 1975

Dear Alicia.

Thank you for the baby clothes. They're beautiful! Did you make them yourself? I am sorry for not writing sooner, but I've been taking care of my baby.

We have named her Bebe, though all of us call her Bimba, since she is so small. She is tiny—six pounds at birth—and wakes up several times during the night. Caring for her has divided the men from the women. I breast-feed her and wake up two times a night. Jassy and I do most of the work. I don't know what I'd do without her. Carlo helps, too—Bebe makes him feel important. He changes diapers and rushes home after closing his shops. Carlo likes to take care of people. But Renato has his head in the clouds and his hands in his pockets. He does nothing but stroll around the apartment saying, "Children are less problem than producing plays." You're right, I tell him—when you have two women tending the crib. But he doesn't hear me. What's most important is that Bebe has made us all remember and have hope. She's our little prayer to the future. We want the best for her, and each other.

I went back to work at Spediamo a week after she was born. Carlo didn't know what to do there without me. It's been okay because Jassy works with me two days a week, on the days she isn't singing or practicing. Bebe often comes to the Spediamo office, too. We have a crib and playthings there for her.

I want to ask you if you mind about me using your address again. We're putting together another large shipment. Your cooperation would really help reduce my paperwork and the hours I spend in the office. Thanks.

I hope this letter finds you in good health. Jassy and I wonder why you don't write. I have included a picture of Bebe in one of the outfits you sent to us.

Truly yours,
Virginia

As usual, there was something from Jassy in the big yellow envelope. This time, instead of music, Jassy sent a letter.

Cara Alicia,
Virginia is amazing! I've learned so much about patience from her. The baby is spectacular. Virginia was meant to be a mother. Me? I don't know yet. Renato has told me, "Have one of your own—bearing a child expands a singer's range at least one note on top and another on the bottom.

Bearing a child will help your career." So I'm thinking about it! Carlo assures me motherhood isn't as demanding as I've always expected it was. But I don't know if I'd ever be as good at it as Virginia is. Still, Carlo is eager. Where are you on this count? Why don't you write or call us? We miss you. Carlo sends his love.

Baci,
Jassy

The women had included a green rattle shaped like a boot and printed with white lettering that said: BEBE RICCI BORN 18 MARCH '75. On the other side of the rattle the lettering was red: CALL SPEDIAMO IN ITALIA 782-9901. Carlo never missed a chance. Bebe's birth had become an opportunity to promote his business.

After I received Virginia's letter, and thanks, I allowed myself to project my senses across the Atlantic again. When I did, I saw the beautiful Bebe asleep in the nursery. Her fingernails were flower petals and her hair was softer than spring grass. Virginia wasn't at home yet. The others were eating dinner—bean soup, bread, and salad.

Sighing, Renato pulled at the crust of his bread. No words passed between the men. Virginia's moodiness had gotten worse since the baby had been born. What difference did money make? Carlo asked himself. Renato loved her. How would he feel if another man wanted to make Virginia his wife?

When Renato left for the Teatro, Carlo complained to Jassy. "Why doesn't Renato pull air into himself instead of pushing out so much around here? His sighing makes it hard for everyone else to breathe," he said.

120

"He keeps a lot in his mind," Jassy answered. "When you're an artist, you create an entire world, a universe within the universe we live in."

"What? You don't think I carry as much responsibility?" It was an old argument between them. "Don't forget—I support the arts, and artists. And what about the lives I ship across the Atlantic to Italy?" Carlo's eyes flashed.

"Doesn't Virginia do that for you?" Jassy answered.

"Where is she?"

The table was left set with one clay-colored bowl and polished silverware.

Carlo ran his fingers through his hair. "Maybe she doesn't like bean soup."

"Shhh. The baby's crying." Jassy checked her watch. "The Bimba's up early. Did Virginia leave milk in the refrigerator?"

Bebe pressed her downy head against Jassy's breast. They sat together in the nursery while Carlo heated the milk. Jassy undid the front of her blouse. "Everything will be okay," she whispered, giving Bebe her own breast.

But Bebe cried more desperately. She was hungry and needing more than comfort. Jassy held the infant closer.

"Don't you worry about anything. I'll take care of you. We all will," she said.

Bebe relaxed. Carlo handed the bottle to Jassy.

When he saw them in the rocker, with Jassy singing and holding the bottle, he wanted to make her pregnant. It was exactly what I didn't want. No, I said to myself, my brother cannot go against what our parents had taught us, and he can't have milk without buying the cow.

In the middle of the night, I was watching the shadow of Bebe's eyelashes on her chubby cheeks and listening to her breathe when I heard Virginia's footsteps in the long hallway. She lifted Bebe out of the crib.

"I couldn't leave," she whispered, taking Babe into her own bed. "I love you too much. You make me afraid to die."

Virginia lay beside her daughter, holding her in the crescent of her curved torso. "I want the world to get smaller and smaller and everyone else to go away," Virginia said. "Why can't I have that?"

Bebe patted her mother's thin cheek. She understood. And so did I. I stationed my spirit beside them like a guardian angel. They were two seeds—one large, one small—tucked against each other. I continued to stand guard in Boston, admiring the mother and her child, and their beautiful storm of grace.

Of course I was unable to drift off to sleep, and while I watched them I began wondering about saints. To be a saint a person had to overflow with grace, and those who entered heaven spewing the most grace could stand closer to God. But once in heaven, the saints no longer need their excess grace, and God recycled it back to earth where it was given away, or sold as indulgences. I had learned the Church distributed these indulgences, like money or blood, to priests, who injected it into souls during the sacraments of baptism, marriage, and extreme unction. That was all right. But what if a person wasn't Catholic? And who actually delivered the indulgences to earth—God, angels, or children? Did it twist and fall down the hole that Mama and Papa said was directly above the Vatican? That night I questioned what I had been taught. I believed excess grace was everywhere and rained all over the world, to all people, and that it couldn't be claimed by any religion.

* * *

Throughout the next year, I did a lot of spying on my brother. It became a habit. I was mostly interested in catching him with Bebe, or Virginia, and I had convinced myself that my ability to see across the Atlantic and peer into Carlo's life was no different from other people's television watching. Usually I tuned into the North End at midnight in the evening, Subiaco time.

It was six o'clock in Boston. Carlo closed his cookware store, dividing the cash from the register according to the presidents' faces. "Hamilton, Jackson, Grant," he said. "Ah! A Franklin, my favorite." He tucked the money into his black bag, and the bag under his shirt. Next he closed the Blue Note, where Jassy no longer worked, and walked one block up Hanover Street to Spediamo. This was when I usually saw Bebe.

While I tickled her with my praise, Carlo counted the cash and reviewed the day's business with Virginia. From what I can remember, Virginia never said anything to Carlo about the Benevolents.

One December evening, after the colored lights had been strung across Hanover, I followed Carlo into Spediamo, hoping to see Virginia and the baby. But it was Virginia's day off, and Jassy was there instead. Usually when Carlo met Jassy, I picked up my sewing, or my English grammar book and stopped watching. But that day I stayed tuned in.

"I have something for you." Carlo handed Jassy a paper bag. "It's the scarf Alicia knit for me when I left Italy," he said.

I was angry! I had run the yarn through my fingers for my brother, not her.

Jassy took the tasseled strip of green wool from the bag. Carlo unfolded it for her to admire.

"The scarf was in the bottom of the trunk, in our bedroom, and so scented with mothballs I had to hang it outside, on the balcony, for a day to make it smell like the North End," Carlo said, watching the expression in Jassy's eyes to assure himself she liked it.

"I don't have a mother or a father, but they watched my sister knit this for me," he said. "If you make it yours, I hope they will watch our child growing inside you." He held out the scarf.

"Certainly, Carlo," Jassy said. Her red hair, cut shorter, curled over her ears. She fingered the wool as she wrapped the scarf over her shoulders. Had I been physically present, I would have tightened the scarf around her neck and choked her. How dare she accept the scarf I made for Carlo!

But Jassy redeemed herself. She always did. "Carlo? After the baby comes, why don't we visit Alicia? You never talk about her anymore." She dropped her arms over Carlo's shoulders.

Baby? I repeated to myself. It was only then I realized Jassy was pregnant and that Carlo was giving a part of me to his lover.

"I hope my sister and I will have learned something from being apart," Carlo said.

I had been stitching holiday costumes for the saints. The needle was still in my hand, and the oil lantern sputtered the last of its fuel. My vision blurred, tears rolled down my cheeks, and I lost sight of my brother. The news of the baby touched me in a way that renewed my hope. I believed Carlo was going to make everything right. He was going to apologize to me, and return peace to our dead parents.

I sent a statue of St. Anne, the patron saint of motherhood, to Boston for Christmas.

* * *

Beginning that New Year, I resolved to emerge from my shell and to extend a touch of understanding to those patients in the St. Scholastica Clinic who were without love. I could tell who they were because no one visited them. Most of them were men. They either stared at the walls, read countless magazines, or watched RAI television. I left them pictures of saints, I massaged their scars, or I simply asked if they needed someone to listen to their stories. I let their fears matter. Their scars, which I had stitched, running down their chests like zippers, were signals they shared with each other, allowing them to begin their life again. "Everyone has pain and don't think you're the only ones in the world with wounded hearts," I said.

The other resolution I made that New Year was to pray extra for Carlo and Jassy. I was sure Mama and Papa had rolled over in their graves, knowing their son had fathered a bastard. Since I had always taken care of my parents' concerns when they were alive, their being dead didn't matter. I was still responsible for both Carlo and myself.

Regretfully, I double-edged my prayers, weighting my brother and his lover's salvation with equal cries of resentment. My brother had won too many pleasures and benefits, I said to God, while I was living by the rules and had nothing. Aren't You keeping score? I asked. Carlo had to be punished.

When I witnessed Jassy giving birth, I was concerned God had listened to only my resentment. But looking back, He could have been warning and reminding us of what was important. It happened in August, during the hot spell that covered the entire Northern Hemisphere.

In Subiaco, stars were falling in the sky. I sat by my window, fanning myself. But hot in Italy isn't as muggy as the heat in Boston. Jassy and Carlo's sweat had soaked through their clothing. Jassy's eyeglasses slid down her beaded nose. It was midafternoon, and they were in Carlo's new blue van, stuck in a traffic jam inside the Boston Harbor Tunnel.

"We're doing Virginia's job. Why did she leave this time?" Carlo knocked the steering wheel with his knuckles. "Every time they have a fight—she leaves. I don't know who to blame—Renato or Virginia."

"Neither. Virginia took Bebe to the Children's Museum," Jassy said. "I told her to take the day off. I said I'd sign the documents."

"Today? Why didn't she go yesterday, or tomorrow?" Carlo shook his head. "Look at you. You should be home with the air-conditioning." Jassy had gained fifty pounds during her pregnancy and there was another five weeks left to go. She had been having difficulty sleeping and walking.

"Don't worry, Carlo," Jassy said. "I can do this for Virginia because she's done so much for me. We'll just sign papers and go back home."

"Are you sure?" Carlo asked. Even fat, Jassy had never looked more beautiful to him.

"We'll be home in an hour," Jassy assured Carlo.

Carlo put his hand on her knee and took his foot off the brake. The van emerged from the tunnel. Carlo dropped a quarter in the toll basket. The casket company was a mile farther, north on Bennington Street and past Santarpio's Pizza.

It was a big, solemn brick building, with one small sign: E. BOSTON CASKET SUPPLY. Jassy had been there before, with Virginia. She told Carlo it was an odd place. "Funeral directors buy embalming supplies, caskets, candles, and grieving-room furnishings here," she said. "The shipping platform's in the rear."

The sun was straight up. The air shimmered with heat. Carlo helped Jassy cross the parking lot. She had a mild contraction, which she blamed on the hot weather. "It'll be air-conditioned inside. A few more steps and everything will be back to normal," she assured him.

Carlo didn't pay too much attention to what was happening to Jassy. He was curious, as I was, to get inside an embalming supply store. In Italy, death is not such a business. We bury our loved ones simply and quickly, as I had done with Mama, and Papa before her. Carlo and I both wondered if wax corpses would be laid out in caskets as display models.

The receptionist, a bald man in a black suit, waved them through the sample funeral parlor rooms—a rose room, a blue one, and a yellow one. At the rear of the yellow room Jassy knocked on a polished door.

"Finally, you're here," Mr. DiMatteo, Boston's Italian consul, said, lifting his eyebrows at the sight of Jassy's huge belly. Also present was Mr. Lozzi, the funeral director Spediamo had hired for the event, and a handsome priest in black who said, in Italian, that he was from a parish in Stoneham. But I later found out he had really been sent from Rome, by Cardinal Ulbaldini, to make sure the shipment was safely packed. I was there, too, but no one could see me.

"*Buon giorno,*" Carlo said gaily. He knew everyone except the priest. "Too bad we're not meeting on Hanover Street to drink wine and tell stories," he said. "Next time." He shook the men's hands. Mr. DiMatteo bumped his heels together and bowed slightly as he shook hands with Jassy.

Jassy's pain came again. I saw her face go tight. She turned from the men and squatted near her briefcase. Holding her breath, she unlatched the case and sifted through the contents.

Carlo also noticed the unusual expression on Jassy's face when she handed the envelope of Spediamo documents to Mr. DiMatteo, who had an equally large stack of papers.

"Please, let's begin," said the priest, who no one knew.

From his briefcase, the Italian consul removed a yellow sash and several official paper embossers. He ducked his wavy hair under the sash and smoothed it over his small chest. Carlo thought, If there were a band, the music would start now.

The group approached the casket. The remains of Giuseppina Bevilaqua, an elderly woman who had died of cancer, were supposed to be inside the zinc casket. The welders, who would seal the casket, lowered their masks and took their positions. The consul sniffed, straightened his tie, and laid his documents in a neat pile on the platform next to the bullet-shaped casket. He handed Jassy a pen. Mr. Lozzi, the funeral director, passed his set of documents to Jassy, Jassy passed her papers to the consul, the consul passed his to the director. Carlo stood behind Jassy, dizzy with the formality. He examined the ceiling of the lofty building. Just like everyone else in the new world, Carlo was not comfortable with death. When I die, Carlo said to himself, I want to be cremated, and for no one to make a parade.

As the others signed the documents required by the Italian government, the consul pressed each paper between his official seals. Then the consul clicked his fingers, indicating to the welders to ignite their torches. Flames shot to the ceiling.

On her tiptoes, Jassy peered into the casket. Then she screamed.

The priest brushed her elbow and quietly asked her not to

look. *"Stia indietro.* Step back, please," he said.

"Mrs. Barzini, what happened?" Mr. Lozzi put his arm around her back. He didn't know Jassy and Carlo weren't married.

Jassy pushed him back. "Leave me alone."

The consul, the undertaker, and the priest moved away as Jassy held on tight to a corner of the casket and howled. Carlo, as concerned as he was shocked to hear such a horrible sound coming from Jassy's throat, stepped forward. "Is the baby coming?" he asked.

"No! Absolutely not! I must have seen a ghost," she gasped, trying to excuse her behavior—and the glimpse of the face she had seen in the casket.

"In the name of the Father, Son, and Holy Spirit," the priest said as the welders bubbled shut the seam on the casket.

But it wasn't a ghost Jassy had seen, and it wasn't Guiseppina Bevilaqua, but a set of staring blue eyes. "Her screaming fit saved the shipment," the priest would later tell me. "No one bothered to look inside the casket. Virginia had kept it secret from all of them, except the consul, who was a Benevolent."

The consul lowered his eyebrows. "Try to control yourself, please. This is a ceremony," he said to Jassy.

Carlo wanted to punch the wimpy consul, but moved beyond the impulse. He watched Jassy. She seemed calm.

Sealed, the casket was dropped into an encasing pine box. The consul wrapped a purple ribbon around the waist of the box, and Jassy pressed her thumb over the spot where the two ends of ribbon crossed. She closed her eyes.

"Let me do it," Carlo said, not taking his eyes off her. "Then we'll go," he whispered. He had witnessed Virginia's labor. If Jassy was beginning hers, Carlo figured the baby wouldn't be born for at least another three hours.

"If the remains of Guiseppina Bevilaqua arrive in Italy, and the seal is broken, she will be sent back," the consul said. He held a long match to a stick of sealing wax.

Mr. Lozzi voiced his agreement.

Jassy screamed again. The contractions were coming one after the other. Her face was turning colors as fast as it was changing shapes. "Oh God! Stop this terrible pain. I can't have the baby now," she wailed.

"Jesus Christ!" Carlo shouted.

A glob of sealing wax dripped on the ribbon near Carlo's thumb. The consul impressed it with a coin-sized seal. "I'm taking her out of here," Carlo said, sweeping his hand from the casket.

Carlo grabbed Jassy. Her hair stuck to her forehead. "I'm all right. I'm all right," she repeated in a whisper. "It's over. The pain has stopped."

As the pine box was being slipped into a plastic case, Jassy turned to walk out of the room. "Carlo, quick," she said. "To the hospital. Now!" she shouted.

Carlo motioned for Mr. Lozzi and the consul to help him carry her. "I think she's going to have the baby," he said.

"No, not here," Jassy demanded. "Take me out to the parking lot, anywhere, not here. I'm not due for a month." Her water broke and splashed over the tile floor.

"Call an ambulance!" Mr. Lozzi shouted as they opened the door to the yellow mourning room.

"What are we going to do?" the consul asked. "Have you ever delivered a baby?" He pulled his ears.

"Don't leave me alone," Jassy moaned. "Please." She couldn't see to whom she was speaking. "I don't want to have a baby in a funeral parlor!"

130

Mr. DiMatteo rubbed his forehead with the palm of his hand. *"Dio mio!"*

The priest was sensible. "If she has to, why not have the baby here?"

"Stop!" Jassy screamed. They were in the rose room. "I can't go further."

Carlo laid Jassy on the sample love seat. "Don't move," he said.

Mr. Lozzi returned wearing a white lab coat and rubber gloves. He carried several bottles of alcohol, a box of towels, and a pair of scissors.

Jassy screamed at the top of her lungs for five minutes. Her fingernails clawed through the upholstered arms of the love seat. Carlo kneeled near her, but she would not allow anyone to touch her. Jassy kicked the priest.

"How long can she go on like this?" the consul asked Carlo.

The priest removed a strand of rosaries from his pocket, handing the beads to the consul.

Very gently, the funeral director lifted Jassy's skirt and snipped off her panties—Mr. Lozzi must have been very thrilled to be working the other end of life. He and Carlo wiped their hands in towels doused with alcohol.

The consul swayed back and forth, reciting the Hail Mary loudly enough for the men to hear between Jassy's screams, which were tapering down to shouts.

Her voice weakened. "At least this is happening in the rose room, and not the blue or yellow room," she said, catching her breath.

Mr. Lozzi caught the baby when it slid out. It was a girl. And then a second baby came. Another girl. Carlo caught it. "Two!" he said. "Two! We have two!"

"God bless," the consul said, crossing himself. It was then

Mr. DiMatteo noticed he was still wearing the official yellow sash of the Republic of Italy. "They have dual citizenship," he shouted, rushing forward to the newborns. "You gave birth to Italians!"

This was not the only gift Carlo's twins received. The priest offered them immediate entry into the Kingdom of Heaven. "I'll baptize them now," he said. "Mr. Lozzi and Mr. DiMatteo will be godfathers." He dribbled water from a paper cup over the twins' foreheads.

"It happened so fast," is all that Carlo remembered.

They handed Jassy her two little ones as the medics rushed her on a stretcher to a waiting ambulance.

I was out of breath. Within twenty minutes, Carlo's children had been born in a department store of death, were granted dual citizenship, and had been baptized. My brother was double lucky. He always had been. All our life he was carrying his own luck and the luck that should have been mine.

After being assured that his daughters and their mother were healthy, Carlo drove home to the North End. Birth, like death, was not news to deliver over a telephone, he thought. Carlo put his head in the clouds and made a wing through the North End, telling everyone that he had fathered twins. "Two girls," he said, his green eyes bursting like grapes. He closed his shops, put double knots in his shoelaces, and didn't hear the parallel news traveling beside him up Hanover Street.

The men were laughing at Carlo. "*È circondato da fiche.* He's surrounded by cunts," they said. "Carlo will serve women the rest of his life. No boys. Poor Carlo!" They puffed on their cigars and spit over the curb onto the sidewalk. "Even if Carlo has money," they said, "he has no sons."

At Spediamo, he waltzed Virginia over the short shag rug. "Jassy's had two babies!" he said.

"Yikes! She was afraid it would be twins," Virginia said, covering her cheeks with her hands. "Just like you and Alicia!"

$T\ e\ n$

Nine days later, I received Carlo and Jassy's birth announcement. I bought the twins, whom they had named Serafina and Cherubina, white shoes at the hospital's new gift shop—at a discount price—and a puppet for Bebe. The girls in the shop behaved as if they knew me, but I had never noticed them before. "Will you wrap these booties for shipment to America?" I asked, covering my nose. I gave them Carlo's address. I couldn't walk to the Subiaco post office myself without suffering a panic attack.

The gifts were never acknowledged. At first I blamed the silly gift shop girls for making a mistake. Later, I found out the package had been destroyed in Rome. There had been an Italian postal strike that month and when the workers returned to their jobs, they burned backed-up mail rather than sort through it.

But before I knew about the strike, I projected my senses across the Atlantic, to my brother's house, one last time.

"Jassy! A package has arrived!" Carlo shouted as he ran up five flights of stairs to the apartment. "It's from Alicia," he said. "I'm sure of it."

Renato, Jassy, Virginia, and the children gathered around the big kitchen table. The women held the babies. Renato held a script. Inside the white boxes that Carlo reverently unwrapped were two gold necklaces with crucifix pendants. The note said, "Congratulations from Cardinal Ulbaldini."

"Who's he?" Jassy asked, swaying the twins on her hips.

"Oh, a big cheese I once met in Rome." Carlo crumpled the note. "I don't know why he sent this to us. I hardly know him."

"He sends us business," Virginia said, but no one listened to her. "It's lovely jewelry. Twenty-four carat." She held the dense yellow pendants on her palm.

"Maybe your sister knows him," Jassy interrupted, tickling Sera's chin.

Renato scratched his eyebrow. "A gift like this is a great honor. From a cardinal, you said?"

The incident sent Carlo searching through the back drawers of his desk at the cookware store. He unfolded a limp carbon of a paper he had signed in Rome, in 1972, the month our Mama had died. He telephoned the Swiss bank number printed on the pages and recited a code to the night clerk who took the call.

"Seven hundred eighty-six thousand dollars? American dollars? Not lire?" Carlo asked. *"Dollari?"* He repeated the question in Italian. Both times the clerk answered yes.

Quickly Carlo ended the conversation. If he asked more questions, the clerk might discover an error made in his favor. Carlo hopped around the back room. "I'm a millionaire," he said. Carlo had $786,000 in a Swiss bank, and the remainder was tucked under floorboards at home and in his safe at the Haymarket Trust. His American dream had come true.

The hours he had spent listening to Renato go on and on about theater, and illusion and reality being whatever someone decided it to be, made sense to him. In his own mind, Carlo had created a world where he was rich. He had smelled it and turned it over in his mouth, always knowing it would become real. Now he owned those thoughts, he said to himself, and his wealth was real.

Careful not to break the spell, Carlo didn't speak a word about his newfound money. He did celebrate the event by buying a run-down warehouse in East Boston, on the waterfront, not far from where his daughters had been born. It was a brick-faced building with steel beam supports across the ceiling. A few of the windows were broken, but Carlo did not repair them because the New England Casket Company was going to lease space from him, and he wanted the souls of bodies brought there to be able to fly outside. He eventually gave Renato a corner of the warehouse to repair sets and store Teatro furniture. Plus, at just about that time, Virginia had lined up a business deal with a construction company that supplied Boston with concrete. They stored their dry mix there.

A month later, after the bank papers were signed, my brother stepped inside his big empty building and shouted his own name—"*Carlo Barzini.*" In Subiaco, I heard the syllables echo in my little wooden house that was so empty of people but full of memories. It made me sad. My brother was living for the future, and I was living both his and my own pasts. I heard him, but I did not look for him. I vowed never to cast my eyes across the Atlantic, though I struggled every day with the temptation to break my vow. If Carlo wasn't going to make amends with me, so wouldn't I with him. Since I believed the Higher Power didn't inspire unattainable desires, I accepted that Carlo and I had broken horns for good. It wasn't so much a loss as it was an opportunity to utilize my energy to make more money.

I continued to attend bypass surgeries. The surgical team now trusted me to electrocauterize the small blood vessels around the semilunar valves. I used the hot tip of a thin needle to sear tissue. I got close-up looks at many broken hearts. I saw they were raw and, when ripped open to the air, some shivered in pockets of yellow fat, some were egg-shaped, and all were the same shade of red. I decided each heart was sacred.

The first week of the next month, the clinic gave me another promotion, and a tiny office with a file cabinet. The administrators were probably hoping I'd stop taking lunch in the supply room. I didn't. The clinic also gave me a raise, which was unprecedented. Little did I know then that they were actually paying me my interest. The clinic owned my house and the land around it, and they were waiting for the day I would die or leave, so they could expand their buildings. Nonetheless the raise, along with the generous tips I received from nervous heart surgery patients who begged me to stitch them up extra carefully so that they could go barechested and not be self-conscious after their operation, added inches to my stockpile.

I cut off my relationship with America. I was born an Italian, and I would live and die Italian. I was not a traitor, or sinner, like Carlo. I was too old to marry, and that was all right. I had my job, my patients, and God was on my side. Heaven was mine—even if I was overweight. Also, since I no longer was tempted to spy on Carlo, I slept more. If you stay awake too often, you lose your dreams. One lovely June night I lay on my cot and asked myself what good my brother's dreams had been to me. I remember telling myself and believing wholeheartedly that whatever happened to me from then on would be my own doing.

Part Two

Eleven

~~~

I didn't expect Jassy to visit. She arrived on my front step in January 1977, on a Sunday afternoon when a waning moon was visible in a dull blue sky. I had been napping, perhaps dreaming, and told myself my eyes had not pried across the Atlantic for over three years. There must be a mistake. Jassy was surely an apparition.

I touched the sleeve of her coat. She was older and more glamorous than when I had first met her, and there was a funny, faraway look in her eyes. She wasn't wearing her glasses. Jassy pulled me close to her.

"Alicia," she breathed in my ear, stretching my name into four slow syllables. I packed more fat on my bones, but I knew she was stronger. I didn't fight. When she spoke, her flesh became as dense as marble, and she smelled clean and magical. She wasn't an angel.

Jassy had come alone. Her white rented car was parked on the road behind the rickety front gate. "Has something happened to Carlo?" I asked.

Jassy shook her head. "He's fine."

No one had visited me—besides the priests who left oil for my lamps and undressed statues on the front steps—since the day my Mama was buried. The few relatives that remained in Subiaco preferred to pretend I didn't exist.

"Your eyes! How very different they are from Carlo's," she said, admiring me. Jassy spoke to me in Italian, flattening the round sounds of my mother tongue with her American twang. "And I forgot you were tall. It's been so long, too long." Self-conscious, I cupped my right hand over my nose.

"Didn't Carlo telephone to tell you I was coming?" she asked. Jassy was perfect, powdered and polished, and unquestionably confident. Her nails were newly manicured and painted glossy red. Her shoes shined. She must have prepared specially for the visit to my house. But I didn't want her to come to me to ask for Carlo's forgiveness. No one could do the work he owed me, not even Jassy.

I stared straight into her brown eyes, which seemed to be lighted from behind. She didn't blink. "I haven't spoken to Carlo since the day I got stuck in the Teatro," I said. I wore that incident like a battle wound, though no one else knew about it.

Jassy was puzzled. "We don't have much time," she said. "May I come in?" She shifted her clean shoes inside my house. I wanted to shove her out. Scream. My heartbeat buried every other sensation. I couldn't breathe. Her being there invaded my privacy. Get out!

She followed me. My hair hung loose and untidy. I guided her through the boarded rooms into the kitchen, which was my room, the only room in the house that had been lived in since 1975. At least it was clean, I remember thinking, assuring myself cleanliness was a sign of my moral superiority. The yellowed walls had been wiped down with a hospital detergent last spring; the chrome fixtures over the sink and on the icebox and cabinet doors gleamed; the big-bellied stove was immaculate and stoked with logs. Only the far corner of the room, where my cot was littered with pillows, blankets, and papers, was an eyesore. Around it on the floor was an arc of undressed statues. I tried to steer Jassy away from that corner.

"Tea?" I asked. Oh no! She was inspecting my room. I circled her, hoping she might feel uncomfortable and sit down.

"Yes," she said. Jassy kept moving, floating around my kitchen. I prayed, my heart beating like a fool's, that she wouldn't step too near the sink and notice her picture tacked on the cupboard. It was the same picture Carlo had sent to Mama and me ten years ago, and the same picture I would carry in my pocketbook to Florence to find her when she disappeared.

Thinking noise would distract her, I rummaged through my sack of supplies. "Sorry. No tea," I said loudly. I put two cans of juice, straws, paper napkins, and a package of pale cookies on the table. "Sit down," I said.

I rushed to help her. I myself was surprised there were two chairs in the kitchen. Jassy draped her wine-colored coat over the back of a chair. I handed her a straw. "Do you want me to unwrap it?" I asked.

"I can do it myself," Jassy smiled kindly, poking the straw into a can of tomato juice. "You're good like Carlo at taking care of people. It must be a family trait."

"I'm a nurse," I said, tentative about her intentions. "I work in the operating room. My patients are hooked up to machines and are never conscious of what I do for them. As soon as I sew them shut, and the surgical team is sure they're alive, the patients get turned over to another nurse who tends them. I don't care for anyone, not really. I just do a job." I glanced at Jassy sideways, suspecting she really didn't believe I did what I did. To her, I was probably a fat old squirrel holed up in a house for the winter.

Jassy responded quickly. "You must be an extremely careful person if you've been entrusted with those tasks. I admire people who can stand near the sick and see their blood, bones, and pain. You have to care, and care about people you don't even know." She paused. "You're a healer, Alicia. Your eyes are serene enough to look into a person's soul and encourage them to go on forever. Not many of us can do that."

I was flattered. "I'm not Florence Nightingale," I said, not wanting to hand back her praise, since praise rarely came to me.

We chatted, floating from English into Italian and back. She showed me snapshots of Sera, Cher, and Bebe, and she cuddled their chubby faces with her fingertips. She told me the adults in their family spent evenings watching the children grow. "They're so fascinating. And Bebe's such a wise soul in a child's body," Jassy said affectionately. "When you play with her, you get the feeling she can outsmart you. Already she's anxious to wear stockings and high heels. Oh, and the twins are outrageous—and funny!"

She filled me in on Renato. His Teatro had won a grant from the State of Massachusetts, but according to her, he was less concerned about money than about the quality of his productions. "Renato's close to attaining a purely individual style that serves his art," she said.

"And Carlo is working on his accent," she said. "After dinner he sits in the front room, in his purple chair, and listens to cassettes of poets reading their poetry. He wears headphones and repeats their words." She said my brother gained a few pounds each winter and lost most of it in the summer. "He misses you," she said.

"And Virginia—last of all Virginia." Jassy sipped her tomato juice. "Motherhood has pushed her to be successful in a way that surprised us all. She's a good businesswoman—

we thought she'd lose interest in the shipping business. But last year, she and Carlo became partners. The shop's still on Hanover Street, and they have a warehouse too, in East Boston. They import construction material as well as export"— she paused—"whatever it is they export." I didn't ask if Virginia and Renato had married, choosing to keep our conversation off unpleasant topics.

"Does Virginia continue to send things to my address in Subiaco?" I asked.

"I don't know what Virginia does. Each of us is busy with our own work, we don't talk about each other's. The children bustle the household, demanding our attention. But I do tease Virginia, time to time, for being so sneaky." Jassy smiled. "She's done so well, I want to know how she did it." Jassy winked at me.

"Is she doing something wrong?"

"I hope not. Why would she? Everyone has their magic, don't they?" She smiled. "I do. I sing. And I'm sure you do, too. It's whatever you do that's special and no one but yourself knows about it."

"You're right," I said, volunteering information I had never shared with anyone but God. I went on to tell Jassy about the corners of luminous material that I sewed back into patients' bodies. "I can see a soul leak out of a wound. And those who lose the most are the people who have more chance of dying. That's the secret side of my job," I confessed. "Open-heart surgery is such a horrible operation, I have to make it more than a mechanical procedure. No one ever sees the patients' faces. The prep team scrubs them down and covers everything but their chests, the anesthetist knocks them out, and then we come in with our masks, carts of tools, and machines." I crumpled the plastic cookie wrapper in my palm.

145

Jassy said she understood the unspoken aspect of my job. "When I perform, I have to be more than I am, more than one person can possibly be," he said. "I have to spread my soul into the audience, so they can feel it. That's what an audience expects. And I get something from my audience. I take the spirit of their expectation and make it my own for an hour or two. I catch their dreams to fuel my own."

We both noticed the sun beginning to drop below the kitchen window. We sat, silent, admiring the vibrant scraping of blue and orange across the square of uncurtained glass.

"It's beautiful," Jassy said.

She was easy to be with, less compulsive and more calm than I remembered her to be. With her, I was able to stop being self-conscious about my nose, my room, and my conversation. I began to celebrate her company. "That's lovely, too," I said matter-of-factly, pointing at Jassy's diamond engagement ring. I was actually very excited to have discovered it, but I didn't want to show the joy to Jassy.

"Yes, it is," Jassy said quietly, curling her left hand onto her lap. I didn't press her for more information. Later, I learned that she and Carlo were to be married when her tour was over.

"Italy is a stopover," she explained. "The New England Opera Company plane landed in Rome yesterday. I took the afternoon off to be with you—but not without a lot of trouble. You're worth it, Alicia. Tomorrow we go north, to Germany and Amsterdam, before touring Poland, Russia, and Czechoslovakia."

"Won't you miss Carlo, and the children?"

"I'm prepared not to," she said, lowering her eyes. "Truthfully, I feel guilty for not wanting to miss them. But singing is as much my life as they are." There was no doubt in her voice. "I love all sides of who I am. And I've taught the children, since the day they were born, that restriction strangles people. I don't want them to know me as someone who dropped her arms and gave up. Carlo has always agreed."

I didn't agree.

It was getting dark. That night, instead of pumping my oil lantern, I switched on the overhead electric lights, surprised that the bulbs hadn't disintegrated in their sockets. The room splashed with a bright glow. It took a few moments for our eyes to adjust.

"Do you have scissors?" she asked.

"Why?"

"It may be bold of me," Jassy was politely apologetic, "but I'd like to cut your hair. You're such an unusual and attractive woman, Alicia. When you talk and move around your kitchen, I see so much vitality. Your face is full of expression. Long, flat hair hides your grace. Shorter, it will have lift." She held the backs of her hands under her chin.

I didn't question her. Jassy was gorgeous, a woman who made the most of a lot. I draped a hospital towel over my shoulders and handed her the scissors Carlo had sent to me one Christmas, long ago. Jassy combed the knots from my hair, pulling a silver-handled brush through it as if my hair were a sheet of silk.

I could hardly bear it. The skin along my spine puckered like a snake shedding its skin. I felt suddenly taller. Jassy knew I needed to be touched more than I needed a new hairdo.

Her hands stroked the back of my skull. I closed my eyes, pressed my lips together and prayed the hateful things I had thought about Jassy in the past hadn't seeped out into the world. The sound of the sharp steel scissors, ripping through my thick hair, filled the room. "You're certainly Carlo's sister," she said. "You both have the same-shaped head."

When she had finished, my waist-length hair brushed the top of my shoulders. I wanted her to trim it yet another inch, but just an inch, and then I'd ask her to take off a bit more, so that she wouldn't stop touching me. I had cared for so many people—first Mama and Papa, then other dying hearts. No one had treated me like a child since I was a child. I longed to be taken care of. Jassy did that for me. With her, I was safe.

"Look." She guided me to the mirror near the refrigerator. "You have such fine skin. You must have earned such invisible pores by staying out of the sun." She was right. I had hidden myself, and not just from the sun.

"Thank you," I said. Neither of us moved. It was awkward to stare into a mirror and have Jassy there behind my shoulder. Just as she had promised, the shorter hair made me look younger and less tired. But I didn't look as good as she did. My forehead was narrow and my nose was so big it overpowered my eyes, which were large and black, and my cheeks were chubby.

Jassy and I split the last can of juice.

"One more gift for you before I leave," she said.

She stood near my cot, next to a small wobbly table, granting it as much respect as a grand piano. She stretched her fingers, hands, and wrists. "Renato has taught me a singer never clasps her hands," she said, rolling her shoulders backward and then forward. She pointed to her neck. "Music sticks in the throat if the notes can't travel down the singer's arm."

Jassy performed "Simple Gifts" for me. "It's a Shaker tune," she said. I didn't know then what a Shaker was, and might have objected had she told me Shakers lived in communes and never married each other.

My wood house picked up the bass in her voice, which

sliced through me, opening a path between my heart and mind.

"'Tis the gift to be simple, 'tis the gift to be free,
'Tis the gift to come down where we ought to be
And when we find ourselves in the place just right,
'Twill be in the valley of love and delight."

The song's power came from so deep inside her, it made me weep for all she was and all she had given to me. I wished I could be Jassy and stand where she stood. That day I learned, for a while, not to envy her. I didn't care that she had Carlo and I didn't, or that she had borne his children, and I had no one. Jassy was totally independent from the others. She had a life of her own, and I wanted her to be my friend forever.

"I have to go," she said.

The emotions of having her visit me and listening to her singing had tired me. "So soon?" I managed to say.

"I've been here longer than I expected. You're such an honest soul, Alicia, like your brother. I love you." Jassy's cheeks were flushed, and she held my hands. "When I finish my tour, you must come to Boston. Carlo wants to make up with you—he's told me that. I'll take you to him—if you'll let me. I know it's hard for you, for both of you. But we women have as great a capacity to love and forgive as we do to destroy. We don't have to be stubborn. There's enough of that in the world."

She kissed my shortened hair, and lingered at the door with her arms around me until I felt free enough to let her go. She had listened to me and invited me back into the world by reminding me of who I was. Jassy had no idea that I was guilty of having conspired against her in my prayers. And I had no inkling we would meet again, in the same house, and that my small house would become hers.

I watched Jassy pull away from the front gate in her rented car. We waved to each other through our windows.

T w e l v e

In the evening, during the week after Jassy's visit, I often admired myself in a mirror. She had told me I was attractive and an original and unusual woman. Unaccustomed to such compliments, I repeated her words to myself as I looked at my elbows and shoulders, and practiced flirtatious expressions and expressions of endearment.

One night, on a Thursday, I held the pink-handled mirror between my thighs and examined my virginity. Never having been so bold, I spread my labial lips. Suddenly a light squeezed out of my hole—a light not dissimilar to the opaque lights I saw in the clinic's operating room. "I'm your virginity," it said, taking a seat at my side. My virginity looked like an angel, but without wings, and with dark hair, not unlike my own. I was relieved to hear the light speak. When I had first seen it, I was sure it was my own soul leaving, making me die for fingering my sexual organs.

My virginity shook its finger at me. "Your brother Carlo is having problems," it said, "and you wear me, like a mask, so you don't have to look for him, act, or do anything. You're an evil and fickle girl for wanting Carlo to suffer! Carlo needs you, more than you need me." My virginity spoke like a well-trained child, full of function and purpose.

"Why do you think his woman came to Subiaco?" it asked.

"Coincidence," I said, arguing, insisting upon seeing things differently. "Carlo isn't in trouble. He takes care of himself," I said. "He always has." And then I bowed my head in shame. What if my vanity and virginity were to betray me, as I had betrayed my brother?

She laughed and disappeared back inside my body.

The next day, and the days after that, when I came home from work, I didn't look in the mirror. I tidied my room, ate chocolates, and sewed costumes for the saints. But the urge to spy on Carlo became stronger, confronting me the way an old habit calls us back to its grip with promises of comfort and friendship. As Lent approached, and with it the season of repentance, trouble rose in my bones, beckoning me to embrace it. I finally looked in on Carlo. I hadn't used my vision in more than three years.

It was Fat Tuesday. I recalled my vision worked best when I didn't think, so I sat on my cot, near the window, counting stars, making my mind go blank. A stab of nausea swept through me—that had never happened before. Immediately I harangued myself, saying if Carlo was indeed having trouble, it would be my fault. I had led him astray with my prayers.

My breathing quieted, and I slumped back on a pillow. Without seeing him, I could already feel that Carlo was miserable and needed to be hugged as closely as I had curled around him in the womb. I tried to rush, to get to him quickly, but my skills were rusty. I urged them forward, forcing myself beyond comfort. *Porca miseria!* Carlo was in trouble! I don't know where I found the energy to make the sign of the cross over my heart before my senses bounced off the brightest star and spread out over Boston.

Carlo was walking up Hanover Street, mumbling to himself. The sun had rolled over the horizon. Streetlights flicked on, and the sidewalk, slicked with rain, reflected my brother's heavy steps. He passed Spediamo, and then back-tracked. A chain and lock bolted the door. He jiggled the chain and pulled down on the lock to make sure the bolt was secure. He was thinking that without Virginia his business would slip away like the rain rushing over the curb into the sewer. Virginia had insisted she would not return.

Of course, Carlo didn't believe her, and he told himself then, as he stood there rattling the lock on Spediamo's door, that she would be back. "Virginia will be back," he said out loud. Hearing himself speak, Carlo wasn't embarrassed. The falling rain was like a wall. "Don't worry, everything will be all right," he repeated. "If she's not back tomorrow, I'll take care of everything myself."

But Carlo couldn't do anything. He didn't know one document from the other, who in Italy picked up shipments, what shipping company sailed out of Boston, how much an ocean-going container might weigh, or where Virginia filed telephone numbers. As far as Carlo was concerned, he was his own fool and suffering the consequences. He hadn't been smart enough to anticipate that Virginia's itchy personality would truly turn against him.

Carlo fashioned binoculars from his folded hands and pressed them against the wet window. Pink, yellow, and white papers were scattered over her desk. Carlo had left the papers in disarray, hoping passersby might look inside and think Virginia would return. And Carlo had been assuring them—the men that continued to call—that she would return. "She always does," he said.

Rain soaked in behind his collar. He could hear the tele-phone ringing inside, but Carlo had nothing new to say be-sides "Next week . . . maybe next week." His customers were growing impatient.

Carlo turned down a side street toward the harbor. Surely

Virginia would come back for Bebe, he told himself. As he walked, Carlo could hear her silvery, determined voice. "I just want to be myself," she had said. "I can't do that here. No one pays attention to me." Her soft hair fell over the sides of her face. "I have to start over, somewhere else."

"Starting over is an American curse," Carlo said out loud. "Starting over is a dream." It was an echo of their last conversation in the Spediamo office.

"I want to give the business back to you," Virginia had said. "I can't make more phone calls. I don't want to ship trunks full of brides' hopes, or cars and motorcycles, boxes of hair dye, hunting guns, or sacred statues."

"Go. Go then," he had said, edging her out, hurt that she didn't appreciate the opportunities he had given to her. Why didn't Virginia respect him? "I can't help you, in here," Carlo said, tapping his forehead. "We each have our own heaven and hell."

"I have what is mine." Virginia avoided his eyes. "And I'm not taking Bebe with me."

"You never do," Carlo had reminded her.

"You and Jassy can teach her more about loving than I am able to do. I can't be a mother."

"You'll be back."

Virginia continued, speaking rapidly, as if she were afraid if she didn't say what she had to say it might never be spoken. "Please, promise to love Bebe when she is older, as much as you love her when she is small."

Carlo wished he had hugged Virginia, and asked her to sit on his lap. Maybe then she would have stayed. But he had stood apart from her, riveted to the floor, empty-handed, and shocked. "How can a mother leave her child? What can I give Bebe that would possibly make up for the loss of you?"

Virginia left.

154

Carlo made his way to the last block of the North End, to Atlantic Avenue. Rain pounded his shoulders. He couldn't see across the street or to the harbor. Streetlights were barely visible. He went back to thinking about Spediamo.

Who would apologize to the men who kept calling every day, twice a day? he wondered. Where could he send them, and the others? How could he save face? Did he have to let go of their business publicly? Did everyone in the North End have to know Virginia had duped him? How many knew he knew nothing?

Carlo slid his hands in his pockets, pinching the lint on the seams of his flannel pockets. He asked himself, if Virginia did come back, how long would it take for him to forgive her? Carlo decided he would not be angry for more than a day. Anger made his blood boil, and he wanted everything in his life to be pleasant, and for years it had been. It would be that way again, he assured himself. Virginia would come back. So would Jassy. She would come home and sing. The children would sit on his lap and listen to her. Then Renato would read to them from Pirandello and play the piano. Carlo quickened his steps.

But the peaceful feeling in his heart disappeared when he saw a body lying on the sidewalk in front of his apartment building. Carlo ran to the rain-soaked figure. It was Renato, and his face was dripping blood. Carlo knelt beside him.

He lifted Renato's hand, tapping it against his own warm cheek. "Renato," he said. But Renato's body was cold and stiff. Carlo listened to his chest. Renato wasn't dead. His heart was in there, slowly banging inside a cave of broken ribs. But who would want to kill Renato? He was harmless. Renato bared his soul, without embarrassment, to whoever entered his Teatro.

Carlo put his lips over Renato's lips and blew air into his lungs. Renato tasted smoky, damp, and like whiskey. But

155

Renato never drank whiskey. He waited for Renato's eyes to open, thinking of the triumphs and despair he had seen in those eyes, wanting to see more. *"Stronzo.* You big shit. *Non puoi morire ora!"* Carlo shouted. "Don't die now!" He thought about how he and Renato had been waiting for summer to make the calamari salad each of them claimed was delicious with the juice and grated zest of a lemon. Carlo cursed them both for deciding to wait. In a city the size of Boston, they could have found calamari any month of the year. Carlo had enough money to fly in fresh calamari from the Mediterranean. Why was he so cheap? What if Renato died?

"Open your eyes," Carlo ordered. Renato was Carlo's friend, teacher, son, and brother. Carlo protected him, as he protected the others. Renato didn't deserve to be kicked and smashed. He wedged Renato's head gently between his knees. "You are like a baby," he said. "I love you like your mother loved you the day you were born. Don't die."

A driver in a passing car stopped to telephone an ambulance from the corner restaurant.

Carlo went with Renato in the ambulance to Massachusetts General Hospital.

"He'll be here at least a week," the nurse in the emergency room said. Renato hadn't got back his consciousness.

As Carlo walked home to the North End, he watched his own feet stumble. The rain had become a hand of fog pushing down his thoughts. Where had he failed, he asked himself? Why was Renato beaten? Virginia gone? Jassy not with him? The children needed their mothers and family. Carlo was sure an angry Lord was punishing him. But for what? It had taken him two and a half decades to carve a place for himself. He had worked hard, with determination and confidence, and he had been honest and had never hurt anyone.

Carlo kicked his own shadow. He was not allowing someone to take it away.

Carlo didn't go home. He unlocked the back entrance to the drugstore, a rickety door he seldom used. In the tiny green back room, Carlo telephoned the contact number for the North End patrol, the Italian guys who watched the neighborhood. Whoever answered said they knew nothing about Renato. "Who's he?" they asked. "Did he pay for protection, too?"

Carlo snapped a plastic eyeguard over his head and slid his wide hands into leather work gloves. On the floor, next to his feet, was a box filled with barber shears and carbon steel knives that local housewives had left for him to sharpen. Carlo had never trained anyone to take over the job of grinding blades on the stone wheel. It was the skill that had given him his first money in America.

He rummaged through the box for the longest pair of scissors. He lifted the black dropcloth from his sharpening stone. Carlo turned on the machine.

"When I first came to America," Carlo said to himself, "I was prepared to sell everything, but no one wanted to buy Carlo Barzini. I was a small man." Carlo opened the scissors. "I delivered coffee and shined shoes. I got sent lower and lower. I didn't become who I wanted to be." Carlo held a scissor blade a hair's width over the spinning stone. "I cut off my pride. It was a good decision. It gave me my own business, made me rich enough to be happy." Carlo touched the scissor blade to the whirring wheel, leaning forward and backward, ripening the dull edge. "I'll go as low as I have to go to keep my family safe," he said.

Carlo picked up a knife. The air around him sparked with flakes of steel flung off from the spinning stone. He sharp-

ened the short scissors last because they were the most difficult.

"It's important to know what you want," Carlo said. "If
you figure that out, you have peace inside. Someone is taking
my peace."

When I looked back on that Fat Tuesday, which was the
same night Carlo found Renato nearly dead on the sidewalk,
I saw that it marked the beginning of Carlo's descent. His
life had caught up with him. For too long Carlo had been
weighing himself down with the responsibility of other people's souls, and no one was there anymore to help him lift his
own. Carlo had to lay his thoughts next to mine and speak
to the same saints. He had to go backward, to me whom he
had forgotten. I was ready to forgive my brother. I had lost
my innocence, and perhaps my stupidity, and finally realized
that my prayers had caused storms on the other side of the
planet.

Thirteen

That same evening as the telephone rang, I bit the side of my cheek, knowing it was Carlo. The ringing stopped. It started again. Rather than listen to the insistent brring-brring-brring, I answered it and feigned indifference, protecting myself in case I was wrong. Maybe it wouldn't be Carlo. But who else would call? I picked up the receiver and stood in the darkest shadow of my kitchen. *"Pronto,"* I said, as if it might be a dry cleaner calling to solicit new business.

Carlo paused, perhaps as surprised as I was to be connected again. *"Alicia, ho bisogno di te.* I need you," he said. His voice was sad around the edges. Any spirals of wickedness I had harbored in my lungs flew out the window. I wanted to comfort Carlo, and I wanted to know how badly Renato had been injured, and if the children were cranky from having been tended to by Mrs. Musetta.

The telephone line went silent, and I didn't breathe into the microphone. But Italian telephones are never quiet. I held on to my end of the receiver while echoes of garbled voices laughed and stretched between us like deaf impostors. I didn't know what to say.

"They've all gone," Carlo said loudly. *"Sono solo.* I'm alone." I didn't reprimand him for not calling me sooner, or for not writing to me himself, allowing the others to write, and sending me secondhand messages through Virginia and Jassy. None of that mattered anymore. "I want you to come to Boston and stay with me," he said with confidence. "Our children need you to care for them." His voice was stronger than I had expected it would be. "I miss you, Alicia. I'm so sorry we've grown apart." Carlo said everything I wanted to hear.

I was gentle. "You need your sister." I had seen Carlo's trouble and knew he needed someone to trust.

"Yes," he said. *"Certamente."*

"I'll come then, to take care of the children," I said.

"When?"

My first inclination was to leave Subiaco that night, in the dark. The next morning I could step into my brother's house.

"I'll come as soon as I can," I promised. "First, I must shop around for the cheapest airfare."

"I'll pay," he said. "Don't worry. Come tomorrow. Go first-class." Carlo paid for everyone. Why not me?

Though I yearned to be with him, my thoughts turned to my money. "Don't you have someone kind to watch the children, until I get there?" I asked.

"Yes, Mrs. Musetta," Carlo said.

"And Renato?" I was baiting him for information.

"He's here, too," Carlo answered, his voice quieting.

"Then he's all right?"

"Sure." I could see Carlo shrug. He was reluctant to mention Renato's trouble, not wanting me to think I might not only have to care for his children, but also to nurse Renato. Or if I knew Renato had been beaten, I might refuse to return to America out of the fear I myself would be infected with its violence. The note I had left on his bed four years ago had said I didn't want to be swallowed up by my surroundings.

After I hung up the phone, I inspected my money, which was stacked like bricks under the sink. The cupboard was filled with hundreds of millions of lire—what my parents had left behind, and the money and tips I had earned while nursing. I stabbed my fingers between the neat stacks of bills. The wall was a receipt for my future. I had planned ahead.

On my cot, I tapped my slippered foot on the wood floor. The kitchen was dark. Wind fingered through the eaves on the east side of the house. "Alicia," I said to myself, "be smart. Jassy said you were unusual and attractive. On the other side of the Atlantic, your money—along with the proof of your virginity—will be worth more than all the lire you have stuffed under the sink and into mattresses. Men will drive to your brother's house and ask to carry you away in their Cadillacs."

Out of the fear and self-knowledge that I might convince myself I couldn't be important in America, I jumped up and emptied a packet of hospital coffee into the basket of my aluminum pot and made a batch of the strongest coffee I have ever drunk in my life. Daybreak and the noise of trucks and cars shifting gears as they climbed the nearby highway ramp crept into the room, and my ears, through the cracks in the cloth curtains.

I unnailed the door to the dining room and tracked over the dusty floor to the back bedrooms, where I checked the family photographs, Carlo's letters from America, my nursing diploma, Mama's rosary, and Papa's watch. I didn't want to forget who I was when I got to America. I packed the few things I would carry with me.

In my old bedroom, I wiped the dust off the faces of the

plaster statues of Blessed Mary and St. Joseph. They stood, a couple, on my dresser, as they had always stood. Nothing had changed with them. But me! Carlo had called me!

I plunged the bottom of a metal crucifix into the straw mattress, which was rolled up and pushed to the foot of my bed. Mary and Joseph would guard my house, and Jesus would punish anyone who entered my room, until I returned to take the holy family to America.

I couldn't sleep. At seven in the morning, I bolted across the field to the earliest mass to be anointed with ashes. Ash Wednesday's smudge was supposed to remind me of my mortality, but as the priest marked my forehead, I thought about all the life I had missed. Yes, I said to myself, it was time to embrace the unknown.

Back home, I filled a huge valise with lire notes, tied a scarf around my head, and, in the center of Subiaco, boarded the bus to Rome. I hadn't ventured beyond Subiaco since the day I had run from America, my brother, and my own brute fear.

Scenery passed. The rolling hills below town were no longer as I remembered them to be—green and lush and rimmed with palm trees. The hills had been terraced and stacked with concrete apartment buildings. The bus passed shops and signs, blinking billboards, and nests of wires that crisscrossed and hissed between poles.

But soon the grand enthusiasm that had dared me out of my house faded. Anxiety crept into my lungs, crippling my breath. I glanced around me at the strangers on the bus and tucked my head lower into the hand that was covering my nose. My throat was too dry to swallow. I prayed to disappear into the plastic upholstery.

As the blue bus neared Rome, the sun shone through holes in the ceiling of clouds, and the noises outside got louder, providing relief from the incessant inner monologue that was repeating to me: "Hide. Don't get out of the bus. Go home."

I lowered my shoulders. The boom of a metal ball ramming a tile roof and honks of cars competing for the right of way soothed my blood. I stopped thinking about myself. If I concentrated, I could pick up the chest rattles of people clearing their throats a block away. But I didn't want to pry on strangers. I persuaded myself to listen to my own breathing, to relax, and to wiggle my feet.

Outside the bus station, I took refuge in a little alley, leaning against cold gray stones until my sweating stopped. I made a deal with myself. "Alicia," I said, "you're not going to give up. You have dreamed about a life for yourself in America. If you want to start over, you can't play second to Carlo, or anyone. Go through with the exchange. If you fail, you must forfeit your money to the church, and join a convent. God doesn't inspire unattainable desires."

I stepped back onto the street. A snarl of warm wind lifted the ties of my scarf from under my chin and beat the silk wings against my face. A path opened. My scheme worked perfectly. I don't know why I was surprised that it did. In foreign banks I turned over my lire for lovely troy ounces of gold, paying $150 for each ounce.

The next day I repeated the same journey, acquiring more gold, and six big diamonds. When I deposited lire in an account that would be secretly transferred to Switzerland, the bank officer made me sign the papers with a ballpoint pen. "Thieves lift signatures made with felt tips and fountain pens," he explained. "You never know whom to trust." He smiled at me because I was rich. I smiled back because he was practical.

On my third trip to Rome, I bought more gold and put it in various safety deposit boxes. I spent several hours in a hotel with my treasures. I didn't walk across the bridge to stay in the only Rome hotel with which I was familiar—the one Carlo had slept in with the Virgin's nose. I stayed on the business side of the Tiber.

"I want a room for an hour," I said to a clerk with a long face. It was a small hotel off a dusty sidewalk.

"We don't allow that kind of business here," he said and continued to tend to his bookkeeping. The clerk hadn't gazed at me long enough to noticed how homely I was. No one could possibly mistake me for a *putana!*

"I'm alone," I said. For once the words didn't frighten me. *"Sono sola."* I was full of the confidence I would soon have to rely on to survive.

The room was perfect. I sat in the center of the bed and bordered the edges of the nubby tan spread with gold. The mattress became a ship and I was a pirate. I weighed each of the gold pieces in my palm, enjoying the timelessness of the sensation. Inside and out, I felt golden and like a child at play. I hadn't laughed in years. Flicking my treasures overboard onto the blue carpet, I licked the gold squares and stuck them to my bare breasts. Then I filled the bathtub with the hottest water in Rome and bathed, blessing myself with the full force of God's graces and the clank of gold on the bottom of a porcelain tub.

My money business was in order. There was one more thing to do before leaving Subiaco. I had to get a new nose.

I found a young doctor—a plastic surgeon rumored soon to be the best in the St. Scholastica Clinic—and cornered him in the physicians' lounge. He was reading a sports journal. I shut the door behind me and held the knob in my hand to be sure no one entered the room while I made him my offer. "I'll pay gold," I said, showing him two polished nuggets. "But we have to do it quickly. Perhaps tonight. I'm in a hurry."

Dr. Scarfone's eyes were confused but kind and hadn't yet been tainted with the power of his own authority. *"Scusi?"* he asked.

"I'll explain." I turned sideways so the young doctor could get a good look at my profile. "I want it redone," I said, pointing to the center of my face where everything about me, except my eyebrows, reached out toward the gray wall. "I can't breathe properly," I lied. "I've suffered long enough. We can operate after midnight."

We used a local anesthetic. I assisted him from a prone position. Dr. Scarfone had steady hands. Along with the gold I paid him, I promised Dr. Scarfone he would never see me again. "I'm going to America," I said before he stuffed my nose with cotton gauze. What joy it was to know in America everything would be different.

The flight across the Atlantic was bumpy. Above us, cosmonauts in a Soviet spaceship were breaking records for days spent in space. I could feel their hovering presence, since our paths coincided for several hours. As the jet approached America, the country protected by the Virgin Mother Mary, the country that promised to bring peace to the world, my heart beat so loudly I feared it would force my soul out of my flesh.

Carlo was waiting. He didn't recognize me. I walked lightly. Since I'd had the nose job just two days earlier, a white gauze mask covered the top half of my face. We brushed elbows. I must have smelled differently than he remembered because he kept looking straight ahead, searching the faces of passengers marching down the exit ramp. Not me.

My new nose worked perfectly. I inhaled his sweet and familiar odor, which had grown older and more ripe. I stopped at his side to place my fingertips under my own jaw, and observed how Carlo's veins pulsed in the same rhythm

165

as mine. His neck was strong, like a bull's. I circled my twin brother in near rapture. His hair was peppered with gray. He was stouter; the lateral step he had taken across the Atlantic had flattened his body, making his profile much thinner than his front or back sides. I wondered if the same would happen to me if I stayed. I forgave him for everything and wanted to clutch his waist, never letting him go. I glanced down to stop my tears and saw that my brother's feet were no longer as delicate as a seventeen-year-old's. In the new world he had to weight himself down in order to stand so proudly.

I pinched Carlo's elbow. He turned, startled. "Where are the little ones?" I asked, although I knew perfectly well where they were. They were with Mrs. Musetta.

"Alicia!" Carlo shouted. "It's you!" He hugged me with such enthusiasm I nearly lost my balance and might have floated upward in ecstasy had he not held me so close. It had been a good decision to wait seven days after his phone call. Justice had mended what had been torn between us. Carlo held on to my shoulder. I possessed no defense against his affection.

I noticed a network of lines crumpling the skin around his eyes. He hadn't been sleeping. He was worried. But inside the worry, inside the green eyes I had missed, and at times hated, there was a spark. What had polished my brother's eyes? I looked away when I thought his eyes might be shining for me.

"Ah! Alicia. You're here," he breathed, brushing the soft back of his wide hand against my cheek. *"Sorellina.* My little sister."

Through the two circles cut around my eyes, Carlo saw my bruised skin, but not my expression of bliss.

"Are you all right? What happened?" he asked. My bruises reminded him of Renato. "Have you been hurt?" Uneasily, he shifted his soft hat from hand to hand.

"An accident," I said, not wanting him to know I had a nose job. It would imply I was not satisfied with who I was. "I fell on the rock path behind our house."

"You look like the Lone Ranger." Carlo tugged the bottom of my gauze mask. "I can't see inside you."

I whispered to him, "You don't have to. I'll tell you everything. Everything will be all right. Won't it, my Carlo?"

He embraced me again, long and hard. His chest heaved against mine. I was still taller than Carlo, and this reminded me that I was the protector and fruit, the person who was to take care of the family. Finally, I reached out, hugging him back, hoping the smell of my perspiration didn't repulse him. It was a sour odor full of fright. Carlo didn't notice. We kissed quickly, like brothers and sisters do, pressing our identical lips, perfect lips, not too thick or too thin, against each other's.

I exhaled. I exhaled completely, emptying the air I had brought with me on the plane from Italy, and the staler air I had been carrying in my lungs since childhood, since Carlo left me. I vowed, from that moment on, we would not be separated again. It was a naive moment. In only a few weeks I would have to buy a return ticket and straighten out the loose ends of Carlo's messed-up shipping business.

Arm in arm, Carlo and I walked out of the Alitalia terminal to the parking lot where we were no longer sheltered from the roar of departing and arriving jets.

Carlo drove his van too fast, but I didn't care. I stared across the seat and inspected his square face. His sideburns were long, his neck had grown wider, and his eyebrows were now as bushy as our father's had been. I forgot every moment we had been apart. "For years I've carried you inside my head, and for years I've talked and listened to you, Carlo," I said. "We've never been separated, not really, have we?"

Carlo was not comfortable with my confession of love. "Love is love," he said. "It can make you stronger or weaker." He dropped change into the basket at the entrance of the tunnel that dove under Boston Harbor.

I glanced up at the two angels, Gabriel and Michael, sculpted on the pink granite archway over the tunnel entranceway. Carlo stopped. He pulled off to the side of the road, slamming the brakes. "We forgot your luggage," he said. The horns of the cars behind us wailed.

"I don't have any," I said.

"That's it?" Carlo pointed to my handbag.

I nodded. I was wearing a black dress, the same dress I had worn to Boston four years ago—but its seams had been let out—and a thick old wool sweater. "I don't have other clothes," I said. "I've worn a nurse's uniform every day for fifteen years."

In the tunnel I counted rows of white tiles. I was silent. Carlo was thinking about money. I didn't have to delve into his thoughts to see the lines of his forehead pressing together. He was deciding how much to give to me and what he might expect in return. I knew Carlo was going to be generous, but not too generous. He wouldn't take care of me as if I were a queen, but I didn't mind. When the time was right, I'd be my own queen.

I interrupted his thoughts. "Caring for people is my business. I'm a nurse, and I'm your sister," I said. "Your children couldn't have a better person to look after them than their Aunt Alicia."

Carlo smiled a broad smile.

Reflecting back on that ride through the tunnel, the way I felt sitting next to my brother must have been how Virginia felt when she was working for him. Neither of us understood how to make other people want us as much as we wanted them.

Downtown Boston emerged before us. I saw the orange clock of the Custom Tower, the Union Oyster House billboard, granite corners of skyscrapers, windowless sides of brick buildings, and the green guardrails of the overhead expressway iced with seagull droppings. It was all familiar. Boston was going to be my home, and I was ready to grab on to its O's and lift my feet away from my old concerns.

We turned the corner and were in the North End. On the first block, next to the small ravioli shop, I saw the big red sign above Carlo's FREEDOM DRUGS. An Italian flag flapped above the sign, next to an American flag. I didn't have to search far down the Freedom Trail to see my brother's other shops: CARLO'S COOKWARE, THE BLUE NOTE, and one block farther, on the right side of Hanover Street, SPEDIAMO. The door was still locked.

Carlo parked the van on Atlantic Avenue. I rushed up the steps ahead of him. The girls were hungry for a mother. I dropped to my knees and reached my arms out to them, but they cowered like little midgets, close to Mrs. Musetta's legs.

"Her face is funny," Bebe said to Carlo. She stuck her thumb in her mouth, turning away from me. Bebe's eyes were a remarkable gold color, and her face was willful and wide, like Renato's. Her hair was light brown and curly, and I had the feeling, looking at her, that she was a marked child. Her beauty was inviting but her wisdom, for such a young person, was offputting. It would be difficult not to make Bebe my favorite.

The twins were beautiful and walking already. They were two sides of a cut apple, both dark-haired and fair-skinned, but their eyes were shaped differently. Cher's were round bowls and Sera's more oriental-looking. Sera was taller, and Cher's nose was more pronounced. At first, both were shy. "My face?" I said to them. "You should see what your faces look like from in here." I smoothed the edges of my white mask and stood up, leaving the children in the front room with their father and babysitter. I walked down the long hallway to the kitchen.

For two days I ignored the girls, providing only basic diaper changing and food preparation services. "She who gives too quickly gives twice," I told myself. Carlo bathed and dressed them and picked up their toys. I watched everything they did. If I was a bit mean, I thought, the children would come to me. I was right. By our fourth day together, the children were in love with me. I kissed their beautiful smooth pink cheeks over and over again.

"Mama Alicia," Bebe called, "read this book."

"Mama Alicia, look at this." Like their mother, Sera and Cher were showoffs. Their hair was as black as mine, and they had the same perfect lips Carlo and I shared.

I turned my body over to them. On my hands and knees I became a bandit horse while the girls took turns standing on my back. I charged down the long hallway. They sat on my head. The twins begged me to carry them upside down like the gong on a clock. I never left the apartment. I stayed inside for a week, both because of my mask and because I wanted to become as much a part of them as their dreams. I slept on the floor on a mat in their room. I loved their soft sweet arms. The children devoured me, and I didn't resist them.

They brought me more happiness than I thought possible, yet that happiness was tainted with self-reproach. At night I cursed myself for being so stubborn and having missed their infancies. In the morning I longed to give them a pill that would keep them small so that I could hold the three of them forever on my lap. I told myself happiness was having nothing change. I didn't want memories. I didn't want anything old, or the future. Happiness was like stone. And that first week in Carlo's apartment was happiness.

Each day I dressed in my black dress, which was appropriate for a single, overweight Italian virgin who had passed the middle of her third decade. But by day seven, I got restless and began poking around Jassy's closet. I borrowed a fringed vest and cowboy boots. At eleven-thirty, Mrs. Musetta picked up the children and took them to the waterfront park, or to the library on Prince Street. Carlo didn't want them to depend on one person. "It's nothing against you," he had said to me. "It's just what their mothers want." I dressed the girls warmly.

When I heard the twins' double stroller bang open on the Atlantic Avenue sidewalk, I rolled up my sleeve, and put on bright rubber gloves. My mission was to scrub a room a day.

The entire apartment was painted different shades of white. The colors had been selected by Jassy before the twins were born. The front room was a bluish-white, to catch the color of the harbor; the hallway was like the inside of a warm biscuit; the bathroom was chalky white; and the bedrooms were ivory, like skin, soft and stark. The kitchen was the same shouting shade of yellow as my kitchen in Subiaco. Carlo had chosen that color. I cleaned the kitchen first.

Second, I cleaned Virginia's old room, which was to become my bedroom. Carlo and I decided if Virginia did come back, she could sleep downstairs, in Renato's room. Renato wasn't around to be involved with the decision. Since he had been released from the hospital, he had locked himself in the Teatro and hadn't come out. I was disappointed. Since Virginia was gone, I was interested in getting to know Renato better.

I scrubbed, scraped, and fumigated Virginia's room. She had left a few pink garments behind. I tossed them into a bag along with *Spiritual Midwifery* and put them downstairs. I

171

heaved the mattress, leaning it upright against the wall, and misted it front and back with an antiseptic. As I wiped the metal bed rungs and wooden slats that supported the mattress, I noticed the statue of St. Anne under the bed, wrapped in a brown blanket. I had mailed the statue to them the Christmas before Bebe was born and was alarmed that the Virgin's mother had ended up on the floor next to dustballs. I cradled the statue as if she were one of the children, apologizing for her ill-treatment.

"You'll forgive them," I said. "I did." Like all saints, St. Anne could see through time and space—and mattresses. I realized she and I had shared the experience of watching Virginia and Renato make love.

I carried the saint into the bathroom. When the children napped, I promised to give her a proper cleaning, scrub the folds of her plaster gown, and brighten her face with Virginia and Jassy's cosmetics. She would soon be positioned in a spot of honor, on my dresser next to my rosary beads.

That night, Bebe, Sera, and Cher slept with me, in my bed, in the room that used to belong to Virginia. Carlo kissed us good night. *"Ciao belle,"* he said, shutting off the light. "Remember, early worms get the biggest birds."

I listened to my brother pace across the front room. I was concerned about him. Since I had arrived, Carlo had become restless. He missed Jassy terribly. When he was near me, he inhaled slowly, wanting to take in the female smell he needed to go on being Carlo. But my scent was not hers, but mine.

I continued to listen to Carlo's footsteps pad on the carpeted floor. When the children's eyes closed, I went to him. "Carlo," I said, "I'm caring for the children and cooking. Renato and Virginia are gone. Spediamo is closed. You have help everywhere else, and too much time to worry about things that have already happened and about people you can't tell what to do."

He stopped pacing to separate a pair of lace undercurtains. Carlo looked out over Boston. The skyline was thick and still, and below it, on the expressway, a stream of cars traveled north, or south, like beads of painted light. It was almost raining. "I wish I were going somewhere," he said.

"Where would you go?" I asked. "This is your home." I didn't want him to leave, not now that I was with him. "Jassy will return."

He shrugged his shoulders. My brother was heavy-hearted. "Thank goodness I made a home for her inside a harbor and not on the edge of an ocean where at any moment our family might fall off the continent into the sea," he said, still looking out the window.

I stood behind, not touching Carlo. On the other side of Atlantic Avenue, the dark harbor water glimmered with reflections of the city and sloshed against broken glass, granite blocks, and patches of land.

The lace curtains fell from the backs of Carlo's wide hands. He wiped his mouth and pulled the heavier overcurtains shut, completely darkening the room. I sat on the red sofa. He stood, thinking about Jassy, tasting her voice, and smelling the folds of her red hair. It hardly mattered that I was in the room with him. He imagined her, lying naked on the purple chair across from my knees, her hands cupped under her breasts, inviting him to her, her knees spread unselfconsciously.

Carlo was driving himself crazy! It wasn't good, for him, her, or the children if he needed her so much. I was relieved when Carlo changed his thoughts and decided to find a spot within his own soul, a button or pinpoint of pure Carlo. He wanted to turn it inside out, for only a moment, to feel what it was like not to want her. But he couldn't do it.

"I'm here, Carlo," I said, interrupting him and my own power to sink inside my brother's brain.

"Alicia," he said, simply and with thanks.

Carlo stopped haunting himself. He sat on his purple chair. His head dropped on his chest.

"Molte grazie, fratello mio," I said, not instructing him, as Jassy might have done, to go sleep in his own bed and not in the front room chair or else he would have a stiff neck in the morning.

Carefully, I wiggled into bed with the girls. Their silken hands and feet pressed against my body. It had changed for Carlo and me. I had someone to sleep next to, and he didn't. It was a greedy feeling. I recognized it immediately. "I don't care that they all loved each other and that I was left alone for so long," I said, harking the gentle edge of my spirit to my tongue. I stared at the ceiling and listened to the children's breathing. I knew I was no longer empty inside. Their trust had seeped into my wounds. I was a full person, and realizing that, I offered a prayer for Carlo and Jassy, and for Renato and Virginia.

I spoke to the statue of St. Anne, who was on my dresser. "Ask God to bring them back together," I prayed. "And I'll stay with them this time."

But then my prayers became like ants crawling on my leg. I only realized I'd said them after the words were on my tongue, and I couldn't imagine where the words came from without my thinking about them first. I couldn't brush them away. I spoke directly to Him: "Reward Jassy," I said. "Up her applause wherever she is. Don't rush her back to Boston. Keep her away until I'm well settled in. And Virginia? If she doesn't want her daughter,

Bebe can be mine. She's almost mine anyway. I'll take Renato, too." I was filled with the desire to have what didn't belong to me, and I didn't want to lose my position as the top female in the North End family.

Fourteen

*B*uon *giorno, signorina.*" Ralph, the owner of the Paradiso Caffè, wiped his hands on the lap of his white apron before sliding a mug of caffè latte over the polished counter to me.

I carried the hot milky liquid to the rear of the cafe and placed it on a mirror-topped table about the size of a large dinner plate. Though Carlo's apartment had not yet been scrubbed from entry to exit, that day I had decided to take a peek outside before I got too comfortable inside. On my first solo venture into the streets of Boston's North End, I was all eyes and overflowing with anticipation of men looking my way. America was the land of the free, and I was eager to exercise my options. No one in the neighborhood knew who I was. Mrs. Musetta had the children, and my raccoon stains were gone. My nose had healed. I was quite attractive, I thought. I wondered how many men would ask my name, now that I was no longer marked by a sharp nose.

After stirring three cubes of sugar into my coffee, I pulled a book from my handbag. It was a recent Maria Callas biography, one that Jassy hadn't finished. She had folded the corner on page 176, and I started there, thinking when she returned I would tell her the ending, and she could fill me in on the beginning. But I was distracted by the conversation of the old men who gathered to gossip in the rear of the narrow cafe.

Impeccably groomed, wearing white shirts and black shoes, the men smoked Perogi cigars and spat in their white handkerchiefs after coughing. They talked in Italian. Nothing about these North End men was especially different from the doctors and janitors I had watched in Italy. Their discussions here were also as glandular.

"You're right. *È un gran coglione.* He carries too much between his legs!" a man with slicked-back hair said.

"He needs an alley as big as Hanover Street for his bowling ball," a curly-haired man laughed. "But all he's got is that little banana warehouse. No wonder he encouraged her to do it."

"But he didn't know nothing. He told us he didn't. The man with big balls is as stupid as the king," a younger man said.

"Ah! But after she left, his trousers got so tight, his hands became the dance partner. Right, Tony?" He slapped the table and laughed. "Big Balls doesn't want us to find her first."

The men laughed. I was tempted to laugh, too, not yet realizing the men were laughing at the same spectacle I was remembering—Renato's flagpole.

They continued, and then I knew: "Renato's feet were always stuck in something secondhand, but he ended up being the one with balls, not Carlo." The mustached man shook his head.

I tilted my ears. Was Carlo the king, and Renato Big Balls?

"Carlo?" The men shrugged and eyed their empty coffee cups. "*È un fesso. Il re di Hanover Street è un buffone.* The King of Hanover Street is a fool. That woman stuck him— they both did. He doesn't know what to do. His hands are

177

stuck in his pockets, too, but because he's afraid to lose money. He's already lost his balls."

My outing was no longer a relaxing one. These old fellows with rocky southern accents knew something I wanted to uncover. I tuned out the popular Italian music coming in on the jukebox, the hiss of the espresso machine, and focused on what they were saying.

A short man held his thumb to his index finger. "Three children from boiled eggs?" He shook his head no. Below the table, the man grabbed his own balls. "The kids all belong to Renato. Who knows how many more he's got running around America—and Italy."

What they were saying wasn't true. Carlo had fathered his children. The twins' feet were exactly like his, and mine, which was proof enough for me. How dare these men deny Carlo what was his! But Renato? Had he betrayed my brother?

I pretended to read, lifting the book close to my face so the men wouldn't notice my scowl. I was repulsed. The old men continued to evaluate my brother's balls. I dared myself to object, but rage caused me to sink into shame. How could I possibly know what was true had I not spied on my brother and his friends? My speculation was no different from the men's.

I looked down at my feet. I was wearing Jassy's boots, behaving as if her belongings were as much mine as hers, or my brother's; and I assumed, since Jassy had given away so much of herself, that she wouldn't mind if I put out my hand and grabbed whatever part of her came my way. She hadn't offered me anything other than friendship and love. Here I was wearing her shoes and fantasizing her beautiful children were mine.

With a paper napkin, I wiped Jassy's coral-colored lipstick from my lips. The old men watched me.

"She's an outsider, an American, not from the North End," the one with an eye patch said after inspecting me with his good eye. "They've been coming here like rats under the tunnel. She's single or divorced, a catastrophe. The rent's cheap in the North End, and it's safe. She's taking a free ride by having our protection and not being one of us."

"Giuseppe, you got it wrong. They come here because they want to be bothered. The Italian man makes the woman feel alive inside. You know what I mean?" The old man with the mustache raised his eyebrows. "It's in our blood. We have passion. The men on the other side only give them promises, and their cocks come smaller than our little fingers. These women want to meet someone like Big Balls."

They didn't suspect I understood Italian.

"Avete ragione. You're right. She doesn't look Italian," another said. "Her nose is too dainty. Italian girls, no matter if they're big or small, they always have"—he pinched the tip of his nose—"lima beans, not peas." He stuck out his tongue and wiggled it vulgarly. The others laughed. "And she's American. Look at the boots." The men agreed. "She's the kind that'll kick and kill until someone takes those cowgirl things off her feet. Be careful with ones like her." They all nodded.

"For sure she's not a virgin." They paused to bless themselves. "No. No American women are. They can't be."

Satisfied at having agreed on who I was, the men started back in on my brother's balls. "We all used to envy Carlo, right? His money. His relationship with politicians. His women. Now we find out the women were slicing his balls, slowly, with their teeth, as if it was a cappicola between his legs." The bushy-haired man ran a toothpick between his front teeth. "One slice after another. Did they think they could get away with it?" The man scratched his crotch. "I'll tell you what's happened to Carlo. They made him like a woman. They ate his balls and his brains. How's Carlo going to run businesses with an empty canoe between his legs and polenta between his ears?"

The thin-haired man knocked his knuckles against the table. "I want you to know I talked to Carlo. He says he can do everything himself. He told me if my cousin wants to move back to Sulmona, he'll open the store just for me and send his stuff tomorrow." The men hushed.

"So is he going to make our shipment himself?"

"Sure. He didn't need the women."

"You don't think he'll leave us stranded? For three weeks the king hasn't done anything but say 'Don't worry, I'll take care of it.' But nothing.

"*Mannaggia mia!* They'll choke us in Rome if we don't get the stuff to them. It's a gift—maybe an Easter present for the pope. Right now they have it in the underground deep freeze. Getting the angel there on time will move our Boston unit to the front. Think of all the grace the cardinal will reserve for us." The man with the pink face got pinker.

Just then, as I was leaning forward to hear their words, suspecting they were smugglers using Carlo's Spediamo as a front, I knocked a spoon off the table. When I bent over to pick up the spoon, quarters spilled from my fringed vest pocket, hitting the tile floor like a handful of loose teeth. The tiny bells of money silenced the men.

On my hands and knees, I scratched the silver quarters from the floor, retrieving them while the men watched.

"The tall one, the redhead, she was supposed to have her own money," I heard the man with the curly hair say. "She didn't need Carlo. The other one needed him more. That's why she took him to the cleaners."

They were talking about Virginia.

"No woman can live without a man to steer her."

"*Avete ragione.* The father is supposed to guide his

daughter until she finds a husband—and the brother his sister. He has to keep her a virgin." They blessed themselves. "But in America the women are greedy, and the men are stupid. They give everything away. It's wrong."

"I raised three girls, and I let them know who is boss. You got to do it, or they become like weeds. It's a female's nature to fight. You got to treat the girls like tomato plants—stake them up and tie them down or put them in a cage. If you don't, who will want them? The fruit gets rotten. And men?" He shrugged. "Hey, what can I tell you? We want to eat, drink, sleep, and enjoy ourselves. Women are supposed to keep everything in order so we can do that."

"A good woman knows what we want. That's why they have to come to us without crazy ideas." The pinkish man tapped his friend's shoulder. "I tell my wife the same. And what does she say? She laughs. 'Why don't you go home to your Mama?' she tells me. 'Mama?' I say. 'She's dead a long time ago and buried in Italy.' 'You got it,' she answers. 'You're in America, open your eyes.'"

They laughed. One coughed and unfolded a starched white handkerchief. "Women make everything complicated. We can't let them do that. We have to save the Virgin." The men blessed themselves.

"Carlo got stuck," said the man with the big nose. He struck a match under his thumbnail and lit his cigar. "We used to think he was lucky! Ha!"

"Renato dumped his sins on Carlo, and that's why Carlo's in trouble."

"Naw! Carlo's got money, and money's what'll save him."

The bushy-haired man dropped his hands to his crotch. "I wouldn't want to be Carlo."

"Me neither."

"*Cazzo!* Will the saints help him out of this one? For sure the Virgin won't help him, unless he helps us." The men blessed themselves and were quiet for a moment.

"When I talked to him, he said he was waiting for a message," the hunch-shouldered man added.

"I don't think he has an inkling of what's going on," the mustached man said. "He thinks Virginia's coming back."

They bowed their heads. One man kissed his thumb.

"Cosa è successo? What happened?" I asked. I put down my book and turned to the men. "Both my ears itch like cabbages full of worms," I said in Italian. "Scratch them for me, please."

The men cleared their throats. Someone coughed but no one spit into their handkerchief. Blood rose to their foreheads like mercury in thermometers. Each pretended I hadn't said a thing. Finally, the bushy-haired man shifted a chair, closing off their circle by turning his back to me.

The men huddled together, straightening their backs. "Spain's in Pakistan tomorrow night," someone said. "The last game of the series. Now why do those Pakistan people think they can play soccer? They've got brown nuts. What good are brown nuts against big balls like the Italians have?"

My eyes sank into my brain like pieces of hot lead. *"Datemi una spiegazione.* Tell me," I said, more loudly. I stomped my foot.

Not one of the men turned. They were pretending I was invisible, and instantly the old pain of being forgotten came back. I couldn't breathe. I bit my tongue and fled out of the cafe, dragging my heavy feet, hoping I wouldn't fall.

On the other side of Hanover Street, I unlatched the iron gate and wove through the tiny Peace Garden in front of St. Leonard's Church. The few thin trees in the garden were bare and brittle. It was cold. The low, mean sky was covered with stringy clouds that buzzed, making me dizzy. Crows clung to the telephone wires above me. My feet crushed the tiny flames of green, tips of daffodils pressing from cracks of the earth.

Afraid someone might be trailing me, I tried the front door of the church. I don't understand why I thought I would be safe inside a church. It was locked. In the rear, I found steps to the basement chapel.

The chapel smelled comforting, like incense and stagnant water, but I wished it were smaller, a closet into which I could fold. Its smooth walls throbbed. I chose a side altar, and knelt on the spongy red kneeler to light a candle. Out of habit, I blessed myself but wasn't truly interested in praying. My prayers didn't stick. God didn't believe my sincerity, and neither did I. But I went ahead, reciting the Hail Mary, while I counted my breaths to determine if I might faint. Fainting would be better than saying more holy words.

I stayed there, in the church, until the sun sank. Then I tied my ratty wool scarf over my head and slumped home.

Carlo stayed late at his stores. He ate alone and prepared his own dinner, a dandelion salad sprinkled with vinegar and oil. "To clean my blood," he said.

He tucked a dish towel under his collar to protect his brown flannel shirt from drops of olive oil. "You're prettier than I remember," Carlo said to me. "I am surprised every time my eyes look at you."

The children were in the nursery playing. "Thank you," I said. I was beginning to understand how easy life must be for girls born with pleasant faces. They went from grade to grade, from man to man, or job to job, their confidence having taken root before their breasts. "Did you hear from Jassy today?" I asked.

"No." Carlo looked away, not wanting me to pry into his disappointment. "Did you buy bread today?" he asked, changing the subject.

I placed a round loaf on the table, along with a package of sliced cappicola that I had picked up at the grocers on Salem Street. I didn't put anything on a plate, as I had been trained to do. American women were athletes, lawyers, riveters, businesswomen, and equals. They could establish or abolish mealtime rituals.

"You must have had a fine day," Carlo said, a bit sarcastically, getting out of his chair to put the bread and a serrated knife on a board. He unwrapped the meat.

I put my hands on my hips, which were still unattractively wide, but I was working on slimming them. "Where's Renato?" I asked.

Carlo wiped his mouth. "Looking for Virginia."

"Is he coming back?"

"Of course. Renato wouldn't leave the Teatro. It's his life."

"Are you sure? Virginia left Bebe."

Carlo glared at me.

"Who will take care of Bebe's future if neither of them come back?"

"Me. And you—if you agree to it. *Non preoccuparti*. Don't worry. They'll come back. They've had arguments before." Carlo sliced a piece of bread from the loaf.

"And your shipping business? Have you closed it for good, or are you going to begin again, without Virginia?"

My brother scratched under his ear. "Why do you want to know this?"

"Because everyone takes from you, Carlo. No one is doing anything for you, but me. And you call me only after they abandon you."

"Alicia, don't speak to me like that. I don't allow a smart-pants voice in my house." Carlo put his hands over his ears. "No one ever talked to me like that. No woman. No man. Don't you start now. I'm my own boss and that's what I am

184

teaching my children!" He tossed the dishtowel around his neck onto the table. "You ruined my dinner. My stomach has turned over."

"Carlo, the men in the cafe want to steal your business."

He lifted his hands. "Everybody in the North End wants to steal my business. Everyone wants to steal everyone's business. They're jealous. That's the way Italians are. You too! No one is satisfied with what they have, and then when they get something new, they don't know what to do with it. They ruin it."

I wanted to scare Carlo, or make him tell me the truth. "The men in the cafe said the women double-crossed you."

"They've been saying the same thing for ten years. It's nothing new. What else do they have to talk about? Men gossip like women gossip. Don't you know that?"

"They said you're going to ship something for them."

"I don't know anything about shipping. I never did. Virginia does everything. It was her job. They'll have to wait until she comes back."

"And if she doesn't?"

Carlo lifted his hands. "You're here three weeks and out of the house for one day and you know everything. You tell me what to do, or you do it. What? What am I supposed to do?" His face was red. He splayed his wide hands on the table and leaned toward me. "Like I said, in America I learned not to make anyone do what they don't want to do. Then everything is better. Don't you come here and change it."

Carlo pushed his chair back to the table, cut another piece of bread from the round loaf and resumed eating the dandelion salad. His eyes darted from the wine bottle to his glass, to the sliced meat, and me. I stacked dry dishes in the cupboard.

When he was finished, Carlo left, leaving me alone in the

kitchen with the dishes and his half-eaten salad.

I thought about what he had said. Maybe Carlo was right. The men in the cafe didn't look dangerous. If I was going to succeed in America, I had to learn not to believe everything I heard. I looked out the window over the sink. Outside Boston's night sky was high and the thin cloud over the moon became a pillow for my ears.

Fifteen

Early the next morning, I carried the metal stepladder into Carlo and Jassy's room. Standing on the top rung, I unlatched the heavy wine-colored curtains from a thick wooden pole. Below me, the fabric collapsed on the carpet, releasing a puff of red dust. There were three windows. I unscrewed the venetian blinds from between the window jambs.

"Alicia, why should you clean, when I can hire someone to do it?" Carlo asked. He stood in the bedroom door, buttoning his shirt cuffs. I looked at Carlo. It was a gray morning, and the windows were so dingy that he seemed to be lighted by the dusk when it was really dawn entering the room.

I shook my head no.

"Why not? I'll send Giuseppe over with a bucket and a brush," he said. "In less than a day the room will be fresh. You won't have to lift a finger." He scratched his ear.

I was determined to scrub the walls, wipe the corners of drawers, and vacuum the mattress myself. "Remember what our Mama said." I climbed down the ladder and shook my finger at Carlo. "She said the woman who lives in a house ought to clean it, no matter how rich or poor or busy she is."

I was clearly criticizing Jassy's lackadaisical housekeeping skills.

I ran the bundles of venetian blinds into the bathroom, dropping the metal slats into a tub of warm soapy water. Carlo followed me. I interrupted him before he could say anything. But I knew he was going to tell me times had changed since Mama had managed her household.

"How can you be sure the toilet seat has really been wiped?" I asked. Jassy had spray-painted their seat gold. "You have to do it yourself." I refolded a towel. "I'm a nurse," I continued. "I know what clean means, Carlo. If you want to throw your money away—or help me out—hire someone to polish the steps in the hallway. I'll clean where we live. It's an honor."

Carlo followed me back into the bedroom to watch me strip the silky pillowcases and roll the stale sheets off his bed. He was remembering Jassy's orange and lily smell, her red hair, and smooth white skin against the dark blue bedclothes that I held in my hands. She had been gone forty days. To him I was taking her away forever, but I was offering him rest and cleanliness.

"I've decided to send out our laundry," I said, folding the sheets into the pillowcases. "A man comes in a truck and picks it up and then he delivers it back the next day." I stuffed the dirty linens into a plastic bag. "I can't do everything."

Carlo shook his head. "You think Mama would have allowed people she didn't know to look at her underwear?" Carlo clicked his tongue sadly. "I'll never understand how a woman's mind works. Do their thoughts ever coin inside to make any sense?"

I defended myself. "I don't know what Virginia and Jassy did, but at the hospital we sent things out. That's what I'm familiar with. I never had to operate a laundry machine—

just a complicated open-heart machine." I tied a knot in the plastic bag. "And it's coincide—not coin inside."

"*È lo stesso*. Same difference." Carlo shrugged.

Bebe's knees were so chubby they knocked together when she ran into the room, distracting us. She raised her arms to Carlo. "Papa!" she said. Carlo combed his fingers through her soft brown hair before lifting her into his arms. "I want my oatmeal, please, with honey."

Carlo kissed Bebe's cheek. He was a gentle man, and I was sorry for letting my teeth grow long with him. "Go," I said to Carlo. "You sit in the kitchen and enjoy your cereal."

He hesitated, surveying the clutter in his bedroom.

"This is the last room to clean," I said. "Leave me alone with it while the twins are sleeping. I promise you nothing will change. I'll just get rid of dust. Besides, I'm sure Jassy will be grateful I did it for you."

Quickly, I moved the furniture to the center of the room and unhooked photos of opera singers, a print of *Moses in the Water*, and a painting of a harlequin from the walls. The pictures left white shadows, which I washed with a sponge. I was sure I could penetrate as deeply into the room with disinfectant as Jassy had done with her personality.

I dragged the red oriental rug and its horsehair pad out to the front entry. A cleaner was picking it up at two. America was wonderful—there was somebody to do everything you didn't want to do yourself, and they came to your house to do it.

Then I got down on my knees to roll the long, thin carpet that ran from one end of the hallway to the other. I crawled into the kitchen on my hands and knees.

"Look!" Bebe shrieked. "Alicia's playing a horse again!"

"*Aspetta*. Wait a minute," I said, lifting my gloved hand. "Stay on Carlo's lap. I'm going to hang this carpet on the balcony. It needs an airing."

189

Carlo had been reading Bebe the headlines in the Italian sports newspaper. "Alicia, you can't put that carpet outside," he said.

"Why not?" I had planned on beating the red-patterned runner with a broom.

"It cost over two thousand dollars," Carlo warned. "I don't advertise my possessions to the world." He gently rubbed his chest with his fingertips. "Everyone on the street will see it and say, 'What? Does Carlo Barzini think he is a king?' "

I pulled off my rubber gloves. "Everyone in the North End knows everything about you anyway," I said, brushing my damp bangs off my forehead. "One long rug won't surprise them. It's no longer than all their tongues."

"No. You don't hang that outside!" he said. Carlo put his cap on his head, his hands in his pockets, and left. Again, I had stepped too far with Carlo. He was like a lamb until some word or deed turned his muscles hard. I would have to apologize.

"Ready?" Bebe asked. "Aunt Alicia? Ready to play horse with me?" She tugged delicately at my skirt.

I held up my finger. *"Un momento,"* I said, running to catch my brother before he turned the corner. "Carlo, I'll do what you asked," I shouted to him from the balcony. I didn't want him to curse me during his day for beating the rug and getting rid of the dust and fingerprints Jassy had left behind.

By midafternoon, when Mrs. Musetta returned with the children, I had scrubbed the ceiling, light fixtures, and the tight seams between the floorboards in Carlo's room. I also folded Jassy's rumpled clothes and was surprised to discover she wore cotton panties, not silk ones, and that her matching peach-colored undershirts had stained armpits—from nervousness, I guessed. Jassy wasn't always as in control as she appeared.

190

While the children played in the hallway, I tidied Jassy's closet, brushing her wool berets and the shoulders of her fur-collared coat, and hanging a long flower-print gypsy dress on a padded hanger. Kneeling, I lined up two pairs of shoes in boxes and her furry slippers under the hanging clothes. I was about to wax the clean square of closet floor, when I noticed that one shoe box was filled with papers, a red notebook, and folded receipts seemingly written in Virginia's childish script.

I immediately imagined the box might contained some love letters. I wanted to read how Jassy and Carlo had longed for one another on paper. And I hoped Jassy might have tucked some of her self-doubts into the red notebook. I wanted to know more about her weaknesses; her strengths were apparent. I set the shoebox on the bed, planning to read its contents after I organized Carlo's closet.

The children continued to amuse themselves. I opened a jewelry case for them. Within the next half-hour I was sure they would demand I tell them a story, or get them cookies, or ask me to pretend to be a prince. While I shuffled Carlo's shirts, I listened to the children's play.

"My hair is red," Cher said.

"So is mine," Sera copied.

The twins both wanted to be Jassy. I prepared myself for an argument.

"I'll decide," Bebe interrupted, taking a string of pearls from Sera.

Sera whined, "Alicia! She took my necklace."

"No. It was mine."

"But I had it first," Cher added.

"*Aspetta.*" I rummaged through the jewels strewn on the floor. "You can all be happy and equally beautiful without worrying about what the other one has. You can be three *bimbe carine,*" I said sweetly, kneeling down to be at the girls' level. "I can't decide—and I don't know how the prince will decide when he gets here—which one of you to take with him."

I propped the big dresser mirror on the floor near the girls. "Watch yourselves," I said. "Look in the mirror."

Then I sat on the edge of the bed admiring them and their reflections, wondering if the women who were their real mothers could possibly feel any differently than I did. I would die for them.

Just as I shifted my attention from the girls to the papers inside the shoe box, I heard footsteps in the outside hall. At first I thought it was the carpet cleaner, who hadn't yet arrived. But no one had rung the downstairs buzzer.

The careful steps climbed upward, passing Mrs. Musetta's apartment. Carlo's alarm clock read two in the afternoon. I listened. It wasn't Carlo coming up the steps. The man coughed. It was a large man. I wondered if it could be Renato. Yesterday the men in the cafe had said he was hiding like a rabbit in the basement of the Teatro. Maybe he had decided to come out. But Carlo had said Renato wasn't in the North End but in another state searching for Virginia. Maybe Renato was back.

The steps got louder and louder. I shoved the shoe box under Carlo's bed. My heart jumped into my throat. Oh, what a dreadful moment! I could smell the stranger, and he smelled of sulfur and cigars. Renato didn't smoke.

I dove across the waxed floor to protect the children.

The man jimmied the lock. He was standing in the door well. "Get your coats," he said.

I looked up at his big nostrils. His hat was pulled down over his eyes. He took a few steps into the bedroom and kicked me lightly on the knee. "You heard me. Get going, lady," he said.

The way the big man moved and the sway of his shoulders

under his shoulder pads told me he believed he was more important than he really was. "You lie to yourself," I screamed, hoping to push him off balance. "And they didn't pay you enough to hurt children."

Confused, the girls huddled in the circle of my arms. "This isn't for real," I whispered to them in my most caring nurse's voice. "By tomorrow you'll forget this man was here."

"Don't be so sure," the man said. "You're all coming with me. Get up."

Bebe, Sera, and Cher jammed against each other, expecting me to shield them from the evil man. Their small sharp chins pressed against my collarbone. I clutched them to my chest.

"Make him leave," Bebe said. She buried her golden eyes in the hollow of my neck.

"*Chi è lei?* Who are you?" My voice cracked. I spoke to him in Italian, suspecting he was from the neighborhood and that he really wanted to hurt Carlo, not us.

"I'll tell you one more time. Put on your coats." The man answered me in English, jabbing the hard toe of his black shoe into my thigh.

"No. You tell me who you are and why you're here. And why you want my children." A primitive instinct rushed through my folded legs. But I stayed seated, clutching the children, rather than kick the intruder. I could see in his eyes that the gangster was cold and heartless. He had killed before. "You watch too many movies," I mumbled.

"I told you to shut up."

"The children's coats are in the kitchen pantry," I said. "Why don't you go get them?"

"I don't like him," Bebe said. "He's got hair in his ears."

"Where's Carlo?" Cher whispered.

The man twisted a handful of my black all-purpose dress and pulled me up off the floor. Only Sera stayed in my arms.

The other children hung below, crying. The gangster had a scar on his right cheek. He put his face close to mine and spat when he spoke.

"The sooner you get your fat ass in gear, the sooner we'll go out, the sooner this whole thing will get cleared up. *Capito?*" he said. "You hear me?" Then he whispered, "If I hurt anyone, it'll be you." His breath smelled of garlic, beer, and strength. The inside corners of his eyes were red. I thought he must suffer from high blood pressure, and I wanted to drive it higher.

"Make him leave," Sera said.

Cher rolled on the floor, pounding the bare wood with her fists.

Bebe clutched my knees. "Don't be afraid," she said.

He put the barrel of his short gun to my nose.

I shoved it away, and the gun fell from his grip.

As it fell, I died a hundred times. I heard the children's cheeks letting go of screams and saw their short lives disappearing like pricked balloons. But the weapon didn't explode when it hit the floor. My children were safe. The gangster slapped my face. I would have begged him to hit me again, and again, if I knew his anger would stay only on me, and not the children.

"Aren't you ashamed of yourself?" I whispered, covering the red mark his hand had printed on my face.

The man stooped to pick up the gun. "I said get going, lady." He stuck the gun to my crotch.

"You don't know who you are," I said. "You're an animal." I pushed the gun away, knelt, and gathered the girls in my arms. I hoped a neighbor might be watching what was happening to us through the curtainless windows and have the sense to call the police.

The man pushed back the brim of his hat. He picked up Serafina. Her eyes were the most frightened. The others

194

would have kicked him. He squeezed Sera's shoulder with one hand, and in the other hand he held the gun to her small chest.

"So you have children of your own?" I asked, reaching out in desperation to the part of him that might have known kindness. "Girls, or boys?"

"Enough shit, lady." I had irritated him, and he lifted the gun, demanding silence.

I wished I had the power to ignite him and blow him away like dust to hell. But the short snub barrel of the gray gun was an inch away from Sera's heart. I moved like a soldier, to the closet, and slid my arms into Jassy's fur-collared coat.

"Now get the kids ready," the man said. When he shook his gun, I heard the bullets inside rattle. "And nothing tricky. Count out loud so I can hear where you go."

I implored him to be careful with the gun and silently asked the children's guardian angels not to let down their guard while I was out of the room. I ran to the kitchen. ". . . five . . . six . . . seven . . ." I took the girl's warmest winter coats from the low hooks in the pantry. ". . . eleven . . . twelve . . . thirteen . . ." They had just learned how to hang up their own coats. My throat closed. I saw their little hands latching the collars of their heavy woolen garments over the wooden knobs Renato had installed for them.

"Keep counting, lady, or the little one gets it."

"Fifteen," I shouted, putting their small gloves, hats, and boots into a string bag. "Seventeen." I grabbed a wedge of cheese and a package of sliced meat from the refrigerator. I stopped counting.

"Do you have bread?" I asked.

"We'll get some," he answered. I grabbed a loaf anyway.

I left the refrigerator door open and spilled ketchup on the floor. It was a signal for Carlo. Our blood was being threatened.

By twenty I was back in the bedroom.

"You carry those two," the big man said. He engaged the safety and put the gun in his pocket. Sera's eyes were glazed. I reached out to take her from him. The gangster stepped back. "I got her," he said.

My words were bald with panic. "Who are you? What do you want?"

"You're not supposed to know, lady."

I considered tripping and falling down the steps, but there were two men waiting on the fourth-floor landing, near Mrs. Musetta's door. One man took Bebe from my arms. She screamed, "I want my mommy!" I felt a tugging in my belly, as if she were being ripped from my body. Bebe stretched her arms to the ceiling, making herself slippery, and I tried to take her back from the man as we rushed down the last three flights of stairs, but the man squeezed her harder when I touched her. I didn't want Bebe to be hurt, and I was still holding Cher.

"We'll be all right, Aunt Alicia, won't we?" Cher asked. I clutched her little body with my own, hoping a crowd swinging sticks were waiting to pound the gangster outside. But when the lobby door opened, wind off the harbor blew into my face, and I hunched closer around Cher, pushing her frightened eyes into my fur collar. We were prisoners of another world now.

They pushed us inside a big black Cadillac that had two facing back seats. When they handed me Sera, I rocked her on my lap. "You're safe now," I said.

Cher and Bebe sat on either side of me. The three men who climbed in back with us were ugly and unshaven, with dirty fingernails, but they wore tailored suits. The car doors clicked shut, and the tinted windows, darker than midnight, locked us inside. I let out a long, high howl as the car pulled away from Carlo's building.

"We'll be all right," Bebe whispered. She patted her small hands over my chest, touching Sera, too. Sera responded. Thank goodness, I said to myself. I had been worried her spirit was ruined.

"Do you think they're taking us to find Jassy?" Bebe asked. "Is that where these men are taking us?"

"I don't think so," I said very casually. I had to be calm. Bebe was already assuming too much responsibility. "Jassy is in Europe. We're going somewhere else."

They kept us in the car until night fell. We hadn't gone any great distance because the surface of the road never changed, nor did the sounds inside the car. We traveled in circles. They had a small potty for the girls. I had to hold my urges. Nonetheless, I shared our meat and bread with the men who had kidnapped us. As they chewed, I prayed they would get whatever they wanted from Carlo and take us back home to him before the morning of the next day. But that's not what happened.

We were led out of the limousine into the inky night and down a flight of concrete steps into the side door of a huge brick building, then down several more flights of steps.

"Don't be afraid, lady." A gangster in a gray overcoat pushed aside a square of fake grass carpeting and lifted open a hatch. A light switched on below and rungs of a stepladder protruded from the square hole.

"Come on down. We're ready for you." A deep voice rose from what I imagined was Boston city sewers.

"I won't go down there," I said. No one pushed me forward. They hesitated, as if I were their sister. The men, six of them, waited, their heads bowed, ashamed to have taken me through a darkened building in the middle of the night and to have made me stumble with them through a maze of basements. They had begun to like me, and I them. I had to remind myself they were criminal.

The children, wrapped in white blankets, were asleep in three men's arms. The men swayed their hips and shoulders, protecting the girls' sleep.

"I won't go first," I said, peeking forward to sniff the air coming out of the hole. It smelled stale, but not putrid. "What if you lock me up down there and run off with my children?"

"Hey, we never thought of that," a man who wasn't holding a child said. The others didn't laugh.

"Shut up, Freddy!"

I got the feeling Freddy was the stupid one in the group, the one everyone used to absorb their own tensions.

"Don't worry, lady. I'll go first," another man said. It was too dark to see his face, but I recognized his voice. Earlier, he had been the one who cried in the limousine when I had sung Italian lullabies to calm the girls down.

I took Bebe from his arms. "I'll carry her down with me," I said. She was the leader, and her natural strength would fortify my own.

At the bottom of the ladder another gangster helped me catch my balance. I wouldn't let him take Bebe, who was still sleeping. I held on to her and faced a huge tube lined with white ceramic tiles, which I suspected were imported from Italy. Though there were no windows, the space felt familiar. It reminded me of the walls and floors of the Subiaco hospital, where I had worked for fifteen years; they had been plastered with the same tiles.

We began to walk. Like the St. Scholastica Clinic, this underworld cavern was well lighted and clean. But unlike the hospital, there were no noises—no squeak of rubber soles, no bells, or machines pumping blood, no microphoned ticking heartbeats, and no rushed conversations. Here there were only echoes of ten pairs of hard-toed shoes. The children were being rolled, having been tucked into three blue carriages with hoods and huge chrome wheels.

Finally we dipped to the right and through long plastic drapes suspended from a roof of earth.

"In here." A man waved us through a second set of curtains and into an immense room with flat floors and round walls. One area was enclosed with a hanging blue tent, which was to be our bedroom. Farther back, in the shadows, was a smaller green-padded tent, which was the toilet. My bladder was aching to be relieved, but first I had to settle the children.

Nothing hid the kitchen. It was equipped with several mini-refrigerators, makeshift counters, hot plates, toaster ovens, and tall open shelves stocked with boxes of pasta, bags of cookies, and cans of tomatoes. A prosciutto ham hung from a metal beam above the sink. Two men in suspenders sat at the central table, carving pears with their pocket knives.

"What took you so long?" one asked.

The other man tipped his hat. Since it was a gesture usually reserved for greeting a beautiful woman, I looked over my shoulder, sure that a female gangster was behind me. But I was the only woman in the bunch. Some girls get used to compliments early in their lives. I wasn't one of them.

"Those little ones yours?" the man asked, admiring me.

"Yes." I blushed and wanted to kick myself for being so obviously starved for flattery. If they knew I was shy and awkward, the men might take advantage of me and the children.

"I'll show them to their room," he said. I followed him to the tent. The floor was scattered with lambskins and yellow cushions. Our cots were sheeted and blanketed. "Good night, *signora*," the man said.

"The bathroom?" I asked, dropping my eyes.

He accompanied me there and back.

Exhausted, I lay on the cot. It hurt my bones to rest. My mind raced. On those anonymous sheets I imagined every awful thing that could happen to us—the worst image being my own and the children's organs in plastic bags being sold to Boston hospitals, and our Barzini blood distributed to strangers who would incorporate it into their own flesh through drip sacks.

But I knew the men I had sat across from in the limousine and the men who had accompanied us into this underground cave wouldn't carve us up. They weren't as dangerous as the man who had taken us at gunpoint from Carlo's house. He was the only dangerous one.

I was sure it was my fault we had been kidnapped. It was because of what I had overheard yesterday, in the cafe. If I had remained silent, none of this would have happened. I didn't deserve to sleep. But I did.

Sixteen

I dreamed about Carlo, seeing him shot dead in his sleep by the same man who had broken into his house to take us. When the gun went off, I woke up sweating, panting, crying for the children, who would be deprived of a fine father, and for myself for never having loved my brother as an adult. Frantic, I called upon my vision, praying I could calm myself down enough to engage it. I rolled over on my cot and found Carlo on Hanover Street, unbundling stacks of *Globe*s and *Herald American*s.

The sky was lead-colored, and on the other side of the expressway, fog blanketed the necks of Boston's skyscrapers. I thanked the Lord and Mary for keeping Carlo alive. He knew we were gone, but not where or why, or who had taken us. I could feel his frustration and sadness. I pulled the blue blanket up over my shoulders and tucked my knees close to my elbows. Carlo wanted Jassy's advice, but he had been unable to reach her. She was performing in Bratislava.

Carlo clenched his jaw. He was determined to go ahead and call the police, even though last night an anonymous man had called to warn him not to contact anyone.

"I saw your sister from my window," the man had said. "She took the curtains down that morning, right? The little ones didn't want to leave. She forced their arms into their red coats."

"Not true," Carlo said, controlling his voice.

"Yes. She even turned to blow a kiss to your building before getting into the car," he said. "The other woman was driving, the skinny blond one. They're working together."

Carlo laughed. The man lied. His sister, an incredibly clean woman, had smeared ketchup on the floor, had left the refrigerator open, and had tracked the red ketchup into his own bedroom. She had done that to let him know she had been taken by force. And Virginia wasn't in Boston. Renato had seen her yesterday, in Tennessee. Besides, Virginia didn't know how to drive.

"Do what we say, or you'll have more trouble than you can catch," the man warned. "You have to trust us, 'cause you got no one else. Don't call the police. Don't call anyone until we get back to you."

That was what the man had said to Carlo. But Carlo was weighing the risks of going against the warning and outside the neighborhood to get us. As he dragged a bundle of newspapers into the store, he mumbled to himself, "Goddamn, why me?"

He dropped the stack of papers and kicked it. He kicked again. He wanted to break the stack apart, the way his life and family had been broken. Ashamed, he stopped. Someone on Hanover Street might be watching him and would calculate his readiness to make an easy deal.

Carlo tucked his chin into his collar and straightened his shoulders. This was America. Opportunity could not be taken away, not for an instant, not from anyone, not even by his own kind. With the same broom he used every day, Carlo swept the sidewalk in front of his drugstore clean of gum wrappers and paper napkins stained with pizza sauce. Inland, the fog was beginning to lift off Boston's buildings. Carlo squinted at the sky, squeezing the broom handle, swallowing, willing the sun to burn through the clouds. March was the worst month of the year, he said to himself. It was unpredictable, long and cold, and the month the old women he knew complained about most.

Carlo leaned the broom against the window of the drugstore. What could he lose? he asked himself. Everything he cared about was already gone. Carlo decided to call the Boston police.

He ran to the back room, to the telephone, and my heart raced alongside his.

For sure my nightmare would come true. The man would break into Carlo's apartment at night and shoot the gun he had pressed against Sera's rib cage into Carlo. But Carlo caught his reflection in the mirror above the grinding wheel and saw that his skin had turned yellow. His liver had coughed up its courage. "Every Italian man, even small men, have some kind of arrangement, an understanding with other men they can depend on. They don't call the police." Carlo spoke out loud to himself. Keeping this business inside the neighborhood would be best for him, the children, and Alicia.

"Is anyone here?" a woman's voice asked. She rapped a coin on the front counter. "I want to buy a newspaper."

Carlo walked out of the back room.

"I could have taken your merchandise," the woman said. "You shouldn't leave your door open like this with no one to tend it. Who knows who would take what?"

The woman was a tourist, not someone Carlo knew. "In the North End, *signora,* everyone is safe." Carlo smiled and took her quarter. He left the store with her and spoke to her husband, a balding man in a neat wool coat, who was waiting for her on the sidewalk. "Your good wife was keeping an eye out for me," Carlo said, shaking the man's hand. "Thank you."

By now the sun was a dull white spot in a sky as gray as the sidewalk. Carlo watched the couple walk arm in arm up the Freedom Trail, past his other shops. Hanover Street split open for them in the same way it was closing in on him.

Later that afternoon, while I was supervising the children's nap, I employed my vision again for a few minutes. I found out Carlo had filed a missing persons report.

He was meeting with the Boston police in the rear of the cookware store. Two uniformed officers stood in front of his oak desk, crowding the small back room. Carlo turned over pictures of Bebe, Sera, and Cher.

"How about a picture of Alicia?" the veiny-nosed police officer asked.

"Only this one," Carlo answered. He handed the police a snapshot. "But she looks very different now." Carlo scratched under his cap. "That was taken when we were six-teen."

"How would you describe your sister?" The freckled officer poised his pen on a notebook.

Carlo paused. "Pretty," he said. "Tall. Round." He nodded his head. "Not athletic, but just big."

"Hair color?"

"Dark brown."

"Eyes?"

"Brown."

"Age?"

"Same as me. We're thirty-five. She's my twin." Carlo pushed back his chair. There was something he wanted to find in the bottom drawer of his big desk.

"Identical?"

"No." Carlo unfolded the *Time* magazine cover of the *Pietà* being hammered by Laszlo Toth.

"What was she wearing the last time you saw her?"

"Black. She wears a black dress every day." With his wide hands he brushed aside a stack of papers and pressed the magazine cover flat on his desk.

"Can you describe her face?"

Carlo couldn't remember.

"Does she have a long face, or is it square?" The younger policeman wore glasses and an expression of indifference.

"Long, I think," Carlo said, trying to remember. He could see my white mask. There was something different about Alicia, he thought. He stared at the picture of the *Pietà* and thought it was my nose that was different, but he wasn't sure. He wasn't sure about anything.

Most of all, Carlo wasn't sure if he had done the right thing by calling the police.

Seventeen

For four days we were held captive in a subway station under construction. The gangsters liked to cook, so we lived by the strict rhythm of meals. Thank goodness the children liked to eat; food endeared them to their captives.

On the first morning, the gangsters served them chicken soup with bread noodles and lots of Parmesan cheese. The girls were so thrilled to eat something other than oatmeal, each of them took second helpings. They sat together in a line, on one side of a picnic table, their napkins tucked under their round chins the same way Carlo tucked in his. I sat opposite them.

"Is Mrs. Musetta coming to take us to the park?" Cher asked.

"Not today," I said. "We're on a vacation. Everything is a bit different." I didn't want to tell them we were in a prison. "But different can be fun. There's plenty of toys here. New ones." I pointed out the many colorful cartons and boxes, which were for me a bad sign. The men were prepared to keep us a long time.

The girls must have felt my concern. Rather than play with games and Barbie dolls, they chose to run up and down the long corridor outside the hatch where we were being sheltered.

"Let's run through the curtains," Bebe said, bending her elbows and making fists. She always won.

The gangsters, who wore white sleeveless undershirts, nodded. "Send Freddy with them," they said.

I ran behind the girls, admiring the flex of their calves.

"Who can go fastest?" I yelled, urging them on. I wanted them to feel free, not trapped, and not to doubt their safety for a moment. If they were unsure of themselves or me, they would get sick. I could handle an illness, but I could never erase the scar of an unpleasant memory.

The second day, I complained about the lack of fresh air in the underground compound. "Can't you open a vent?" I asked, sweaty from having run after the children. "Scentless gases could kill us." I fanned my neck. "The children are getting pale."

The men at the picnic table put down their playing cards and shook their heads.

But a few hours later, right after lunch, three cages and five birds arrived underground.

"What are they?" Sera asked.

"Birds, of course," Bebe said. "Canaries."

"But why are they in cages?"

"They're pets," I answered happily.

"Birds aren't yellow. They're supposed to be black. Why are we here where there's no sky?" Cher asked. "When I close my eyes, it gets darker than the back of my mouth."

"I don't know," I said calmly. I tilted my head. "Ask them. They might think we like it here."

Bebe approached the kitchen area. "Misters, we don't want to stay with you anymore," she said.

"What? Aren't you enjoying yourself?" A tall man who

was washing the lunch plates turned to answer her.

"I want my daddy."

"Can't you pretend we're your Papas?" said another man, as he swept the crumbs from under the table into a dust bin. "You're used to more than one, aren't you?"

And more than one mother, I thought, not at all insulted.

Cher shook her dark hair. "None of you can be my daddy," she said.

"Why not?"

"Because I don't like you, that's why." She wrapped her soft arms arms around my neck.

"And you're bald," Bebe added. I had to hide my laughter. Bebe had a basic understanding of how words dented people. The twins didn't have the same talent.

"Take us out of this place, Aunt Alicia." Sera tugged my sleeve. "Why do you let them keep us?"

The children trusted me, and I was helpless. But I had to be a positive example of womanhood. I confronted the men.

"It's time we set things straight," I said assertively. "I want to know where we are and how long you intend to keep us." I put my hands on my hips, but I might as well have been shooting bullets into an iron.

"Want to tell her, Freddy?" The man who was sweeping the floor laughed. "She can't go anywhere, can she? Not like the other one, the blonde who slipped away." The man who addressed me had black hair and a matching mustache. "We gotta get your brother to do what we want. Then we'll let you go."

Freddy dried his hands on his apron. He was the kindliest of the men. "We're under 'arvard Square," Freddy said, not pronouncing the *h*. "Where we're standing is going to eventually be a station where the trains pick up passengers. We're breaking in the Red Line that's going from the square farther out into Cambridge and Somerville. But we're on strike. We won't go back to work until this whole mess with Carlo's been worked out." He pointed at the earth ceiling and whispered, "The construction bosses think we're striking for more money, but we're really striking for spiritual reasons. We have to wait for a go-ahead from our real boss—if you know what I mean." He winked at me. "Don't think for a moment that all we do is dig tunnels. We got big hearts and big ideas." He tapped his forehead.

The other man continued to whisk dirt into the dust bin. "Right above us is a museum—the Fogg. Over there is the Harvard library. That-away are some stores. And about two miles over your left shoulder is the Charles River. Three thousand miles away is Rome." He scratched under his belt. "We're keeping you until your brother does what he owes the Benevolents. Carlo's stalling us."

I thought how miserable it would be to lose my own treasures sacked away in Rome. "You must be asking him for more money than he can give you. Lower your price," I said, "then Carlo will help you."

The men blinked. "We haven't asked Carlo for money," they said, somewhat stupidly.

"How much do you think he has?" Freddy asked.

"If you don't want money, what do you want?" I asked.

"We want him to do what he always does for us," the other man said. "We warned Carlo not to contact the police. He'll get us all in trouble if he goes outside." He paused.

"But, hey, Carlo's in on it, right? We can't go down without him being pulled in, too," he said. "What more can I tell you? No woman could do it all on her own, behind our backs—and Carlo's—and leave us holding an empty sack." He held a cup out to me. "Want some coffee?"

I shook my head no. "Are you Mafia?" I asked.

Freddy and the other man grimaced. "No way," they said.

When the espresso took effect Freddy told me they were

members of the Benevolent Society. "We ain't killers, we're doing this for the Virgin," he boasted, blessing himself. "We love the Virgin. We'll do anything for her. And we've got brothers all over the world—in Chicago and Seattle. The Mafia wouldn't do nothing for the Virgin. They commit crimes for money, not us. We're clean. We have to be to carry her on our backs."

I laughed. "But with money you wouldn't have to be digging ditches!"

"Tunnels." Freddy corrected me.

"Why not ask Carlo for money?" the other man said.

"No way. This is a done deal, for the Virgin, and our boss in Italy. Carlo's been in on it with us from the start."

Though my next statement earned me special treatment, I have often regretted making the announcement. "I'm a virgin," I said loudly. Although I considered my chastity a prize, and something worth parading in America, I was ashamed to have confessed it to the gangsters. But at the time I was willing to try anything, hoping they would listen to me, take money from Carlo, and let us go.

There was a long pause. Freddy and the other two men exchanged curious expressions, lifting their ears and eyebrows.

"You're a real virgin?" Freddy asked.

I nodded. He stood.

"It's against Benevolent rules to involve a virgin in our business. We can't kidnap one! We can't eat with one—or sit on the same chair without blessing it first. We give them our respect. Right, Carmen?" The men made the sign of the cross.

"Alicia." Bebe tugged my hem. "I thought we were going!"

"Sh-sh-sh," I whispered to her. "Help me by playing," I said. "Maybe we will get out soon."

I sat at the table and the men stood around me. *"Voglio una spiegazione,"* I said, commanding their allegiance. "Tell me."

"There's reason behind our digging the subway," Carmen explained. "We take side trips and make connections. We take back things that don't belong to the people who have them and send them to Italy, where they belong." He paused. "Maybe we could show her," he added.

"You've said enough, Carmen. We're sworn to secrecy." Freddy pressed his lips shut with his fingers. He might have been the sweetest of the gangsters, but Freddy was also the most suspicious.

"Show me what?" I asked, staring at Carmen.

"The Virgins," he glared back. When called upon to be rebellious, Carmen was not unlike many other Italians. He hated authority.

Freddy whacked Carmen on the head. "Shut up, I told you." He took Carmen's empty espresso cup and rinsed it in the sink. "We got work to do," he said. "Let's go."

The shifts changed.

The twins kept busy, making clay castles on the clean floor.

When the new men came in, Bebe moved closer to my knee. She sucked her thumb and listened.

"Hey, lady, here's a magazine." A familiar-faced man dropped a copy of the French *Vogue* on my lap. "From the newsstand upstairs," he said. "They didn't have anything Italian, sorry. I thought you'd like the pictures." He smiled. I wondered if he had a crush on me, or if he had heard the news—their prisoner was a virgin.

The man began preparing our dinner. "What are you hungry for today?" he asked.

"Don't think about me," I said. "The children are more

important." It was exactly what men liked to hear women say.

"Polpettine? Tiny meatballs?" the man asked Bebe. "Special for the little ones?"

It was a day full of gifts. Another man, in for the evening shift, brought me knitting needles, hairpins, and red yarn.

"What am I supposed to make?" I asked.

"I don't know. Just knit. Isn't that what women do?" he asked. "How about socks?"

That night, while the children danced to accordion music, I knitted and cursed and prayed to the saints. I asked St. Christopher—even though he was a defrocked saint—to curse the future steps of the men who would wear the socks I was knitting. I was losing my composure, laboring for breath, and sweating. I thought all men wanted women to be virgins and prisoners who were interested only in fashion and sewing.

"We should give her back," I overheard one man say. "A virgin shouldn't be seen by so many men."

I sat in the rocker, flashing the long needles in my hands, keeping an unpleasant expression on my face. No man had ever wanted me. And now, not even my kidnappers wanted me. As I rocked, I saw the men revere me as if my bones were charged with a heavenly electricity, making me glow from within like a low-wattage saint. They had stopped admiring my physical grace; instead they saw only my holiness, my sacrifice, and my purity. I preferred their lust.

When it was time to bathe the girls in the buckets, I stopped the rocker. "No one needs to wash tonight," I said. The children were relieved that I had finally spoken. The twins, who hated getting wet, were jubilant and changed into their pajamas without my help.

I dragged the rocker into the tent and put the girls in their cots, tucking their soft-boned shoulders under silver blue blankets.

"Aunt Alicia, you look sad," Bebe said.

I smiled. They were unfamiliar with my brooding, and despair frightened them. "I can't be sad when I'm with you." And it was true. "I'm unhappy when I think too much about myself," I said, tapping my chest. "I promise I won't get lost inside here tomorrow. All my life I thought little ones like you would surely be more helpless than the sick people I took care of in the hospital in Italy and be more work than my own parents. But you're more wonderful than wonderful. You are you."

Comforted, they shifted their heads on their pillows.

"I won't let you fall asleep with a stone in your heart," I said, touching their foreheads. "Think about angels, and clouds, and count as many shades of blue as you can imagine." I listened for the little kicks that indicated their muscles were sleeping. "I'm so glad to know you," I whispered, watching their eyes close and their breathing shift to dreaming.

I myself was too tired to sleep. I rolled my hair to the top of my head, sat on the rocker, and brooded, wanting to get what was left of my bad mood out before the morning. Near my foot was a soup spoon. I picked it up and saw my reflection in its bowl. I curled down the corners of my lips to make myself look mean. At the same time the spoon mirrored the glint of a golden painting, tacked to the tent wall behind me.

Quietly, I found the flashlight and held its beam on the golden-framed picture of a Madonna and child circled with tiny adoring angels. The faces were flat and lacked perspective. I touched it, feeling the fine ridge between the painting's gold-leaf background and the flesh-colored face of the Madonna. Her skin was smooth but ancient. My hand seemed to drift backward through time as I slid it across the face. In a huff, I turned off the flashlight and sat down in the rocker. The Madonna and child was yet another gift from the men who worshiped virgins.

I closed my eyes and attempted to find Carlo. The last two days of our imprisonment, I had been unable to find him. Because of my bad mood, I couldn't clear my mind. I knew Carlo wasn't dead because I had overheard the Benevolents complain he was pulling their balls and not coming through with the shipment scheduling, though he continued to promise he would. "Carlo's scared to look dumb," one of the gangsters had deduced. Half their goods were stuck unpackaged in Carlo's warehouse. Several times they had asked each other, "What if we get caught?"

That night I couldn't find Carlo either. Instead I prayed for him, asking the saints to give him guidance. He was all alone. And I asked the good Virgin to speak inside the gangsters' thoughts and convince them money was good enough. With money, they could find someone else to help them. I couldn't last another day in the tunnel.

As I rocked and prayed my stomach rumbled. A painful spasm of gas exploded in my bowels. I had to go to the bathroom.

I stepped outside the tent. Usually a man accompanied me to the toilet. But tonight, I insisted on privacy.

"I've eaten too many grapes," I said, assuming he'd understand my urgency. "Please, allow me to sit alone."

Now that the men knew I was a virgin, my integrity was invincible.

"Go ahead," a man who wore an eye patch said to me. I recognized him from the Paradiso Caffè. But I didn't have time to question him about what he knew and what the men had been saying that day. I was ready to burst. I walked to the toilet. My entire body thumped with freedom, knowing I was going to be able to let go and have a good, healthy shit. I hadn't done that for four days.

The toilet tent was at the far end of the underground compound. I stepped inside and sat down. Everyone deserved moments they can share with no one else but God, I said to myself.

When I finished, rather than proceed directly back to my tent, I snooped around behind the toilet. I knew the Benevolent men wouldn't come looking for me, being concerned I had fallen asleep or gotten lost. Men sat so long, they made careers on toilet seats. Nurses know.

The area behind the toilet was damp and unfinished. I clicked on my flashlight. The beam found a polished wooden chest large enough to be a coffin. I lifted the lid. The placard inside the chest read CASSONE: A BRIDE'S HOPE CHEST. My mood lifted even higher. I was delighted. Maybe one of the Benevolents was going to fill the chest with fine white linens and propose to me.

I flashed the light farther behind the toilet tent. Wood beams divided the black dirt floor into squares. About ten feet from where I stood, the tunnel descended. I pointed the flashlight beam down the hole. The light reflected back the red eyes of several rats. I almost screamed, giving away my clandestine activity to the Benevolents, who were probably keeping an ear out for my call. But as I made a quick movement of my hand to cover my mouth, the flashlight picked up the glint of my favorite metal—gold.

I lifted a translucent plastic sheet draped over a wooden crate behind the bride's hope chest. I squeezed the flashlight under my armpit and pulled a square painting out of the crate.

It shimmered. Pressed over its surface was a thin sheet of

gold. There were figures on the painting, too, but I couldn't make out who they were. The placard read THE BAPTISM OF ST. JOHN.

Ah, Jesus's cousin, I told myself. I closed my eyes for a moment, wanting to remember what I might know about this saint, besides that his head had ended up on a platter. But the rapture of the beauty under my palm infected me with a clean emptiness. I couldn't think of anything else but consuming more, to know each of the paintings in the crate as intimately as I had just known St. John. I didn't need the flashlight.

One by one, I flipped through the paintings, being careful not to knock or chip them. I caressed their thick, golden frames, and pressed my cheek against their smooth and sandy surfaces. I did not need to see their beauty with my eyes. My heart sprouted wings, and I dipped out of the present and into the past and back again, into the part of time that exploded with creation. There was no evil, or jealousy, or feelings of possession. It was in a whirlwind of pure beauty and perfection.

I swooned sideways, leaning into something hard, not caring if it was a gun that had poked me. I told myself I had just lived beyond what most humans experience. I turned to meet my fate.

When I switched on my flashlight, I saw it wasn't a Benevolent with a gun but something the size of a person, covered in plastic. I lifted the sheet to see a marble statue, a few feet shorter than myself. I knelt to touch its feet and gown, which fell in crisp V-shaped folds. It was an angel. I stood, running my hand over short wings which were unmercifully worn. Each time the angel had attempted to fly away, its wings must have been shaved. In her right hand the angel held a rope. Her left hand was missing.

"We gotta get her now." I heard footsteps and panicked.

"Can't we wait until she's finished?"

The distant voices were coming closer. I managed to crawl back into the toilet tent.

"No, dummy! We can't watch the eleven o'clock news tonight. We gotta do it now." The men's loud voices quieted.

One of them scratched the sides of the canvas tent. "Psst," they said, without getting too close. "Alicia, are you finished? Sorry to rush you."

There was a long pause.

"We've got good news."

"We're going to move you tonight."

Again the gangsters transported us through the secret subway corridors quietly and with admirable gentleness. They put the children inside the hooded carriages with chrome wheels. This time they sat me in a wheelchair and blindfolded me.

As they tied the black mask around my forehead, each man slid his palms over my shoulders, cheeks, and ears. I wondered if my eyes had been covered to hide their affection, or had I become their Virgin and good-luck charm?

One man undid my bun, slowly pulling out the hairpins. He passed them around to the others as mementos. They washed my dirty knees with warm washcloths. As they groomed and said goodbye to me, I clutched the padded arms of the wheelchair, torn between screaming out for the help I knew wouldn't arrive, and wanting to return their affection.

"So you lowered your price," I said as they strolled me to the exit.

"We told you it's not money we're after."

I understood what was more important to them than money. They had the paintings and the statue, and they wanted Carlo to return them to Italy. I remembered touching them all and what an ecstatic sensation it had been. They didn't belong underground, alone, or hidden in a basement. Their beauty, woven into gold, paint, and stone needed to be seen by many eyes to release sweetness.

The temperature changed. The men covered my lap with a blanket. We took a ramp up the tunnel. I heard the rush of water and detected a stale, fishy smell.

"We're near the river," I said.

They put us into the car and we drove under the expressway that separates the North End from the rest of the city of Boston.

Eighteen

Astrong full moon and streetlights fingered through the North End alleys.

"So, Alicia, you have a house in Subiaco?" the gangster across from me asked. He was one I hadn't met. In the tunnel I had heard the others whispering about him, saying he had been sent in by the crew from the old country.

"Yes," I answered. I could feel the other men were disturbed by his question.

"You left it empty, you said?" the same man asked, avoiding catching my eyes.

"Yes." I was cooperating because I wanted to get home. I was sure Virginia had returned.

"Not much else around your house, is there?" another man asked.

"A church, a cemetery, a hospital," I answered, used to being asked about Subiaco. My memories about Italy were fresher than theirs, and during the four days in the tunnel, the men had often asked me questions about what they had left behind.

"Where exactly is it?" the man asked.

"My house sits on a field on the backside of a rocky hill. In the spring—right about now—the field fills up with delicious dandelion greens." I kissed my fingertips. "Why do you need to know this now?"

"Just making conversation," the man said. As we drove through the North End, I was feeling a bit melancholy about leaving the gangsters.

The man asked one final question. "No one goes to your house, then, while you're gone?"

"I do have one neighbor—Lena," I said. "But she keeps to herself. I was very much alone when I lived in Italy."

Rather than proceed directly to Carlo's building, the long black car cut up Copp's Hill, past the Old North Church, and down Clark Street. The driver was cruising the streets to see if Benevolents were still standing guard in dark door-wells.

"Hey, Luigi's gone home," the driver said, pointing to Luigi's spot near the Green Cross Pharmacy on the corner of Clark and Hanover. "It must be clear."

"Clear of what?" I asked. "The police?" I was nervous now.

"The police are gone," a backseat gangster said.

I shuddered. The last thing I wanted was to be caught in a car chase or shootout with these men who masqueraded as competent criminals and drivers.

The mood in the car changed. The driver, frightened by the police talk, pressed his foot on the accelerator. He continued to speed through the North End. "Slow down!" I screamed. He needed someone to tell him what to do, and the men in the car were not taking control. "Turn right here," I commanded. "The Benevolents might be good at digging tunnels, but you're ignoramuses in cars."

I stared out the car window at the rows of stout brick buildings lining the perimeter of the North End. "Stop here," I ordered.

"Where are we?" Bebe asked, groping to get closer to me.

"Home," I said. The gangster to my right got out of the car. I slid across the leather seat and pulled myself right back into the car. Being held captive in a cave for only a handful of days had caused my agoraphobia to return. I could only step outside, I told myself, if the raw eyes of heaven didn't look down at me.

Bebe nudged Sera and Cher. "Get up," she said softly.

I asked the gangster beside me if I could have a blanket. "I want to drape it over my head, like a tent," I explained. "We aren't used to the sky."

"Use your coat," he said gruffly.

The limousine door opened again, letting in a stream of yellow light from the gas streetlamps. I squinted and draped the wool blanket over my head.

"Wait a minute, lady." The man behind the door, who had been sitting next to the driver, grabbed my sleeve. He had a scar on his cheek. "I told you, you can't take nothing from us," he said. "You got enough upstairs." He pulled the scratchy blanket from my hand. "I'll give you a warning." He was mean, and the only Benevolent who did not adore my virginity. "I know what you know," he said. "You saw the stuff behind the toilets. If you tell anyone what you saw, or what we have, I'll get you. I'll get you good. *Capito?*"

"No, I don't," I said. I had been defiant with this gangster from the first day. He was the one who had taken us from Carlo's. He twisted my hair, forcing my face an inch from his. I remembered his ugly breath and wanted to drive my shoe into his shin and my knee into his balls. This was the same man who had held a gun to Sera's chest.

"Next time we won't give you or the kids back, and we'll ruin you," he hissed. "You won't be a virgin. We were nice this time. Right?" He sprayed my face with saliva when he spoke. I had to make a deal.

"And Carlo?" I bargained. "If I keep my word, will you leave my brother alone? Never bother him again?" This man would kill Carlo rather than kidnap him.

"Not Carlo either," the gangster sneered. "But maybe you'll have to come back and help us. We'll keep it all in the family, okay?" He laughed. "You can be an honorary Benevolent. Deal?"

He smelled like pepperoni, but I kissed him longer and harder than I needed to, to seal the deal. I wanted to get away, and I needed the blanket. I hoped distraction would work. My method was successful.

I hunched over the girls. Wind sucked the blanket against our backs as we stepped from the car to Carlo's building. The front door was locked. The black limousine sped out of the North End. I pressed the buzzer. We covered our ears. Above us, the cold air amplified the stalling engines of a jet approaching Logan Airport.

All of us waited impatiently. We wanted to fly up the steps, or through a window, to be squeezed in Carlo's warm arms. Finally, Renato peeked his wide face through the small pane of glass on the lobby door. He lifted his eyebrows under a white bandage. He didn't recognize me, and he couldn't see the children.

The little ones pressed their shivering shoulders against my knees. When I had first met Renato, I had been fatter, my nose sharper, and I had worn my hair wrapped tight around my head like a halo. I reminded myself Renato's was the only grown man's penis I had ever seen that wasn't attached to either a sick or dying man.

Renato herded us into the lobby, checking up and down

Atlantic Avenue before shutting the outside door. "How did you get here?" he whispered.

Renato saw the answer in my eyes. I wasn't going to talk. I had made an agreement, most likely with the same Benevolent who had beat him a month earlier. Maybe Renato had made promises, too. He shifted his droopy eyes to the children.

He knelt and touched his cheek to their cheeks. Their foreheads made a circle. He picked up Sera and Bebe. I followed him up the steps, carrying Cher. Smiling, she dragged her fingers along the wall.

Being close to Renato excited me. His hips swayed inside his corduroy trousers. His feet were bare and long-toed and similar in shape, I thought, to his penis. His T-shirt hung on his broad shoulders in the same way I wanted to hang on to him. His musky scent wound round me like a rope. I wanted him to like me. But I knew it wouldn't be easy. He was intense and cautious, a man women loved to love, but he was also not interested in spreading himself thin.

I glanced out the hall window, over the sloped roof of the restaurant across the street, past the piles and docks and old brick warehouses to the dark harbor. I wanted to tell Renato his overdedication to the theater had made Virginia run away, and that he shouldn't do the same thing to me. Then I told myself I was ridiculous, that Renato would never look twice at me.

"Welcome home," he said, bowing slightly as I entered the apartment. The children ran ahead, down the long hallway to the kitchen. Renato kissed my cheek and took my coat. I was more interested in being near him than in seeing my brother.

My throat was dry. I swallowed. "Has anyone heard from Jassy?" I asked. He shook his head no. "Where's Carlo?"

"In his room."

Out of the corner of my eye, as Renato folded my coat, I saw him survey me and scratch his rib cage with his thumb. "Alicia. Carlo's lovely sister," he said, very respectfully. "How long has it been since we've last seen each other?" He didn't know I had been an audience to his and Virginia's secret act. If he had I would have been too embarrassed to look at him.

I shrugged.

"Are you hungry?" he asked.

I said no, hoping I would have an opportunity to eat bread with Renato later. I wasn't accustomed to having my mind so stirred by a man, and I felt stupid but unwilling to be otherwise.

The first room we passed, on the left, was my room. The door was ajar. Renato's tassled shoes were near the threshold. His books were strewn on the floor and stacked on the dresser at the feet of St. Anne. The bed was rumpled. There was no sign of Virginia.

"We didn't expect you tonight," Renato apologized. "I'll move my things out right away."

"We?" I asked, barely able to get the word out of my mouth.

"Carlo and I," he answered.

"Virginia didn't come back?"

He shook his head.

"How long have you been here with Carlo?" I asked, wondering how long he had been in my bed.

"Four days." He motioned for me to continue on down the hallway to Carlo's room. "Since the day you were kidnapped."

I dropped my eyes.

"Are you all right?" Renato touched my shoulder.

"Yes," I lied. I wasn't all right. My stomach ached. It

ached about being home, and not being home. It ached about wanting Renato and for thinking about my desire when I should have been thinking about my brother. And under all the confusing feelings, mostly I ached for Carlo. I had come to America on a crusade, determined to straighten out my brother's life, behaving as if my own ideals were the right ones and as if God listened only to me. But when Renato touched me, I forgot everything. I was an idiot, but a strong idiot who could force herself to stop being stupid. I turned into Carlo's room.

He was flat on his back, his head slightly elevated on a caseless pillow. He didn't return my smile. I knelt next to his bed. His eyes were as flat as the blanket and his skin as gray. He had pinned a cotton diaper around his neck to keep it warm. The room smelled of camphor and was in the same disorder I had left it in the day the children and I had been taken underground. Long sheets had been tacked over the three windows.

"Can I get you some water?" Renato asked Carlo. Renato genuinely loved my brother. He had left his theater in other people's hands while he took care of Carlo, got him meals, and answered the phone.

Carlo hardly lifted his head, moving his flat eyes no more than his bones. I could see that while I was gone, Carlo had looked into hell. I was sorry he had to suffer. Renato shut the door, leaving the two of us alone.

Carlo whispered to me, "Knowing the children are safe will make me better." He wanted to believe himself, but his voice was too distant to have any impact. The huge purses under his eyes were dark and abandoned.

I covered his hands with my own. Carlo was heading toward death. He needed me.

"Mama and Papa both told me dying was like being a ripple around a stone thrown in a lake," I said. "They kept going out and out with the ripples, until the ripples became so insignificant they disappeared. They said sometimes a ripple got interrupted, so they couldn't disappear, and had to wait to begin again. Barzinis die quietly," I said. "We don't need orchestras, or gun shots, or anyone to push us out of our life." I tried to make Carlo see the connection between what he was experiencing and what had come before him. "Mama and Papa were old and sick and prepared to die," I said. "You're not."

"Why didn't you tell me about Mama and Papa sooner? Why now? I wanted so much to know what they were like after I left. You pushed me away," he said.

"Mama's and Papa's lungs collapsed and that was that," I said, building an urgency in my voice. "And once they died, I never heard from them again. Mama promised she'd continue talking to me. Papa said he'd send me a signal, too. But I got nothing. I prayed and prayed to them, and my words went into a black hole. Then I prayed to saints, asking them to find my parents and remind them of their promise to me. But nothing, no sign, came. Mama and Papa hadn't earned a heavenly voice. And I'll tell you, Carlo, you aren't a saint either. You're an ordinary man. You'll disappear, unless you fight, and no one will know you were ever alive."

Carlo stared at the ceiling. His eyes, still flat, hadn't changed. Had he been listening to me?

I moved quickly. With a great heave, I reached my hands behind his shoulders and forced Carlo to sit upright. I swiveled his body. His bare feet dangled to the floor.

"Don't forget I'm a nurse," I said loudly. "I've not only seen it happen to Mama and Papa, but to strangers, too. Even if you haven't got a disease, you can make yourself die. If you will yourself to die, you die without grace. You'll get no indulgences. You must begin below where your last life left off." I held the bottom of Carlo's skull firmly under my hand and spoke close to his face. "It might as well be called suicide. God won't let you into heaven if He's not the one who calls, and your family will carry your weight even though you've ripped yourself away from them."

"You're crazy!" Carlo shouted, swatting at me with his wide hands. "You always were!" He kicked my shins. "Get away from me!"

"You haven't seen anything," I shouted back. "You weren't there. You don't know. You ran away from it, but you can't slip through the crack now. You must earn your next life—like Mama and Papa did. While you're alive, the past howls to hold on to you. Only when you die can you truly begin again. But, Carlo, now is not your time. Do you understand? It will only be worse if you leave now. Don't be foolish!"

Carlo's eyes weren't flat anymore. He growled and punched. I was the stronger one, and quicker. I held his arms at his side. I had won him back.

"*Strega!*" he screamed. "You ugly witch!"

"More! More!" I said. "Tell me more!" I wanted Carlo to scream.

"I wish I'd never asked you to come here. You've brought nothing but bad luck to this family."

"Me? Me?" I repeated. "You think it's me that brought you bad luck? What about that redhead? Redheads are daughters of the devil—Mama told us that. They're too independent. They don't listen to anyone but themselves. They're bad apples. Mama never allowed one to step into our house." I was furious. Why couldn't Carlo remember what we had learned, what had been so important to us when we were children? He had cut off the ground he stood on.

"Don't talk about her! It's your fault our family has no peace," he said.

227

"Carlo, I'm not the one who is crazy—you are. You tried to be someone else. You left. You left us. You left me. Then, years later, when we are grown people, you have the nerve to drag me into this circus with rings everywhere and nowhere to go," I said. "It's not the way it's supposed to be. In America no one cooperates. It's not right. No one rests," I said, punching my fists into my own hips, daring Carlo to continue our fight. "Everyone chases their own ideas."

My brother didn't have the energy to go on. I had called Jassy the daughter of the devil and the source of his misfortune when she was the source of his hope. He was hating me. As well he should have been. I was wrong. I softened. "Who am I to tell you what is right or wrong?" I loved Carlo so much. More than anything I wanted to mend our distance. "I'm so sorry, Carlo," I said. "We have so much to say to one another, so much to tell. Let's not be strangers."

I let go of his hands and put my head to his chest, against the familiar rhythm of my birth, his heart and mine, and our mother's and father's echoes.

Carlo hesitated before he dropped his own head over mine and pressed his ear on my cheek. I had what I hadn't had in seventeen years: someone of my own blood to know me, to hold me without possession and with all the feelings of possession in the world. And he had the same.

Renato put the children to bed and packed his things into a duffel sack. When he left, Carlo and I were sitting on the red love seat in the front room.

"I'll be sleeping in the Teatro," Renato said.

At dawn, Carlo drew open the curtains and lifted the blinds. As the horizon lightened to purple and then to a soft orange, we watched a thick cloud lick over the harbor.

"It's the earth's private time," Carlo said. "I've watched

this moment every morning since Jassy's been gone. It's my way of staying close to her."

I stood next to him at the window. The outlines of water, concrete, and sky caressed each other. It was quiet. No seagulls, pigeons, or jets crisscrossed the milky dawn.

"I thought I had lost you," Carlo said. He loved me, too. He put his hand on my waist and guided me back to the love seat. "And if I lose you, I would lose the children, and Jassy. How could I have explained it to her? It would have ended between us—and everybody. People can't live together when ghosts of children keep them apart.

Carlo held the soft belt of his robe in his fists and twisted it. "I knew nothing, and they squeezed tighter and tighter. What could I do? They insisted I make a shipment for them. I couldn't do it. I would pay for someone else to do it. 'No,' they said, 'it has to go through Spediamo. You made the deal.' 'What deal?' I pleaded. 'Don't play dumb,' they said. 'You can't back out now.' " He became silent, lost in his own thoughts.

I leaned against my brother's shoulder and remembered the shoe box in Jassy's closet. I went to find it, but the box wasn't there.

"Alicia, I went to get money to give to them so they could buy and do whatever they wanted." Carlo said. "But my money was gone. Who took my money?"

"I have my own money," I said.

"Not you—I didn't think you."

"Who?" I asked.

"Whoever gave it to me might have taken it back," Carlo said.

In a turn of our heads the light shifted. For a few seconds it was lighter inside the room than outside.

"Virginia. I never should have trusted Virginia." He

cupped his forehead in his wide hands. "She was too blond, too jealous, and she knew too much. The way she moved was too sharp. I was the fool. Her smell was sweet, and she spoke so softly, handling the babies as if they were magic inside skin." Carlo shook his head. "When she asked me for a percentage of the shipping business, I wouldn't do it. I made so many mistakes with that business, from the first day. It broke me." Carlo raised his hands to his face. "All along, I was telling myself Virginia was a woman who couldn't and wouldn't do anything without my approval. I repeated those words to myself. I didn't want to give up anything. She didn't either."

Carlo's eyes pinched shut before he covered his face again with his hands. "In America, if you want to make money, you can't think of anything but yourself. When you get it in your hand, you have to run. That's exactly what she did. And she learned how from me. I don't know where she is. Renato said she went to the middle of America, to the heartland—Tennessee. We aren't sure." He looked into his palms. "To save you, I told the police you and the children went with Virginia, that you really hadn't been kidnapped, that I had made a mistake."

"That's all right." I smoothed my hands over his shoulders. "A mother won't leave her child unless her shame is unbearable and she knows someone will love her child more. Maybe she didn't believe she was a good mother. Maybe it had nothing to do with you."

Carlo spoke in a hushed voice. "But she stole. How could she steal from me?" He folded his arms over his chest.

"I can help you, Carlo," I said, draping the edge of a blanket over his lap. "If you need money, you can have mine."

Carlo shook his head to erase the rattle of my generous offer. He was accustomed to taking care of people. No one gave him anything, and he preferred it to stay that way.

He brushed his hands through the air. "They didn't want money. They wanted Spediamo. I asked them why Spediamo? What were they sending to Italy that no one else could ship? They laughed. 'What do you think—blue jeans? Disco music? Hair coloring? Bleach for the ladies' mustaches? Pearl Drops toothpaste? Come on, Carlo, don't play dumb. Would we kidnap children for junk?' "

"Have you heard from Jassy?" I asked.

"No," Carlo said. "I think she's still in Czechoslovakia."

"You love her," I said.

"I loved her from the first moment. There's no one like her. I want my children to be just like their mother."

I sat silent with his words.

"I've got to go open my stores," Carlo said. He limped out of the front room, down the hall to the kitchen to make his oatmeal.

I climbed into a hot bath and lay in the claw-footed tub, submerging every inch of me under hot water, washing away the sights of guns, underground caves, and men in aprons. Then I closed my eyes and Jassy appeared inside my head. She was singing the same Shaker tune she had sung to me a month ago in my kitchen in Subiaco. She called to me with her long arms. Her eyes were wide open. It was eerie. Her image was so strong I was sure it hadn't arisen from my own brain. Her voice was hypnotic. I refused to listen. My brother gave her enough attention; she wasn't going to get mine, too.

I bent my knees and slid my head up the curved back of the tub. I remembered the tall gangster holding the gun barrel to Bebe's soft chest. We had survived. I remembered the underground cave, my tent, and the treasures behind the toilet. I pressed my hand into my stomach. It didn't ache anymore. And instead of the doughy belly I was used to touching, my hand pressed into firm flesh. I had lost weight in the

231

cave. The food had been fine, but I had pushed it around my plate, existing for four days on bunches of grapes, spitting the seeds on the floor, never bending to pick them up.

I remembered Renato had been sleeping in my bed while I was gone. I wondered how strongly the pink sheets would smell of him when I climbed between them to rest.

Nineteen

The children slept through to dinner of the next day. Still in their pajamas, they wedged next to the adults around the kitchen table.

"I want the same *polpettine* we ate in the dungeon," Cher said, referring to the meatballs the gangsters had prepared for them. She squeezed her head onto Carlo's elbow.

"What? You don't like my spaghetti anymore?" Renato asked. "Plain with butter?"

"We like *polpettine* better now," Sera said.

I was the only adult to laugh. The children were teasing Renato and Carlo, hoping to warm them, but the men were unsure about how to bridge the time they had been apart.

"The gangsters spoiled them," Renato said, pouring himself another half glass of wine. "We'll have to be strict to straighten them out." His forehead was still wrapped with a bandage. By now the wound would heal better if exposed to air. I wondered if the bandage was there for my sympathy and hopeful attention.

"Better spoiled than dead," Carlo said softly, running his wide hand through his hair. I was concerned. My brother was too miserable to be aware of how his words affected the children.

"Yes, and better alive than morose," Renato added, elbowing Carlo as he cleared his plate. Carlo had not eaten. "What? You only eat *polpettine*, too?" He mimicked Cher's little voice.

The children laughed. This time so did Renato.

The phone rang. Renato put the plates on the counter and answered the call. "Long distance," he said, covering one ear with his palm and stepping into the pantry to hear more clearly.

Carlo's face brightened. We all thought it was Jassy. And the children, feeling the excitement, began to speak more loudly. I had to shush them twice. But they didn't listen. Renato was right. The next few weeks, we would have to be a bit more strict.

"What? Could you repeat the message, please?" Renato said. "Our connection is bad." Maybe it wasn't Jassy, I thought.

Renato stepped out of the pantry and shook the telephone receiver before putting it to his ear one more time. His wide face was drawn tight around his strong cheekbones, making his skin spotty, and his ponytail seemed to pull back on his stark expression. He motioned for me to step into the pantry with him.

"The person hung up," he said.

"Who?"

"It was a woman, not Jassy. The woman was afraid. She could only whisper."

In no time Carlo was in the pantry with us, moving in like a bull. "What's going on?" he asked.

Renato turned to face Carlo and delivered his lines without emotion. "Someone just called to tell us Jassy has disappeared," he said.

We were as shocked as eyes frozen in the instant the lights of an operating room are switched on.

234

"Who was this person?" Carlo shouted. "What kind of joke are they playing on us? Don't they know I've had enough?"

I shooed the children into their bedroom, making the excuse that I missed their toys and wanted to visit them. Renato put his arm around Carlo and walked him to the front room.

A half-hour later, Carlo knocked on the children's door. He smelled of whiskey but wasn't drunk. His eyes were red from having cried. "Who wants to sit on Big Papa's lap and listen to a story?" he asked, brushing his forehead with his wide hands, as if to wipe away his fears. He smiled, knowing the children's innocence would relieve his suffering.

"Tell us Jassy's stone soup story," Bebe said, plopping her round *culo* on the floor between Carlo's knees. She surveyed the twins' faces, daring them to oppose her position. "It starts out in a kingdom where two people have only a stone and a pot of boiling water, and they ask the other people to bring peas and carrots."

"Yes, the stone soup story," the twins echoed, not arguing over whose legs would lean the closest to their father's.

Carlo switched on the night lamp and began: "One morning, a long time ago . . ." He and Jassy had told the children the same story at least a hundred times. They never tired of it. But tonight he was speaking more slowly, as if he wanted to hear his lover's voice beside his own.

I left the room. It was better he was alone with the children. Expressing sentiment wasn't Carlo's strongest feature. And he was needing to be loved by the little ones.

Renato had gone to the theater. I envied his anchor. No matter who disappeared or left, Renato could escape in his work. I straightened the kitchen, washing the dinner dishes by hand rather than stacking them in the dishwasher. I sponged warm soap over the plates, remembering the disturbing phone call our family had just received. Renato had thought the woman who called must have been a singer from the same opera company as Jassy. But why would the woman be frightened?

I rinsed the dishes. Jassy could have run off with Virginia, I said to myself. The two of them might be languishing on a beach in Tahiti enjoying Carlo's money. Or, like me, Jassy could have been kidnapped. But I resisted seeing Jassy being carted away by men who would admire her as much as they had admired me. So I imagined her alone, as alone as I had been in Subiaco.

It didn't suit her. Jassy came rushing out of my head like an unplugged tire. Her spirit swirled around the yellow kitchen. With a broom, I tried to swat her out the window, but she was determined not to disappear. Jassy was looking for someone. It wasn't me.

"I can't blink, or I'll lose everyone," she said in her low, bravado voice. Jassy was speaking to herself and not to me. Her spirit had a large head, and her face looked as if a plastic surgeon had done a hack job on it. I dried the sweat from my palms.

Jassy's spirit bounced down the long hallway and back into the kitchen before slipping under the french doors into the nursery. I quietly pulled a chair close to the nursery door and stood on it. I was barefooted and didn't want her spirit to sneak out of the room and into me through my feet. It was impossible to shake off a soul if they got you that way.

Carlo continued talking to the children, as if nothing unusual had just happened. "Time is everywhere," he said. Carlo lifted his arm and pretended to catch time. "Nothing," he said, rubbing his thumbs over his fingers. "No one can catch it. Time finds you. That's why if Jassy had stayed here with us, she would never miss anything, right?" The children laughed. "But she had dreams to catch. We all do. You, too."

Carlo's voice had picked up its usual pace. I wondered if my imagination had cooked up the ghost. Maybe nothing luminous had slipped inside the nursery. I waited another few minutes before pushing on the door. The knob wouldn't budge. I heard Jassy laugh. She was laughing at me!

"Wait a minute," I said out loud, rattling the door but creating no sounds. Jassy wasn't letting me in. Quickly, I jumped back onto my chair.

In a whisper, she sang a lullaby:

"Sweet and low, sweet and low, wind of the western sea.
Low, low, breathe and blow, wind of the western sea.
Over the rolling waters go, come from the dying moon and
    blow
Blow him again to me
While my little one, while my pretty one sleeps."

I listened to the end. Hearing Jassy sing, I was reminded how wonderful she was, and how safe I had felt when I was with her. I pushed the nursery door open.

The girls were asleep in a heap on the pink carpet. Carlo was on the rocker in a daze, his lips curled in a tentative smile. I shook his shoulder to startle him. His eyeballs showed only white and his breathing was half–shut down.

And I saw Jassy, or at least the shadow of Jassy's ghost, standing behind Carlo. Her eyes were pulled back, as if she had no eyelids. Her head was three times bigger than her body.

I shook Carlo's shoulder. "She's come to take you with her," I hissed as loudly as I could without waking the girls. I pointed to Jassy's luminous head. "Her eyes are stuck! She'll take whoever looks back at her!"

But Carlo screamed when he saw me, even though Jassy was the monstrous presence in the room. "What are you doing here?" Carlo asked me. "Aren't you with Mama?"

My brother was traveling backward in time, toward his own birth. If he had gotten there and had re-experienced being in the womb with me, he would have died.

T w e n t y

The next morning I telephoned my brother at the drug-store and Renato at the Teatro to tell them I was leaving. "It's better I go. We can't wait for someone to come to us and explain," I said. "You stay with the children."

"I'm sure her schedule was changed," Carlo said, denying the events of the previous night. "Let's not get too excited."

I feared Jassy was dead, but not really dead. She was in limbo and wanted Carlo and her children to keep her company there. I was convinced this was true because Jassy hadn't been baptized, which meant she couldn't go to heaven where Carlo and the younger Barzini souls would eventually be admitted. To solve the dilemma of her eternal loneliness, I planned on redeeming her broken soul. At the Vatican, with my gold, I would buy her indulgences, specifi-cally grace slotted for the sacrament of baptism. Then Jassy could become God's bride, and leave Carlo alone.

"Maybe she's still in Bratislava. The show's been a tre-mendous success. That's why she isn't contacting us. No, she hasn't disappeared," Carlo repeated. He wouldn't allow himself to think she was dead. But he hadn't heard from Jassy since the day before the children and I had been kidnapped.

Jassy was supposed to have arrived in Florence two days ago. All day I had called the theater where the New England Opera Company was performing. No calls were returned. The hotel where Jassy had written she would be staying didn't know who she was. I didn't tell Carlo about the dead-end phone calls when he came home for lunch to say good-bye to me.

Carlo didn't touch his food. I had prepared a plate of mortadella sandwiches with sliced tomatoes and sprigs of watercress. In the past ten days he had lost twelve pounds. The harmonica valve on the kettle whistled. "I'll make the tea," he said. "Chamomile." Carlo had given up coffee, hoping his body, deprived of caffeine, would relax.

He placed our most fragile cups and saucers on the table next to the teapot. I set out a plate of cornmeal and raisin cookies next to the teapot and dusted lunch crumbs into my hand. The brightness of the day slanted into the yellow kitchen through the venetian blind slats.

Carlo took a cookie. It was a good sign. His appetite might be returning. "More?" I asked.

He tugged the napkin out from his collar and shook his head no. His green eyes wandered around the yellow kitchen as if he had never sat in the room before. "For so long everything was perfect," he said. His shoulders lifted and dropped. "If someone has hurt her it will be my fault. I gave her too much freedom to stray too far from home. In the North End, it was all right for her to be independent. I could keep an eye on her when she didn't know. Goddamn peninsula," he said. "Italy killed her. I'm being punished."

"By whom?" I asked.

Carlo glanced at the ceiling and said something that surprised me. "God," he said. Carlo had never been concerned with God before.

"No." I shook my head. "It's life," I said. "Don't worry, it will get good again."

Renato, a Band-Aid taped to his forehead, rushed into the kitchen. He didn't want me to take the trip. "I'll go," he said. "The people you'll have to deal with are bound to be dangerous."

My journey was unquestionable. I had been the one who had prayed against Jassy, and I was the one who had to pick up after my prayers. "I'll be just fine," I said. The men who had kidnapped me had turned out to be quite manageable. I suspected my skills would be as trustworthy on the other side of the Atlantic, no matter whom I had to stand up against.

"Authority always works against us," Renato warned. "Don't trust anyone." He gave me more advice and left.

Carlo put his wide hand over mine. The dishwasher groaned. He compared my sturdy and scrubbed hand to Jassy's long, smooth, and polished one. "If you were her, and I had a second chance, I wouldn't allow you to go," he said.

"But I'm not her, and you're trading me with the hope I'll bring her back." I was determined to keep my position in his family. My brother had to depend on me. I would either bring Jassy back, or free her soul, which seemed more likely. In either case, we had to confront our losses and continue. "It's time to call a cab," I said.

Carlo pushed himself up from the table. "Are you sure you can talk to people?" he asked, aware of my trouble with strangers. "Maybe I'm the one who should go." Carlo couldn't go anywhere. His face was a canvas of white skin over white bones. "You haven't had practice with big shots," he said. "Make them laugh first, then they'll help you." He didn't sound confident, but I listened anyway.

"Carlo," I said softly. "Be good to yourself while I'm gone. Renato is helping in the stores. Buy a chicken today. Make yourself soup with lots of garlic and crushed red pepper. And rest."

Carlo headed out of the kitchen, his hands stuffed in the pockets of his wrinkled trousers. He turned. "I hate to send another woman into the world alone," he shouted. "I stand on sand."

I tapped the table with my knuckles. "It's only those who don't leave their homes who find life easy. But it's really indifference they're after. The world doesn't know they exist. Believe me, those that hide don't escape suffering. Their minds become tortured. An internal war is as bad as any pain of the flesh."

Eight hours later, I landed at Da Vinci Airport in Rome. The weather was like summer. Beyond the wire fence surrounding the tarmac, palm trees bowed in a breeze scented with oranges and artichokes. I touched the tip of my new nose to convince myself I was who I was.

"Can't you do it for less?" I asked Cardinal Ulbaldini. He had grown to be an old man with a round head balanced on a skinny neck that appeared to be even thinner because of his loose clerical collar. The broad line indenting the center of his chin had deepened, the sign of a person who both pushed and pulled to get what he wanted. "After all, this pope isn't Italian," I said. "Can't the rates come down?" I spoke to him in English, believing that this language gave me more authority.

He poised a fountain pen over a sheet of parchment. "It's been the going rate since 1292," he said dryly. "The price for clearing a soul through limbo hasn't changed. We adjust it according to the rising cost of living." Ulbaldini scratched the deep clef in his chin. "If she died without baptism, you need to purchase the sanctifying graces set aside for that sacrament by saints who died with an excess. That's the only way. It's easier—and less expensive—to buy a marriage or an annulment, you understand, than a baptism." He sat in a thronelike chair behind a black marble table.

Around Rome, Cardinal Ulbaldini was known as the Church's best businessman. I had specifically requested a meeting with him. As soon as I saw him, of course, I realized he was the same cardinal who had paid my brother Carlo fifty thousand dollars in 1972 for the photos of Laszlo Toth whacking the *Pietà* with a hammer. I might have avoided Ulbaldini if I had known that, thinking the cardinal might charge me more for his services to make back some of the money he had paid out to Carlo. I shifted in my seat.

"How do you know how many excess graces a saint has earned?" I asked. "And where do you store them?" It was the mystery I had often contemplated. I was sure someone high up in religious ranks, like Ulbaldini, could answer it.

"The pope decides," he replied. "And excess graces are stored inside a church. Why do you think we go there to worship? Why do you think there are paintings of saints on ceilings, and statues of saints in vestibules? Why do you think the pope lives in Rome? It's because Rome has the largest collection of statues, carvings, and paintings, and therefore the biggest stockpile of grace—both sanctifying and actual—than any other place on this planet. Italy vibrates with holy art. We house religious rapture. No place else has as much. Grace belongs here. We have to keep it here. And you—why don't you know this? You said you were Catholic. What did you learn in school?"

The cardinal was a businessman and a zealot. "Then you understand how important it is to redeem her," I said.

"Jassy's soul will block spiritual traffic above Italy if her soul is left lingering in limbo, and above Italy. But can't you lower your price?"

"Let me tell you how to do it for less." Ulbaldini sympathized with the financial aspect of my negotiation. He pulled several folders from his file case. "Here," he said, pointing to a picture of St. George spearing a dragon. "You can invoke St. George, St. Ubaldo, or St. Anthony for the passing. These saints have set aside special compensations to serve those on earth who have died without peace. Hiring a newly ordained priest to do a Vatican mass will lower your costs, too. Understandably, a mass offered by the pope costs the most. Candles are always extra."

"But I want something special," I said. "How about the Virgin? God's mother collected more indulgences and graces than anyone besides God Himself. How much do the Virgin Mother's graces cost? Since they are so abundant, aren't her graces less expensive?" Ulbaldini didn't intimidate me. Underneath the trimmings and sacrifices he had made to lead a holy life, talking about money excited him.

"We have no accounts set aside for the Virgin to do simple passings of unbaptized souls into heaven. You see, by the special virtue of her Assumption, the body of Blessed Mary was glorified and taken to heaven. Her soul never left her flesh. You remember that from your catechism, don't you?" he asked, shuffling the pictures of St. George and the others back into their folder. "Presently, we invoke the Virgin's graces only for those who are alive and suffering terminal diseases, such as cancer and leprosy. And she's quite expensive—after all, she is God's mother."

I remembered Carlo's advice. He told me to humor people who had power. "So, doesn't God's mother feel out of place in heaven having a body when no one else does?"

The tassel on his red hat shook as the cardinal laughed.

"The mysteries aren't for us to understand, only accept," he said solemnly.

Ulbaldini reviewed my application. He shook his head. "There's no way around it. You're going to have to pay an extra thousand for a baptism. She was a grown woman. The Church welcomes everyone, but children and the living are the ones we prefer."

"Her children are baptized," I said. "So am I and so is my brother Carlo. We live as a family. We want peace, Cardinal. That's why I have come to you. My brother gave up everything to get his children back from kidnappers. Then he lost Jassy. Have sympathy for us."

Ulbaldini pushed his half-glasses up his birdlike nose and checked over my application again. "Carlo? Carlo Barzini, you said? Carlo from Boston? He's your brother?"

I nodded. Ulbaldini had unveiled my little altar.

"He's a short man," the cardinal said. "Green eyes. Moves like a wrestler."

"Yes." I couldn't lie to a man of the Church. I leaned forward, wanting to squash my brother's name out of the air.

"Fine man. He's been doing the Church's work for years," the cardinal said, winking at me. "Why didn't you tell me you were his sister in the first place?"

I dropped my arms, the sides of my mouth burned, and I was ready to spit fire. I didn't know then about Carlo's deal. I did know I didn't want Carlo to be involved. Redeeming Jassy was to be my act of contrition.

"Carlo is a sweet and generous father," I said, pulling my eyebrows together, trying to discourage the cardinal's continued winking at me. "He doesn't know anything about me coming here."

The cardinal snorted before he laughed. "Carlo understands: 'Give to God what belongs to God and to Caesar what belongs to Caesar.' Yes, I certainly admire Carlo." Ulbaldini tore my application in half and began to write, with his fountain pen, directly on the parchment. "Carlo deserves a big favor." Ulbaldini wobbled his big head on his skinny neck. "I'll do this for him myself." Ulbaldini was going to baptize Jassy for free. "It's the least I can do, considering the circumstances." The cardinal assumed an intimacy with my brother that I was sure didn't exist. I hated him. He was a bald man pretending to have hair.

I sat back in the uncomfortable chair. "Nothing free is good," I said quietly. "Let me pay for at least half of the sacrament."

Ulbaldini blotted his signature. He winked again. "I'll take care of it by tomorrow." He indicated where I should sign the document. "Do you have her birth certificate, passport, or driver's license?" he asked.

The ritual would be worthless to me. No sacrifices had been made. Jassy's spirit wouldn't respond. The transaction was over. I stood up.

"What's wrong?" the cardinal asked, tapping the parchment. "Sign here."

I ignored him.

"You're not an opportunist like your brother," he said.

"I told you, Carlo doesn't know I'm here."

"Oh?" The cardinal stood beside me. "I thought you said he wanted to come himself. I would have loved to have seen Carlo. He's helped us so much—that is, until this last month." He crossed his arms over his chest. "But he could have just called me if there was a problem." He paused. "Alicia, maybe you could help us. How soon will you be going back to Boston?"

"I'm not sure." I reached for the cardinal's hand, bowed, and kissed his ring. "I hope the pope doesn't mind you offering to give away the Church's services."

"God bless you," Ulbaldini said. "I'm truly sorry to know

246

Carlo's girlfriend died," he said in a hushed voice. "How did it happen?" He scratched his cleft chin.

"She was an opera singer," I said. "She disappeared in Florence."

"Beautiful city. Almost as crowded as Rome." He touched the center of my forehead. "Is that where you are going next?"

"Yes," I said.

"Let's keep this between us," he said, draping a hand over my shoulder. "Like in confession. Come back if you change your mind. God will bless you."

Later, I found out from Ulbaldini's assistant that the cardinal hadn't known about Jassy's disappearance. But after my visit he began suspecting a connection between the missing shipment, the death, and my urgent visit. No one but a handful of the Benevolents knew what had happened, and they wanted it kept secret.

I took a train to Florence. It was a somber city, dark when I arrived, and the Florentines, dressed in shades of brown, slid through the shadows of their avenues and extraordinary monuments. I buttoned my raincoat and proceeded, according to my map, south to the center of the city. I didn't want to take a room near the train station, but a less expensive one in the older section of town.

While I walked through the cool night, noisy with automobiles, I eavesdropped on a few conversations, noticing that Tuscans didn't slur their *s*'s. Above me, the night sky was hard, the darkness sharp, and beyond the amber glow of the city the stars were clearly defined, like tips of lightning. I was able and happy to be alone because my brother, the children, and Renato expected me to return to them.

The clack of my red cowboy boots on the worn cobblestones reminded me of my mission: to find Jassy and put her to rest. I didn't need Ulbaldini. I would stop talking to God and instead listen for His instructions. If I found her, I myself could perform the sacrament.

Around the next corner I spotted an old hotel with a new neon sign, LA DANZA. I checked in.

"*Signora,* we have a trattoria in the front," the proprietor said, checking his watch. "Customers can enter from the next street over, or through the rear of the hotel." He was a slight, proper man with a stiff mustache. He pointed to the glass door behind him and quickly adjusted a red carnation that had swiveled sideways in the vase near his elbow.

"We serve the most exquisite beefsteak in Florence." He pressed his index fingers and thumbs together. "Grilled in the fireplace, sprinkled with olive oil and garlic, and laced with a sprig of rosemary." I thought it was a speech he made to anyone who arrived at the hotel before eight-thirty.

"Thank you," I said, taking the room key. Rather than ride a remodeled elevator to the third floor, I walked up a narrow marble staircase so worn from centuries of use the risers looked like faceless smiles.

La Danza wasn't a four-star hotel, but the towels were linen. I splashed cold water on my face. With my head cradled in the crack of the linen towel, I thought about Carlo and how he and I used to hug each other and laugh whenever Mama grilled steak. We were always eager to eat meat. I was hungry.

They served roasted red potatoes with the steak. The meat was thin, about as thick as a finger and curled slightly on one edge along a thin rim of springy fat. The meat released a clean straightforward taste enhanced with needles of rosemary and tiny discs of garlic. I drank jewel-red chianti. The waiter took my plate and returned with a pea and endive salad, salted and drizzled with olive oil. I dipped a crust of chewy bread into the oil. The greens were newly ripped from the earth. I turned down a plate of grapes. Espresso came last.

"Excuse me, miss, do you want sugar?" a man interrupted. He spoke to me in slow English. "One cube or two?" It was the end of the restaurant's day, and the man was filling sugar bowls.

"Two," I answered in English.

He had kind eyes and wore the white shirt and short hat of a cook's assistant. He went back to his work. I watched him load the sugar bowls and blow out the candles on the rear tables. Twice he turned to smile at me. Once I smiled back. His brow was hesitant. The third time he approached my table and removed his white hat.

"Signora, each evening, before I go home, I have a cup of coffee in the kitchen. Tonight, do you mind if I join you, for company?"

Because I had indulged in two glasses of wine, or because I didn't want to go up to my room, or because Florence was my father's town and in it I could trust the men, or because the cook's assistant seemed so innocent, I said yes.

My heart throbbed up my neck and jaw into my ears. But I suppressed its red sound, becoming passive and polite, struggling to make conversation in simple English sentences. He thought I was an American. His name was Umberto.

"Where do you live?" he asked.

"Boston," I answered.

"Cold. Right?" He hugged himself.

"Yes."

"Do you like it?" he asked.

"Not the cold," I said, though I hadn't known a winter in Boston.

"Are you married?"

"No."

"Why not? You could stay warmer."

"American girls are different," I said, relying on what I thought Jassy and Virginia might say.

Because the trattoria was dimly lighted, I suspected Umberto was interpreting my awkward shyness for a certain kind of cold-blooded American reserve. But that trait didn't work against me. I had the distinct feeling that Umberto wanted to melt me. I was right.

"I will show you the real Florence," he said, "not the Florence for the tourist. And when I come to Boston, you must show me the real Boston," he laughed.

I agreed to go on a walk with Umberto.

I scurried to my room for my coat, stopping to rinse my teeth. I considered the upcoming hour a rehearsal for becoming a true woman. I ran a brush through my hair.

The front street was well lighted and busy.

A half block down the sidewalk, he took my hand and put it inside his jacket pocket with his own. I lingered on the sensation of the soft flannel that lined his jacket pocket, and the sinewy ridges of bone on Umberto's hand. My knees buckled. Our palms were both sweaty. The fluttering feeling in my stomach and the pulse between my legs were uplifting. Was this how love began? I asked myself.

Our eyes met. I didn't know how much meaning I was projecting onto him and how much emanated from Umberto. I refused to truly care. This is a special evening, I said to myself. Enjoy it.

We proceeded down Via della Pergola. Umberto was tall, his shoulders were broad; he stepped straight and had a freshness about him that was confusing me. Perhaps it was because he was as innocent as I was, I later told myself, when I replayed our meeting in my mind.

"Where do you live?" I asked. I had to repeat my question.

Umberto lifted his foot and tapped his heel. "I was born in Umbria, the bottom of the boot," he said. I was surprised I hadn't detected southernness in his accent. We were among a small crowd of people, mostly couples at a corner, waiting for the light to turn red. I saw the girls were doing most of the talking.

We crossed the intersection, and I moved my elbow in closer to Umberto's. I was nervous and would have preferred to be silent, but since the women around me were carrying on the conversations, I forced myself to talk, too. Since he had said he didn't understand much English, I repeated the word exercises I had practiced with Freddy, one of my kidnappers, in the subway cave under Harvard Square. I said words with *h*'s, *k*'s, *g*'s, and *th*'s, sounds foreign to Italian. "They Keep Kleenex," I said. I lined up more sounds. "Heave Ho Helter Heroes Kill Home. Go. Gone. Going. Think Thatch Hatch. Jimmy Carter?"

He swayed his head and smiled. We walked a few more blocks. "So many of us want to find a place to belong," he said in Italian. I pretended not to have understood. "We've both been lonely." My heart warmed to Umberto.

But I wondered what I was doing that made me seem lonely. I wasn't. I felt terrific. Could I possibly have been swimming in it for so long that the emotion saturated me? When I had been truly lonely, stuck in Subiaco, I spoke to saints and the sick, and watched Carlo and the others, cursing, envying, and living through them. Believing it impossible, I had rarely dreamed of holding a man's hand. Umberto clipped my forearm against his own. He glanced at me without begging me to look back at him. I stopped talking and attended the sensations of my arm pressing against his ribs.

251

In the Piazza San Giovanni we admired the magnificent striped bowl-topped Duomo, "designed by Brunelleschi," Umberto said. Nearby couples kissed each other between columns. The outline of my lips brushed against the night.

Gently, Umberto removed our hands from his pocket. He kissed my palm and threw the kiss into the sky. It was my first. I quickly devoted it to any saints who might be watching. I asked the saint to add the kiss to their stockpile of graces and send it back down to the Vatican. It was a pure one. I closed my eyes, ready for more.

But Umberto gestured toward a relief sculpture of a fractured Madonna and child spotlighted over the west archway of the Museo Opera.

"My darling," Umberto said in Italian. "You are wonderful, beautiful, a perfect woman. I do this for your honor." He blew the Virgin a kiss and grabbed my arms, turning me like a dancer to face him. *"Potresti aiutarci a trovare l'angelo?* Will you help us find the angel?" He said these words in the most sonorous Italian, and as if he had to say them.

Then Umberto tenderly rubbed his chin against mine and walked his lips across my cheeks. Our lips slipped against each other's like two pieces of silk.

"Do you hear it?" I asked when we stopped.

"What?"

It was magnificent. I had heard the music of angels.

He touched my wet lips with his finger and continued kissing me. When his tongue touched my earlobe, I nearly fainted. In his awkward passion, Umberto unbuttoned the top buttons of my raincoat and stroked the side of my neck with his trembling hand.

But the angel voices kept me on my toes. "Look up, look up," they sang.

Umberto touched my breast. It was a gentle but possessive

touch, a touch that reminded me who I was, and who he was. We were strangers. I came to my senses. I removed his hand from inside my coat.

"I've never done this before. I want more of you," he said to me with absoluteness. I later learned that this is what happened to men once you got their passion going. They lost their restraint.

Umberto kissed me again, as if he were starved. He hugged me tightly. I had to do something. I pushed him away and held his face in my hands, three millimeters from my eyes.

He was handsome, a dark man with stern eyebrows and white teeth, and not as young as I had first thought. His eyes, which were different shades of brown, expressed innocence and longing. The kindness I had seen in him earlier was simmering in discontent. Like myself, Umberto wanted more than he had. He said it was me. "You can have me forever," he said in Italian. But I wasn't supposed to understand him.

I kissed him slowly, tasting his dreams, losing my sensibility.

But not completely. I opened my eyes and looked up, following the crisp folds of the sculpture of the Madonna's robes and veil. At her elbow, near her child, was a hand, just a hand, carved from the same block of marble.

"Look! The hand!" I said to Umberto, pulling away from him. I lifted my palm, bending my fingers slightly, to imitate the gesture.

Umberto grabbed my wrist and braceleted his fingers around it. "The angel behind the hand is missing," he said. "After the war they took her from us, without paying anything. For years we tried to get her back. When we found her, we lost her. We lost everything," he said. "You must help us complete the Virgin. You'll do it, won't you?" He said all this in Italian.

We walked back to the La Danza, confused. He slid my hand inside his jacket pocket. The sensations I had continued to soak me with the pleasure many saints had renounced. That night, I was sure I wasn't a saint, and I was willing to cash in any grace I had accrued for a night of carnal joy.

"Ciao," I said. It was the first Italian word I had spoken to Umberto, and I said it during our very last moment together.

"Think of me, Umberto, whenever you feel lonely in Boston," he said in careful English. "And the angel," he pointed into the sky. "Don't forget her." Umberto saluted me. "Send her back to us, if you can."

He was as reluctant to leave me as I was to leave him. We stood on the sidewalk under the hotel awning as awkwardly as two children who had outgrown their clothes. Probably if I had invited him to my room, he would have come up with me. But it was better for both of us that I didn't.

"Thank you," I said, shaking Umberto's hand again. He bowed to kiss it and stayed in the lobby while I rose above him, in the elevator, like the Virgin, with my soul and hymen intact.

In my room, I undressed and felt pity for myself and my naked body. Facing the mirror, I stroked my own breasts with my fingertips, wishing I had not been so shy with Umberto. And why hadn't he been more insistent? So many men say they wanted virgins, but none were taking me.

I lay alone in the dark, alone and forgotten, listening to the night, hearing time pass. The greatest misfortune is loneliness, I thought. It has no past or future. The whole problem of my life had been learning how to break out of it, and how to communicate with others. Being chaste had brought me nothing. I believed I had grown too good at talking to saints, and to the dead—but I couldn't share a table with them. They didn't kiss me. I didn't want to join them in eternal life, as I had wanted to join Umberto.

Twenty - One

"Believe me, no one in the theater will be helpful if you drop in on them," Renato had advised me before I left the North End. "Artists need privacy to re-create themselves." I telephoned and set up an appointment. "And remember . . ." I heard Renato's precise voice continuing to instruct my brain. "Assure the manager no one remembers the bad shows, only the good ones."

The Teatro della Pergola's door handles were brass. I stepped inside the quiet theater. Jassy had been last seen there, onstage. I looked around. It was modern, decorated in the classical style, and its size was good, I guessed, for opera productions. I proceeded through the red lobby and down the carpeted slope, past hundreds of plush golden chairs.

The manager, obviously nervous about my visit, was up front, near the orchestra pit, coiling electrical wire into a neat circle. "She wasn't pouring on the volume, so her voice was quite beautiful when the platform dropped," he said, leading me to a chair. The manager was a carefully combed, bearded man in his late thirties with a stomach that slouched over the waist of his brown trousers. "Her chest register had character and there was a bloom on the high notes," he said, touching his throat. " 'The American Sensation' I called her—all sweetness and spitfire." He shook his head but didn't continue with an apology, or regret, about Jassy's disappearance.

"As I mentioned on the telephone, Jacqueline Porter was my sister-in-law," I said, holding a tissue against my nose, exaggerating a sniffle. I couldn't fail. In order to save Carlo and the children, and with them myself, I had to convince the manager to tell me exactly what had happened to Jassy. I wiped my nose again.

"People don't vanish," I said. "But she did. The hotel doesn't have a record Jassy was there. Her signature was lifted off the register. But you say she was here." I pointed to the stage.

The manager folded his arms over his belly.

I continued. "The Italian police, the government, the opera company, her family—no one knows where she is. Not even the journalists are curious—can you believe that? We don't know whose hands are in the bag. Of course, there is every reason to suspect criminal activity. But who are the criminals?"

I turned toward the manager, who was sitting next to me. "My family has had a recent string of bad luck," I said. "Last week, I myself and our children were kidnapped but released. No one paid to let us go. We hope the same might be true for Jassy. So far no one has contacted us, except a frightened actress who fears the same fate faces her."

I wiggled the arm of the chair between us. "We both know Italians disappear every day," I whispered. "People are snatched off the street by the Red Brigade, Mafia, Green Movement, neo-Fascists . . . and Benevolents." I glanced sideways to see if the manager reacted to my inclusion of a religious group's name. He didn't flinch.

"Italians are a possessive bunch," I continued, surprised that my tongue was able to keep pace with my thoughts for such a long time. "Some of us steal what we think belongs to us, or punish neighbors who have what we want for our own." I paused. "Jassy's an American. And a singer who isn't famous—not yet."

The manager said, "You're right. It was a crime of professional jealousy." He rubbed his beard. "Singers aren't too proud a breed to hurt one another." The manager wasn't giving me anything. I had the feeling he was grabbing anything to say to make me go away.

"What might be worse," I said, pulling a tightly fanned hundred-dollar bill from my sleeve, "is if Jassy has decided to run away. What if she herself wanted to disappear? Maybe she has stolen money, maybe she has a lover? Why should we suffer and worry endlessly?" I scratched the tip of my nose with the money.

Again, the manager folded his arms over his big belly, tucking his hands under his armpits. He watched me intently, not knowing what to make of me. I could be a government agent investigating yet another opera scandal, I could be someone sent from Rome, from Gioacchino Tommasi, to find out if the Teatro della Pergola manager was following orders, taking bribes, commonplace *bustarelle*, owed by anyone who ventured behind the stage. Or I could be who I said I was, the singer's sister-in-law.

The money was crisp. He looked at it, waiting, reminding me of a surefooted goat. I wagered he was the type of man who might buy a magazine with pictures of nude women, but would feel guilty the next morning and throw it away. I had nursed men like him in St. Scholastica. How could I convince him I was trustworthy? He had to help me. There was nowhere else to go.

I unlatched the buckle of my handbag. "I have a picture of

Jassy," I said, tucking the American money between my fingers like a cigarette. "It's an old picture, taken when my brother Carlo was courting her." I handed him the faded snapshot that had been tacked above the sink in Subiaco for over a decade. "She was always attractive, even when she was younger," I said.

The manager took the photo but not the money. "She had character," he said, flicking his fingernails on the picture. "Even here her eyes stare out from the paper as if she had known she was headed for stardom." He shifted his eyes to the stage, as if Jassy was standing before us. "She had such a beautiful, tricky, twittery way with her voice. When she sang, she held the audience in her hand," he said.

"Let me show you more." I emptied the contents of my handbag. A rosary fell onto the floor, along with several other religious souvenirs I had bought in Rome from nuns who sold papal-blessed knickknacks to tourists. My green Italian passport dropped with a thud along with a handful of small silver coins, my return airplane ticket, a yellow packet of chewing gum, a miniature mirror and small hairbrush, and my wallet. We crouched on the floor, and I spread out my gear.

"These girls are hers," I said, unfolding a photo of the twins. "My brother claims that having the twins expanded Jassy's range. So the children say they gave her her career." I whisked the rolled-up hundred-dollar bill over the twins' photo. "If I don't find Jassy, I'll be the woman they call Mama. And her, too." I passed him a photo of Bebe, and with it the hundred-dollar bill. "They probably won't remember the woman who gave birth to them."

The manager rose from his knees, and I swept my belongings back into my handbag. I congratulated myself. I was getting better at making bribes—my first bribe being to the surgeon who had redone my nose. For a moment, I wondered if he ever thought about me, and quickly, I pulled my mind back to Jassy.

"Can you imagine how awful it is for a family to lose someone?" I said. "Every time the telephone rings, or someone knocks at the door, no one says anything. But it is always noisy in our house because we are waiting. We don't allow ourselves to really live, to breathe, or to take long walks." I stood close to the manager and shifted my handbag over my shoulder. "You're a man. Men have so many responsibilities! You must understand how difficult it is for my brother to work and be a sensible father when the woman he loves has disappeared. You can understand his pain, can't you? He hears her voice. He sees her when she isn't there. And he has the children's hearts to consider. Carlo doesn't know what to tell them about Jassy." I tapped my hairline. "What should he put in their brains? Fear? Or is it better to pretend she never lived, and he never loved her, so that the children will not feel abandoned?

The manager was listening. "I can hardly believe Jassy would involve the opera in a scheme," he said softly, rubbing his beard. "Or that a jealous person would hurt her. She was a devoted artist, a queen in the theater. I agree. She was taken from this theater by force."

The manager was going to spill the beans, and I was ready to catch them. I tucked his forearm around mine and patted his hand. "Jassy loved opera as much as she loved her family," I said. "She wouldn't have hurt anyone. She wouldn't threaten your reputation, or leave her family stranded. Tell me. Who took her?"

The manager went back to his office and returned with a pair of eyeglasses, which he gave to me. They were wirerimmed, gold, and Jassy's. I cradled them in my palms as if they were nuggets of magic.

"I'm sorry," he said. "The glasses are all I have. I have no idea who took her." He told me what he knew.

"Moments prior to the end of Act Two of *La Cambiale di Matrimonio,* Jassy went down the trapdoor, just as she was supposed to do, just as Rossini indicated in the score." The manager made a wide, slow sweep with his arm, scooping air with his left hand. "In Act Three, she never came up." His lifted arm dropped. "The platform did, but Jassy wasn't on it. The orchestra stopped."

He was sympathetic, not covering up. "Something was wrong. She was too professional to miss a cue. Even if her leg had been broken, Jassy would have continued with her role." The manager shifted his shoulder away from mine. "I want you to know, no one speaks of disaster in the theater. It breaks our luck. We're a superstitious bunch."

He continued. "I rushed around the back of the stage, checked her dressing room, and the bathrooms. Nothing. Even her makeup kit was gone." He shook his head. "No one saw her go. No one saw anyone come into the theater. We tried to keep the show going, but—as you know—her understudy was afraid the role was jinxed."

"And the other actors?" I asked, nodding.

He let go of my arm, straightened his posture, and refused to think about what was sinister and complicated outside his theater. My time was over. The unexplainable could lie like a stripe next to the obvious, the fabricated, and the fantastic. None should penetrate the other. I, on the other hand, wanted these worlds to merge.

"Please, go on," I urged.

He returned the hundred-dollar bill to me. "I don't know anything other than theater and opera," he said. "I do my job. I've been here ten years. The glasses are all I have to give you. I found them under the gearshaft that moves the platform up and down. Take them and go."

261

I tucked the money back into his shirt pocket. "Will you do me one more favor?" I asked, wedging into what remained of his kindness.

"What?"

"I want to stand onstage, on the platform where Jassy was last seen in the Rossini opera. Will you lower me down?" Wherever she might be, I hoped to use my vision to connect to Jassy—if she were still alive, that is. It was my only chance.

The manager checked the time on his black wristwatch.

"I'll ask for nothing more," I assured him. "And I won't go to the FBI, or the American Consulate and cause you more trouble if you do this one last thing." I batted my eyelashes at him and hoped he hadn't noticed how awkward I was at flirting.

He brushed the front of his shirt, passing his thumb over his pocket. "I'll turn on the lights," he said.

The stage was bare except for a few unpainted flats. Heavy velvet curtains draped each side of the proscenium. On the floor strips of gray duct tape marked the edges of the descending trap. I turned to face an empty house.

The three hundred seats were vacant. Nonetheless I was thrilled. Spotlights pointed directly at me, warming my skin. I felt taller than I was. I could hear blood spin through my veins and arteries and felt loved, beautiful, and powerful. Being onstage stretched a moment into something longer. Death was impossible.

I immediately understood Jassy's addiction to performing, but I couldn't imagine myself being a performer. I was clumsy. My voice was ordinary, and my legs incapable of taking a breezy step. I satisfied myself by swaying from side to side, thinking about Jassy, hoping my audience wouldn't mistake me for her. She had been blessed with more than she needed to be human, I thought. And perhaps that had been her curse.

"Ready?" the manager shouted.

The square on which I stood separated from the surrounding stage. As I slowly descended, I waved to the absent audience. And for every inch larger I had felt standing on top of the stage, being underneath it made me feel small.

The chilly beige substage smelled freshly painted. The only other theater I was familiar with—Renato's—was a mess. I had assumed every theater was the same, that disorder was an artistic necessity. But here, in the Teatro della Pergola, order seemed a necessity.

With the lining of my raincoat, I polished the lens of Jassy's glasses and circled the shaft of gears that controlled the trap platform. I cleared my mind. When I was pleasantly blank, I slid the warmed glasses over my nose. The first glance through them rocked me with nausea. Jassy was nearly blind. Critics had marveled about her faraway gaze, saying it was heavenly. But it was her bad eyesight that caused her to look angelic, not her acting. How had Jassy maneuvered herself around a stage?

The small room became quiet and bewitchingly chilly. I didn't know what to expect. "Come on!" I challenged. "I'm ready."

At that moment, a coppery taste filled my mouth. I saw a shimmering reflection of Jassy in the room. It was the same image I had seen two nights ago in the children's nursery. The head was enlarged and the eyelids were clipped open. If Jassy had existed in this form for two days without blinking her eyes, I thought she must be furious.

Her ghost settled in a corner, disheveled, skeptical, and anxious. Not encased in flesh but air, her image was at once as flat as a sheet and dipped back into a deeper dimension. And for as much as I was repulsed by her big head, her gaping eyes and random formlessness, I knew I had to inhale Jassy and share my flesh with her.

"Jassy, I'm Alicia," I gently said. "Carlo's sister. I don't know what happened to you. None of us do. I won't hurt you. We just want to figure out how to help you rest." It was the invitation Jassy needed. Her spirit jumped into me, jolting my body against a wall. Immediately I realized that the difference between inhaling her soul and inhaling a soul in the St. Scholastica operating room was that I had to contain it. There was no wounded flesh to receive my exhalation. Jassy was inside me.

My head ached. I had never imagined a single person could possess so much vastness. I couldn't feel where Jassy stopped. She was big—a heave and a quake, and I was so much less. And she didn't smell dead but like oranges and lilies.

And like smoke, we rose to the stage and the last moments of her last performance. The house was full. Our torsos were pressed into a tight blue bodice that displayed our round breasts on a shelf of lace. Singing, our voices raced like wind, round and round each person, appealing to their appreciation of beauty, urging them to hope and to want, and asking them to give us their expectations so that we might be even better.

The words rushed through Jassy. Her arms stretched up. She was breathless but was able to continue. Her music, not propelled by lungs, throat, lips, or will, rose by the absence of those things. Jassy had mastered hollowness.

When the back of her throat became numb, I gave her mine. I couldn't feel our differences anymore. She and I were together. Her blood raced past my ears. I lost myself. She was stronger. The audience applauded as the platform lowered, and I saw men near the small crawl door on the left side of the substage. They clutched Jassy's clothes in their arms, her wine-colored coat, and her makeup box. They crouched like ducks behind a litter of props, expecting her.

I can't see how many there are. I grab the rope but it's greasy. There's no way I can climb back onstage. They push me against a wall and jam a wet handkerchief into my mouth. Will they kill me? My neck hurts—and my back. They pin my arms together so roughly. They have a bag. For my head? It's coming. Help me! Now it's dark.

My legs kick. I struggle to pull loose but I'm stuck. They punch my side to make me stop struggling. I bend to the pain, a horrible pain, but my cry stays stuffed inside my mouth. My hands ache.

They swing my feet off the ground. I squeeze my thighs together—goddamn them—arching like a twisted thread. Something rips. In a second they wrap tape around my ankles and up to my hips. Through the gag I suck in air, a corner of sweet air, before they tape the bag tight around my neck. It's rough. I feel their hands on my bare shoulders. They tape my wrists. Worse, one of them blows foul gas in the bag. It makes me sleepy. I see icicles.

Sleeping, I was heavier than they expected and stiff as a corpse. It was a tunnel they pushed me through. I can still smell the earth. Someone forced my shoulders and another pair of hands grabbed my knees at the other end.

They were quick and laid me on my side in the cold trunk of a car, I think. Or was it a coffin? They buried me alive. They shut the lid.

I lift out of her flesh, but stay close, and see where they have taken Jassy. The road is newly asphalted, smooth and loud. The sign says AUTOSTRADA DEL SOLE.

She kicks. She wants to smell the North End in the morning, see herself feeding the children yellow and white boiled eggs, and she wants to listen to a record with Carlo before she falls asleep.

She had one more chance. *If I sing.* If only I sing, she says to herself. *I can stay alive.* But the bitter gas bubbled up from her stomach. *I couldn't spit it out.* It pushed me farther out of Jassy. It backed up behind her nose. *Bitter. Bitter. Bitter. And my feet became lighter than my shoulders. I had no choices left. It was dark.* The end?

I keep listening, feeling her head sink down. *Come, come cradle me. You are on your way, too. With me. Is it you, Alicia? I'm still here. Come. It isn't so bad. A puff from me and you'll be on the other side.*

I saw her then, for a stark long moment. Jassy was on her side, in my bed in Subiaco, her eyes peeled wide open. *Please.* She reached out, wrapping her cold arms around my waist, tugging me close, pulling me into her like a pillow disappears between a sleeper's knees. *The others will be saved.*

I screamed.

"Such a scream!" The theater manager shook my shoulder. "*Signora! Sveglia!* Wake up! *Sta bene?* Are you all right? What happened?"

My head on my knees, I curled around my chest, slowly daring to gaze beyond the bend of my elbow. The lower corner of the screens, stored on the right side of the room, were numbered with black chalk. The manager's black shoes were polished. There was order around me. I wasn't in Subiaco, in bed with Jassy.

"Shall I call a doctor?" he asked. "I thought someone was choking you. Your scream was a struggling one."

I didn't respond. My jaw locked. I hugged myself and inhaled the scent of my own skin, burying my head deeper between my elbows.

Cautiously, the manager patted my upper back. "I'm

266

sorry about your sister-in-law," he said. "Really I am. I wish I could tell you more than that she was a wonderful singer. It was an accident, I am sure."

I rolled onto my stomach and pounded the floor. "I don't want to go with her," I said, my voice hoarse from having helped Jassy sing. "Pray for me, not her."

The manager stood up. *"Piacere, signora,"* he said. "You need more than I am qualified to give you." He straightened his brown tie.

I pushed myself upright, retrieving the air that had been sucked out of my lungs. I blessed myself.

"Do you want a priest?" he asked. "Or a cab?"

I blew my nose.

"How about a cigarette? I have cigarettes upstairs."

"You didn't tell me everything," I said to the manager. "Why did you paint this room after Jassy disappeared? It smells fresh. Did you have to cover fingerprints? Is there an exit door behind that stack of flats?"

"Signora, non so nulla. I know nothing. Please." He held up his hand like a stop sign. "I'll walk you to the door."

The rest of the day, I hid in the cold churches of Florence, going from one to the other, speaking to no one, not even to God, hearing only the pain of being nothing and belonging nowhere. I longed to be one-dimensional, to lie on a piece of paper, and disappear when folded. Only then, I believed, would I be safe. But a blessing of strength found me. I had sense enough to know my desire to vanish was my madness. If I died, or if I didn't die, I could not destroy who I was.

Darkness came like oil down a funnel, and a shrinking moon buttoned the sky between Florence's clay-topped spires and grand striped domes. I found myself seated on a stone bench at the edge of the Piazza del Duomo, in the same piazza where twenty hours ago I had taken my first kiss.

I counted the cathedral bells as they rang out nine times.

Nine was the number of completeness. I thought about Carlo, my brother. How could I be so stupid to believe, for my entire life, that those first nine months we grew together in a womb had joined us forever? Strangers can weave into your spirit as closely as your own blood. Just as Jassy had pulled me into her, she had pulled Carlo, and Virginia had pulled Renato. And we had all pulled the children into our souls.

I was a complete person. I was Alicia, and I could love Umberto, or Renato, or any other man, in the same way Carlo had loved Jassy. Or I could be alone. Love rules without rules. Carlo didn't have to marry before I did. We didn't have to supervise each other's mating. I could cut myself loose from the past, just as Carlo had done, just as the angel had cut herself loose from the Madonna and child.

At that moment, and not before that moment, did I truly put together the broken pieces of my story. Last night seemed so long ago, but I remembered Umberto had kissed me and asked me to help him find an angel. I thought he had been speaking about me. But now I knew he was asking for the angel in the Harvard Square subway, the angel in the crate behind the toilet tent, the one I had touched, with crisp folds in her dress and clipped wings.

I told myself I didn't want anything to do with reuniting the angel with her hand and with the Madonna and child. Already, getting the two pieces together had caused disruption and destruction. It would be better if the angel were buried inside a subway station never to be seen again, I said to myself. Perhaps it is best to leave the broken and damaged to repair themselves, otherwise the mess that is made can be worse than the intention to celebrate them. The Benevolents had wanted to return the angel for their glory, for beauty, and the Church's grace. But in their passion to worship the Virgin and correct the mistakes of the past, they had bungled the life of the living.

T w e n t y - T w o

"I don't want to drive anything made in Italy," I said to the garage mechanic. His brown mustache had been recently singed by a short cigar.

"Sure, *signora*." The mechanic nodded. It was after business hours. I had caught him before he locked up his shop.

He handed me the keys to a blue Chevrolet. Then he unzipped the thigh pocket of his grease-fingered jumpsuit and deposited my lire there. "I suppose you won't be returning," he said, patting the thick wad of money I had given him.

The car lurched out from between the parking lot stanchions. I had only been behind the wheel of a car a few times before my father died. It was almost ten o'clock. The traffic wasn't too bad, but my driving was still horrible. I circled the block surrounding the La Danza Hotel. When I slammed the brakes and gripped the steering wheel, I found it impossible to coordinate the relationship between my braking foot and the accompanying sensation of being flung through the windshield. Cars behind me blared their horns. I got used to the noise. I had to find Umberto.

I stuck to the inside lane, panicking at every intersection. I was lucky to get an easy parking spot right in front of the La Danza Hotel.

Umberto was sitting at a table near the glass door. Seeing him again made him real to me. I enchanted myself remembering the warmth of his skin and his sincere passion.

But wait. Who was Umberto talking to?

The men at the table sitting with him wore black suits and silk scarves and held stiff-brimmed hats on their laps. Umberto was wearing a suit, too. Already, he looked older than yesterday. Tonight someone else was filling the sugar bowls. I squinted to read Umberto's lips.

"I don't know what happened to her," he said. "She left nothing, no clue."

He looked nervous. Umberto wasn't good at lying. I had written my North End address, folded it into an envelope, and had given the envelope with his name on it to the cook at the restaurant.

When Umberto leaned forward, I saw the other man. He had a wide cleft in his chin. It was Cardinal Ulbaldini! Not only that! I saw that Umberto was not the same Umberto I had kissed the night before. The Umberto sitting at the table with Ulbaldini was wearing a white collar around his neck. *Gesù Cristo!* I said, blessing myself three times. The man I had undressed in my mind, and had made love to in my sleep, was a priest, or maybe more. Maybe he was a monsignor.

I dropped onto the floor of the car and laid my stomach over the hump between the passenger and driver sides, pounding the carpeted floor with my fists. Umberto had tricked me. He was not an innocent waiter, or a bungling Benevolent, but a merciless killer and kidnapper who had played a grand joke on my brother, his family, and me. I was the virgin they had all used, not cherishing me, but raping my true emotions and dreams. I wouldn't allow them to win. They couldn't trick me or take away the pride I had collected and the belief in my own beauty.

271

I told myself I could never go back to my little house in Subiaco and hide like a dog that couldn't bite. Knowing what was waiting for me there enabled me to sharpen my teeth. The house was no longer my own. Furious with constructive rage, I jerked the car out of its parking space, and sped out of town.

On the outskirts of Florence, near the entrance to the autostrada and under an umbrella of cypress trees, I stopped at a twenty-four-hour roadside shrine set up by the Sisters of the Immaculate Heart of Mary. I was overjoyed to have found it. In Italy common people like myself can find God everywhere, not just in churches, or through priests.

"Excuse me, Sister," I said, speaking through a window to a pair of nuns inside the shrine. The nuns took donations and dispensed prayers and small indulgences, like spiritual insurance agents, to travelers heading toward Rome.

I spoke fast. "For most of my life I have hidden myself in a room in Subiaco, promising to save myself for the future, and now that the future has arrived, I know my last task, before I can step through the door to freedom, is the task of a holy woman. Please help me. I have money," I said. "Please. Let me wear your clothes."

The nuns led me through their ticket booth to the inside vestibule. There I exchanged my raincoat, black dress, Jassy's cowboy boots, stockings, and two hundred dollars for a nun's garments. Nearby I saw a huge box filled with other women's street clothes, obviously exchanged for the same habit I was wearing. I was touched to know that others, like myself, must have been pushed to do holy deeds.

I confided in the older nun, telling her I was a nurse and had held hearts in my hand, but had not known who they belonged to. And I told her about Umberto, and how I had been willing to destroy everything I believed I valued for a moment of pleasure. "And I made a promise to God," I said.

"I told Him if I failed, I would give up my worldly possessions and become a nun."

"Everyone makes promises," the old nun laughed, her eyes loose under her lids. "If no one was jealous too much life would be lived." She patted my head. "Too many connections would be made and no one would understand that love requires dependence, attachment, and always threatens separation."

I maneuvered the car around the shrine's gravel parking lot, and as I was about to pull onto the road, I saw Umberto pass by in a car. I put my foot on the brake. There was every reason in the world to fear he was after me. If he knew where Jassy was, he might get there first and destroy her, my hope, and me.

His car slowed down and backed up. In my blue veil and white collar, I looked like any other woman who had taken the vow of chastity. And closer up, Umberto didn't look like who I thought he was either. He had long sideburns, a thin mustache, and was wearing an ascot.

But later we found out we had both been wrong. It had been me, and it had been Umberto. Both of us were disguised. He was running away from Florence and from Cardinal Ulbaldini, who was pressuring him to find me and to find Jassy.

I pulled the Chevy onto the autostrada, leaving tire tracks on the road. I was a virgin on the run, and I knew exactly what I had to do.

Twenty-Three

I arrived in Subiaco just before the green tongues of grass on the sides of the highway were about to yawn for sun. Rather than take the exit nearest my house, I drove one stop farther, taking a left off the ramp and winding around a narrow road up the hill to the center.

Other than the town statue honoring Gina Lollabrigida, there was no one to wave to in Subiaco square—not that anyone would have recognized me in a nun's habit, with a new nose, and behind the wheel of a Chevrolet. Still, it wasn't my nose and clothing that made me different from the person who had left Subiaco a month ago. It was my eagerness. I wanted to be let loose and to experience the joy of being where everywhere and everyone is now. For too many years I had done penance for my brother's pleasure and my own stupidity.

The main street descended. I glanced across the limpid river. Several miles away, on my right, the orange stacks of the paper mill poked out of the gorge. I wound around a rocky hill and passed St. Benedict's cave, a site that had once comforted me. Now the cave made me anxious. Next to the cave was a monastery with a spire, and when its shadow hit the hood of my car, I rolled down the window to allow the dark air to rekindle all that I knew. What lay ahead of me was my last job as a nurse, a citizen of Italy, and the old Alicia Barzini.

First, I drove to the St. Scholastica Clinic. The key to the supply room was on the third-floor station in a matchbox under the television. I held the key in my palm and tucked my hands deep into the loose sleeves of the nun's garment. The janitor, Giovanni, was taking a cigarette break near the stairwell.

"*Buon giorno*," he said respectfully, not recognizing me.

I lowered my head and continued down the white-tiled hall to the supply room, which had once been my haven. I remembered how I used to sit there, devouring stolen chocolate, cheese, and leftovers from patients' dinner plates.

I worked quickly, filling a laundry bag with reels of gauze, boxes of cotton, alcohol, dozens of candles, two jars of honey, formaldehyde, morphine, a hypodermic needle, and a tank of oxygen. I dragged the heavy bag into the elevator and across the parking lot. The sun was beginning to bleed into the sky.

In Boston, it was the middle of the night, and as I drove the longer route back to my house, I hoped Carlo and the children's eyes were closed and that in their dreams none of them were searching for Jassy. If they were, she might take them with her.

I parked the Chevy behind the house, near the propane fuel tanks. I longed to inhale the scents of dandelions, hillside juniper, green peas, and fans of lettuce that under normal circumstances in March would greet my nose. I expected sweetness was not what I would smell. Rather it would be the stinging stench of rotting flesh. I pulled a surgical mask over my nose, stuffed it with sage leaves from the side garden, and tied a scrub apron over my nun's garment.

As I picked the herbs, I noticed several gallons of oil had

been left for me, tucked behind the rosemary bush. It was the oil the Subiaco Benevolents supplied me with to fuel my lamps when I sewed costumes for their statues. I wondered if I had pulled the local branch into the larger scheme of their brothers. If I had, were they willing or unwilling participants? If they caught me at home, would they kill me? They hadn't meant to kill Jassy. Everything is easier the second time.

My hands shook. I wiped my mouth. If I died right then I was afraid I would not possess my own afterlife, just as I had not possessed the life I was living. But I could not abandon Jassy. She was trapped between limbo and the clouds, and her broken soul deserved the freedom to begin again.

The back door lock had been broken. My long blue skirt snapped as I stepped inside the house. Jassy was in my bedroom, still dressed in the fancy blue bodice she had been wearing onstage in Florence. Her body had stiffened into as uncomfortable a position as I was sure her soul was stuck in. She was lying on her side, atop the bare metal springs of my childhood bed. Her back faced me; her swollen elbow jutted back from the curve of her waist. Her neck was twisted to the right, and her legs were bound together in gray tape. The bag had been taken off her head and left on the floor.

I didn't walk around the bed to face the eyes I knew were open. I stepped in closer to her, feeling so much like the black flies buzzing against the glass pane of the closed window. With one hand I caressed the thick belt of rosary beads around my waist, and with the other hand I touched Jassy's red hair. I expected it to be brittle and to break from her scalp. But it filled my palm with softness. Her hair was as slippery and alive as my own. Everything outside of death is vanity, I said to myself. I kissed the rosary beads and touched the crucifix to the center of Jassy's forehead.

"Hail Mary, full of grace," I said, pressing my own eyes

shut. "The Lord is with thee. Blessed art thou amongst women and blessed is the fruit of thy womb."

Very gently, with trembling fingertips, I traced over her forehead to find her eyelids and to close them over her eyes. But her skin was crisp and didn't budge. I prepared myself to try again.

When I kissed my own fingertips, I saw they had picked up a grayness from Jassy's flesh. Her death was leaking out of her into me.

I ran out of the house to the field where I rubbed my hand in the earth, wiping death where it belonged. I prepared myself for a battle. Jassy wasn't going to slip out of her life as easily as my Mama and my Papa had. She was a kicker.

I strapped the oxygen tank I had stolen from the hospital onto my back, dropped a clear plastic mask over my face, snapped on a pair of latex gloves, and dragged my equipment bag into the room. "Honey will melt the shock out of your eyelids," I said. "Honey will transform your eyelids into flower petals."

I dripped golden syrup over her face, which wasn't gray or bloated. I noticed Jassy's body wasn't decomposing either. The moment she died she must have experienced an increase in blood pressure, due to fear, I told myself. Fear was preserving her.

While the honey sank in, I readied the rest of the house.

Papa's tools were in the cupboard. On my hands and knees, I hammered long nails into the footprints of kidnappers, murderers, gangsters, art smugglers, and the bungling virgin worshipers who had brought Jassy's body into my house. Their mistake would cost them more than sleepless nights. I would mark their feet with stigmata.

I scattered straw throughout the house and scattered bullets from Papa's gun and holster in the straw. I turned the mirrors, so no corner of Jassy's soul would be tempted to

277

hold on to her flesh. I set up Mama's statues. St. Anthony, stuffed with alcohol-drenched rags, went on the dresser in my bedroom. St. Joseph was put facing the door in the dining room. And in the kitchen, on top of the old tin tabletop, I lined twenty wax St. Benedicts next to twenty St. Scholasticas.

Back in the bedroom, I poured the gold pieces I had sealed inside the statue of the Blessed Virgin into a canvas sack. I propped the emptied statue of the Virgin in the bend of Jassy's knees while I cut open the tape encasing her ankles. She was five days dead, I guessed, and still supple. Her veins took an injection of morphine. Only the impious would question this. Jassy's soul was so big it had made a special connection with the Other World, not being completely in or completely out of the earthly one. Her body didn't smell either. I took off my oxygen mask.

Using a hot-water bottle as a makeshift drip sack, I pumped her stomach with formaldehyde, figuring when the room was hot with fire, she would explode. I soaked the straw mattress under her hair with propane from the outside tank and sprinkled the black Benevolent oil throughout the house, over the straw.

Finally, I stretched a braided, gas-soaked roll of gauze from the Chevy's gas tank into the bedroom where Jassy lay. I shut the curtains, sprinkled sage and clumps of oil-soaked straw everywhere, and tossed handfuls of dry black beans over my shoulder, knowing the beans would help Jassy's spirit slip through to the other side. I made one last pass through the house before going into Jassy's room to close her eyes and to tell her I was going to give her a second death, and with it a chance at eternal life. Just as I was about to cut her arm with a razor scratch to release blood and with it her fear, she screamed to tell me to move aside.

"One death has been pain enough for the life I've lived," she said.

I had never heard a corpse talk, though I had often prayed for that experience. I told myself Jassy had always been a determined woman, and quite bull-like with her dreams, so why shouldn't she resist my actions. I assured myself my will was as strong as hers.

"Souls can begin again." I said. "But you haven't let yours go. You died with your eyes open." I spoke tenderly. "It was a horrible death. I'm sorry. I can't bring you back in this direction." My instinct told me bodies who had died violently could grab any emotion and make it ugly.

"Don't try to fool me, you witch! You want to destroy me." Jassy's words pounced on me. "Life is precious. You want mine. I won't give it to you." Jassy moaned a frightful moan that rumbled and thundered and darkened the room so much that I couldn't see the hand in front of me.

"Calm down. What you are experiencing now is not death," I explained.

"What do you know? Birth and death are no secret to me. You know neither directly."

My knees buckled. "I'm not waiting to be born, nor wanting to be who I'm not. I'm Alicia Barzini, a thirty-five-year-old woman who can create and destroy. I believe in myself as much as you believed in yourself." I moved forward in the darkness.

"Jassy," I said, "Your soul is stretched too big. There are holes in it. You've got to get small to begin again. Go back to being the size of a seed."

I moved my hands above her corpse, searching for the statue of the Blessed Virgin which I had left propped next to her body. I found it and held the statue upside down, with its hollow hole near my nose. In my other hand I grasped the prayer book which I had taken from the night table next to my bed. "Come get me," I said. Then I glued my tongue against the roof of my mouth so that Jassy wouldn't slip into me, I sealed my lips, and I inhaled.

Instead of allowing it to enter my nose, I guided Jassy's spirit into the hole at the bottom of the statue. I quickly covered the hole with the prayer book, and carefully wedged the statue of the Virgin next to Jassy's corpse.

I baptized Jassy, salting her lips and pouring what oil was left inside a golden gallon tin over her body.

"I bless you in the name of the Father, Son, and Holy Spirit," I said. "You have renounced Satan and all his deeds. You can begin again."

The words comforted me as much as they coddled her soul. The room brightened. Her death may have been difficult, but her rebirth had been simple. I spoke for her. She was now contained inside the statue of the Virgin and within the safety of a womb. In a moment I would release her into the air, the medium the dead sustained themselves in during their journey to heaven.

I carried the statue to the window. "Keep your eyes shut," I said, "and you'll go on the most magnificent trip you've ever had." I lifted the window, then the prayer book, allowing her soul to escape. A pack of flies, collected on the window, left too, scooting off toward the few white clouds in the still gray sky.

A tremendous wave of relief filled my heart. I could go to Boston and be with Carlo, the children, and Renato. I imagined them all sleeping, and their heads sunk safely on feather pillows. For an instant I drifted into the same softness, sensing what I had to look forward to.

I turned from the window to admire Jassy's body, curled up like an infant's and slippery with oil. She was newly baptized and pleasing to God. I slid my hand over her bare shoulder, and it was only then that I allowed myself to be sad. Never before, with such force, had I felt the love that bound me to dust, to the call of birds, and to the labored rhythm of my breathing. Jassy was gone. No one would hear her. Her work had given her so much pleasure, and she had died with it, not with people. I admired her. Jassy fiercely believed nothing could stop her—not anyone else's dreams—and she believed she could change anything. If I could have a part of her, that would be what I would choose, not her beauty, her voice, or her talent for organizing people.

When I heard sniffling, I was so startled my back teeth could have marked a coin. I was sure someone had come to get me. But before I ducked under the dusty bed to hide, I saw tears drop from the corners of Jassy's eyes.

"I was dreaming about Jassy, statues, and babies who flew like cherubs without wings. I'm empty, so empty. I have no one."

"It's Virginia," I said, recognizing her delicate voice. "Are you dead, too?" I asked, thinking I'd have to perform another baptism.

She was not crying for herself. "I wanted to punish the Benevolents for being so arrogant as to think they could own the past, when I could not own my present. I wanted to punish Carlo for not paying me enough. And punish Renato because I had stopped loving him." Her silvery voice rose from deep inside Jassy's body. "How lonely it is to bring your broken pieces together. It would have been easier for me to stay fractured. But look, look what my selfish behavior has done to Jassy."

"Ah," I said, finally making sense of how Virginia had come to be in the room with me. "You were dreaming about Jassy, and she brought you here."

"I didn't want to steal. I didn't want to sneak. I didn't want this to happen. I was sorry for the future, and when it came I didn't know what to do."

"Why didn't you just complete the shipment?" I asked. "You could have collected the money, sent the angel, and left."

"I couldn't humiliate myself anymore. But look what my pride did. I should be dead, not her."

"Maybe she'll take you with her," I warned.

"No one wanted me to die," another voice said. It was Jassy's. She had come back and was speaking from inside the corpse, too. "My death was an accident."

"It was my fault," Virginia said, with resignation.

"It was mine," I rushed in, sitting on the bed next to the corpse. "For ten years I prayed God would punish Carlo by taking Jassy away. I wanted to make everything right, by my rules."

"So you believe this happened because of your prayers?" Jassy asked.

"God listens?" Virginia asked.

"Yes—I think so," I said, quite confidently.

"Be quiet, both of you," Jassy interrupted. "We're small parts of something so much bigger. Don't either of you take blame." Even dead, Jassy took control of a situation. "Listen here," she said, "we have a few things to clear up. Let's go as fast as we can."

Virginia laughed. "It's so good to be so close to you, Jassy. This is our last time? Hey, maybe we can finally figure out what Carlo meant when he said two minds had to coin inside."

"I maintain it was a pronunciation problem," Jassy said. "He meant coincide."

"Maybe, maybe not." Virginia wasn't going to argue. "It's not so bad inside your head," she said. "So much

282

order—like neat shelves. But it's not how my brain works."

"You carry so many numbers inside yours!" Jassy said.

Both women expressed their sorrow for missing knowing each other as they grew old. "I died young and stayed beautiful," Jassy said. "But you have a chance to give something back to the world."

The sun was moving into the sky, and the fumes from the gas and oil, which I had splashed inside the house, were beginning to make me dizzy. "I've got to go," I said. "I'm the only one here with a body. I don't want to be surprised by a visitor."

"We'll zip out as soon as you leave something behind," Jassy said to me. "After all, we're giving you our men and our children."

I removed my Mama's ruby ring from my finger and slipped it on Jassy's oiled knuckle. "It's yours," I said. "It belonged to Carlo's mother, and before that to our grandmother."

"What about Virginia?" Jassy prodded.

"There's nothing of value left to give," I said.

"Yes, there is," Jassy corrected me.

"My gold?" I lifted the canvas sack, which was strapped to my wrist. "It's just money." I shrugged.

"Give her your magic," Jassy said.

I opened the valve on the oxygen tank, grabbed my bag of gold, lit the candles on the dresser, and ran. In the kitchen, I turned on the gas stove and headed off to the highway. As I ran down the road, the sun spun out of control, and the ground rippled like dark waves. By leaving Subiaco I was choosing to live. Though the past tugged endlessly, I knew my task, like Carlo's before me, was to cut its tentacles and keep intact only the core.

At the ramp to the highway, under a billboard for Fiat, I got into a stranger's car and tucked my nun's skirt modestly under my knees. "I'm going to the airport," I said. "Will you give me a ride?"

The house exploded, filling me with a vapor of lightness. I didn't look backward, but kept the image in the back of my mind. Nothing could really be destroyed.

Twenty-Four

"Sister, is it the custom for nuns to hitch rides?" the driver asked. He was on his way to Rome.

"According to the new rules, it is," I answered.

The kind, overweight man drove ten kilometers out of his way to drop me at the Leonardo Da Vinci airport. "We're here," he said, nudging me.

I carefully shifted the bag of gold from my lap and held it under my arm like a football, not wanting the contents to rattle. *"Mille grazie,"* I said.

Inside the terminal, I took my place in the back of the line leading to the international counter. When someone tapped my shoulder, I nearly died in my nun's shoes. I was sure it was the Benevolents—or the Italian police—come to handcuff me. I had assisted murderers, burned my house, stolen from the hospital, lied to my brother, replaced my nose. There would be no redemption for Alicia Barzini. I would never get out of Italy, to America, let alone be admitted to heaven. I could never start over.

They covered my mouth with a hand and dragged me backward into a corridor. I wrapped the strap of my sack of gold around my wrists. No matter what they did to me, I told myself, I would hold on to my money. I might have been born poor, but I would die rich.

The stiff ring of the nun's collar cut into my throat, choking me. I was ready to get it over with right then. But death was not ready to catch me.

"Alicia," he said. "You're a brave woman." It was Umberto. Was it possible my journey was going to have a happy ending?

"Did you kill her?" I asked.

"No," he said. "I found out the same day you did."

Then Umberto worked his hand under the back of my nun's tunic and pressed me against his chest. We kissed more than once, not caring that we were displaying affection in a public place, and were both dressed in clerical clothing. I heard the laugh of the child inside me being overcome by the moan of a woman, and I wasn't afraid.

"They don't know where we are," Umberto said. "But they still want the statue. If we give it to them, I can stop being a priest, and you can stop being this." He tugged my veil. Umberto had found his virgin.

"But we'll wait until we're married," I said, hesitating under the formidable burden of freedom.

Umberto agreed. "Of course," he said. "We'll enjoy breaking our vows together."

We arrived at Atlantic Avenue at dinnertime on the Saturday evening before Easter. When we walked into the yellow kitchen, Carlo was seated in the same chair where I had last seen him sitting, five days earlier. The white napkin stuck inside his collar illuminated his sad face.

"Where is she?" he asked. I didn't need my sixth sense to know he was miserable.

At the stove, Renato, his back turned to us, stopped piling spaghetti on blue plates. I stopped to look at everyone.

286

I remember at that moment the Barzinis and Riccis—even the children—seemed larger than life to me. Each of them was bigger than Jassy. I squeezed Umberto's hand to make sure he was real, and it struck me deeply that I was no longer on the outside waiting to be invited in. I was one of them.

"Hey?" Bebe asked. "Why is Aunt Alicia wearing those clothes? And who is that man with her? Is he a priest, or just dressed up like one?"

Renato wiped his hands on his red apron as he inspected us both with his wide-set eyes. He shook Umberto's hand. "Sit down," he said. "Eat with us."

"*Dov'è lei?* Where is she?" Carlo asked again, more urgently. He hadn't budged from his chair to shake Umberto's hand. His green eyes were drained of hope. I suspected his seeing me with Umberto was a reminder of his loss. I vowed not to allow my happiness to interfere with Carlo's grief.

I put my finger over my lips.

"Tell us!" Cher said. "Where's my mother?"

"Where is she?"

"Why doesn't Alicia answer?"

"Shhh," I whispered. "Jassy's gone to sleep for a long, long time. We won't see her again, and that'll be sad for us. Jassy allowed us all to dream. No one was ever so generous. We'll have to learn how to be big people without her."

Bebe ran to the window. "Is she up there? Does she see us?" she said, pointing to the night sky.

"She's in Italy," I said. "She couldn't come back with me. She's with your *Nonna* and *Nonno,* your grandma and grandpa."

Carlo pushed away from the table.

I followed him into his bedroom, thinking that for years I had known everything about my brother. My vision— whether a blessing or curse—had allowed me to peer into his life. At times I had empathized with him, but mostly I had been jealous of his good luck, and desired to either destroy or possess what he had. Rather than learn from what I saw and merge his success into my own behavior, I had stood on the opposite side, isolating myself. I was stubborn. Worse, I had condemned his happiness, believing only then could I take back my own. And now that I had my own, and his was gone, I was scared inside because I knew how lonely Carlo felt. I wanted no one to know that emptiness. Jassy was dead.

But he had me and I had to tell him the truth. Seeing my brother was as miserable as I had wished he had been without me, I slipped backward. I wanted to erase my strength. I wanted to change everything back to the way it had been before I had set foot in America, before there was a need to conceal what I had prayed for and what Virginia had done to him, before Jassy had died. At one time I might have believed God was on my side, protecting my righteousness, and that I could say and do anything because I was under His wing. That day God was testing my courage. I was on my own.

"There was an accident in the theater," I said to Carlo, being as much a messenger of the dead as of the living. "No one dies, not really," I said, but Carlo wasn't interested in philosophy.

His eyes blinked hard. "Why didn't you call me?" Carlo sat in the stuffed chair at the foot of his bed, his elbows propped on the chair's worn pink arms.

"You know how Italians are," I offered limply. "The police, the opera company, the hospital—no one could decide what to do, or whom to call. When I got there, it was too late. They said I had to make a decision about the body, quickly." I sat on Carlo's bed. I had no idea what he was thinking. My connection to him was gone.

"How did she die?" Carlo's questions were direct.

I panicked. God was making me think, giving me time to decide what Carlo needed to hear.

"I did what I thought would be best," I said, smoothing the wrinkles from the blue spread on his bed. I paused, remembering how Jassy had once lain where I sat, beside my brother, and how she had rested for the last time on my own bed in Subiaco. Her absence would ache in us for a long time.

"What was that?" Carlo pushed me to talk.

I folded my hands in my lap. I was waiting to hear a voice, any voice—the voice of a saint, or Jassy's voice. Even my own voice would do. Someone had to tell me what to say. I waited. Nothing came. I asked myself if I hadn't learned something from watching Carlo and Jassy. Hadn't I learned to be kind, to be myself, and at the same time protect everyone? Hadn't Jassy kicked on her way out, and after her soul had been released hadn't she forgiven everyone, even Virginia?

"They asked me if I wanted to put Jassy's body in a crate and ship it inside the belly of a plane back to Boston. I didn't think you'd want that," I blurted. God was giving me time to think.

"This is her home, Alicia. Why wouldn't I want that?" Carlo was too worn out to be angry.

"Who knows how restless her soul might have been sealed inside an airplane? Maybe it would have escaped before it got here," I said—but I was really thinking about how restless my brother's soul might become if he knew Jassy had lost her life in the trunk of a car; or how I was going to live knowing my virginity, which I had once held up like a halo, was the reason they had kidnapped Jassy; and that Virginia had been shipping religious statues and artwork to Italy through Spediamo and siphoning money from his cash registers for herself because Carlo had not paid her enough attention, or salary. Nor did I want to explain the Benevolents to my brother. I wanted Carlo to respect his neighbors, and not suspect that every unemployed man standing in the dark doorwells of the North End had had something to do with Jassy's death. "Don't worry about anything," I said, soothing Carlo with his own favorite words. I couldn't tell Carlo the truth. I got up off the bed and stood behind his chair to massage his shoulders.

"Stop, that won't work." Carlo brushed my hands away. "You're doing this to punish me. You've never forgiven me for leaving you with Mama and Papa. You never told me why they died. You've refused to tell me where they're buried. They've haunted me, and you have never lifted their anger from my shoulders. Now you want Jassy to haunt me. There's not enough room in here for me anymore! *Ho troppe cose per la testa.*" He rubbed his temples. "I'm carrying too much in my head."

"Carlo, how did I know what was going on in your mind? All these years I wanted and resisted being close to you. I didn't really understand you, did I?" It was more a question for myself than for Carlo. "I thought I knew everything."

"Nothing!" Carlo asked. "You were on the other side of the ocean, cut off from everyone. And you wanted me to join you, to live my life beside you, crying." He touched his chest. "I won't let you do this to me again. I want to know everything. Start with Jassy."

I told him she had been accidentally hit in the head in the basement of the Teatro della Pergola in Florence and that the government wanted to cover up the incident. "There is a ring of Italian smugglers digging tunnels into the basements of museums and churches. They are stealing precious goods from basement storage vaults." I explained that Jassy's

290

death was kept quiet in order to capture the smugglers. "They were Mafia," I whispered. "I didn't want Mafia coming after us. Mafia are brutal."

Carlo was listening to my story.

"We have to tell ourselves, and the children, that Jassy died singing," I said. "She died in the theater. We should be so lucky to end so quickly and in the place we have worked so hard to get to."

I put my hand on my brother's shoulder and this time he didn't brush me away. "Virginia had nothing to do with Jassy's death." I continued with my story. "It was coincidence that Jassy died after the children and I were kidnapped. We were kidnapped because Virginia was about to ship something illegal, but I'm not sure what she was shipping. I think it was dangerous, something from one of the universities across the river—either MIT or Harvard—something like genetic germs, or chemicals. The children and I were taken into the tunnels below those universities, that's why I know. They had something crated in boxes down there. The boxes were heavily guarded. I couldn't go near them. Whatever it was, it was something designed to hurt people.

"I imagine Virginia had second thoughts about what she was doing. She was getting involved in something subversive and too big to handle. Maybe she was helping terrorists. She didn't know, but she wanted out. She didn't want to involve Spediamo, or you. She wanted to protect our good name, and the name of all Italians. She left them stranded, thinking they'd find someone else. They refused. That's when you came in. They wanted you to complete the shipment without her. It's good you didn't."

Carlo was believing me. He relaxed into his chair.

"There's one more thing," I said. "About Jassy."

"What?"

"Jassy died with her eyes open. Remember what Mama told us? She said if a corpse is left staring, the soul looks for a partner. Jassy was looking for you. I closed her eyes so you both could rest."

Carlo sighed. Perhaps he was wishing she had found him.

"Mama and Papa also taught us to respect the dead," I said. "I took her to them so she wouldn't be lonely. Jassy is buried in the field behind our house in Subiaco next to our parents, who always loved you." I took Jassy's glasses out of the pocket in my long tunic. "This is all I have of Jassy to give to you."

Carlo carefully slid Jassy's gold wire-rimmed glasses into his shirt pocket and leaned back into the stuffed chair. "Thank you," he said. My heart ached for Carlo, and for myself for having lied, but I knew I had done what was best. I trusted God would forgive me.

I stood behind Carlo for a while, smelling the terror of his loss. It was an acid smell, similar to the odor of an old grapefruit. If I had told Carlo the truth, he would be stinking of death. In two years' time the smell would have penetrated him completely, and he'd be cold on a slab in a hospital.

I closed the door behind me, leaving him alone, knowing he would be broken, without a beginning or end. For a while, Carlo would be the lonely one. Before I joined the others, I hesitated in the long hallway, wanting to turn, to go back to Carlo, to wrap my arms around his chest and synchronize our heartbeats one more time. If I went backward, I wouldn't have to go forward.

That night—and all nights until I married—I slept in the upstairs bedroom across the hall from my brother. I was prepared for Carlo to need to talk, or to cry out for comfort.

The children might be restless, too. My happiness about having found Umberto became secondary to my respect for Carlo and the children. I wanted them to need me, and they did.

Easter passed without celebration. The lilies, sent to our house by neighbors and Renato's actors, were more funereal than joyous.

Monday morning I knocked on my brother's door. "May I have your keys?" I asked. I was going to open his stores and manage them until he was able to go out.

"Here," he said, pressing a large cold lump of brass and steel into the palm of my hand. He gave his keys to me, without instructions, without warnings, and without a trace of mistrust in his eyes.

For a few days Umberto was patient, amusing himself with walks along the Freedom Trail and into Boston to see the city's department stores.

By the fifth day, Umberto had seen enough. After dinner, when we were alone for a few minutes, he caressed me on the love seat in the front room. We were both eager to explore one another but had also been programmed not to violate our flesh. It took time.

Until we were married, Umberto slept in the downstairs bedroom, in the room below mine. That night, at midnight, when everyone was sleeping, Umberto tapped on his ceiling with the handle of a broom. I squatted above him and knocked back softly, rapping my knuckles on the floor. After five minutes of this playful signaling, our taps became more erotic. It was the wildest Saturday night of my life thus far. Realizing how self-contained and frustrated I had been, it was easy to imagine that Umberto's wooden broom handle was his penis, and the floorboards below my squatting hips could open wide enough for the handle to enter my virginity.

The next morning, when I walked into the kitchen, Renato was preparing the girls' breakfast. I was embarrassed. I didn't know if he had heard Umberto's and my activities, which had continued into the dawn hours.

"Alicia, you did good in Italy," Renato said, raising his strong eyebrows.

I sat down at the table. Even though my flesh would know only Umberto, I was grateful for having been primed by Renato. I expected more from sex than the usual virgin.

"You took the shoe box, didn't you?" I asked. "That's how you knew where to find Virginia."

"Considering Carlo's condition—I didn't want to give him more reason to be sorry," Renato said, sitting next to me. "I went to Virginia to get Carlo's money back."

I asked. Renato didn't shift his eyes away from me. He stirred his black coffee. I knew he liked it strong. "Where is she?"

"On a commune in Tennessee, a place called the Farm," he said. "Virginia hates communes, but she can't be alone. When she saw me, she said I was nothing to her. She hated me. I had to leave her alone, forever, so she could go on with her new life." Renato folded his arms. "Alicia, she wasn't the same person. She was distant, her hair was short, and she had changed her name to Diane. Since it was clear she didn't want me"—he lowered his big eyes—"I told her if she gave me the money, I'd destroy the other papers. I didn't want trouble in our family.

"But Virginia insisted she didn't have the money. She said they took it from the other side, because Carlo had reneged on a deal. She was lying. Her eyes were so desperate—but I couldn't understand what she needed money for. On a commune? But I thought I should give her a chance—six months. If she doesn't come back by September, I'll turn the papers over to Carlo."

"Did she know Jassy was dead?"

"Not then, how could she? It was before it happened. But I had the feeling she was waiting for Jassy to come get her, to tell her what to do next. That's how their friendship worked. Jassy was always bailing her out of something. And Jassy needed Virginia, too, to prove to herself she was strong, a hero."

We sat silent for a moment.

"Did the Benevolents beat you?" I asked.

"I don't know. They didn't say who they were." He leaned back in his chair. "They wanted to know where Virginia was. I didn't know."

"I think it's over now. Carlo has had enough suffering. We have to protect him."

"Carlo knows Virginia took the money. He's not stupid, but he doesn't want revenge, and he's considering me and Bebe. He wants her to return what she took as much as I do. It will restore his faith, and mine."

I told Renato it was because of the shipments Virginia was making that Jassy was dead, and it was my fault, too. "They gave me back to Carlo and took Jassy because I was a virgin," I said.

Renato held my hand. "To buffer ourselves we dwell on beauty," he said, "and we fall in love. But neither love nor beauty washes away violence. We are human."

Renato placed a bowl of oatmeal next to my spoon and filled my coffee cup. We both were aware that I might have given him my virginity had I flown back from Rome alone. That was our secret, but it was not the only secret I would carry.

Twenty - Five

~~~~

I kept busy overseeing several of Carlo's businesses, and with my nightly erotic voyages with Umberto. I was in love, and how wonderful that was! But I was also grieving with Carlo, who was long-faced and struggling. Still he was the boss, and I asked for his approval before buying anything that cost over fifty dollars. He agreed to allow me to take over Spediamo.

I bought a few red brocade armchairs and a matching sofa, and hung an abstract painting on the golden walls. The North End office was going to be my headquarters. I planned to continue importing construction material, exporting household goods, and managing the several international business ventures Virginia had initiated.

I uncluttered and straightened her files. My first order of business was to complete the Benevolents' final shipment. Umberto helped. There were reasons not to leave it undone.

Over the past ten years Umberto, who had been Ulbaldini's assistant and the Benevolent Relocation Department coordinator, had researched what artworks had been stolen from Italy and tracked down their whereabouts in museum basements. Nothing was ever formally written down. Since he had received the Spediamo papers Virginia sent, Umberto knew how to arrange the documents, the correct names to list on shipping logs, which embossed paper to staple to the front of the logs, and exactly how to list goods on bills of lading so that the customs agents would not be suspicious.

"*Così l'ha fatto lei.* This is the way she did it," Umberto said to me as he reshuffled the papers. Most often we talked in Italian to each other, though Umberto did have a basic understanding of English.

As he punched the papers with a staple, I noticed that beneath the buckle of his belt, his penis had become erect. It seemed to rise at such unpredictable moments! I rubbed my belly against him, both of us eager to explore sensations we had neglected. In his three-piece suit, Umberto was more handsome to me than he had been in a priest's frock or waiter's uniform, and he was extraordinarily attractive because he was all mine.

"Are you wearing my gift?" he asked, sliding his palm under the waistband of my skirt.

"Yes." The previous day Umberto had given me silk underpants, which he had presented in layers of pink tissue. We stood near my desk. I allowed him to fondle between the slippery fabric of my panties and my hips for as long as it took for both of us to want to fall down on the floor.

"Stop," I said. "Someone might peek into the window and see us."

Though I had forgiven my brother for having lived in sin and for having fathered children outside marriage, I was determined to be as intact on the day of my marriage as I had been on the day of my birth. This decision to remain pure and to give myself only to Umberto created an enjoyable tension between us. We were perfect for each other.

"I can hardly wait until this is over," Umberto said. He staples the Spediamo documents, and we went back to work.

That May, the Spediamo container we shipped from Boston to Rome, the one containing the angel and her attending artwork, slipped through the scrutiny of Italian government officials at the port of Livorno and was lifted directly onto a red Benevolent truck. Before going to Rome, the truck driver drove through Subiaco square and past my old house, which was a heap of ashes. It was part of my agreement with the Benevolents. I wanted the dead and the living, Jassy and my parents, to see the shadow of the statues and paintings that had left them behind and had taken me to the new world.

"And what about me?" Umberto asked as he reviewed my story. "Tell them you negotiated for more than a truck parade through Subiaco."

I did. Cardinal Ulbaldini himself got the pope to sign Umberto's release from the priesthood, and with the generous cash they paid me for completing the shipment, I bought a thousand indulgences for my new family. Since we had all been baptized, and provided we died bearing only venial sins on our souls and not with the stains of the mortal sin of murder, we would go directly to God and line up for the next round of life.

The Subiaco branch of the Benevolents agreed to bury whatever bones they found in the house ashes next to the fence, near where my parents lay covered with earth. And they agreed to build a Barzini garden over the graves, whenever they expanded their clinic.

On May 19, Umberto and I were married. Carlo, Renato, and the children left us alone and checked into a hotel. It was quite a night. We both enjoyed destroying the symbols of our virginity and suspending its puncture until our marriage bed was wet with both our sweats. It was then we began smelling alike.

In September Umberto began studying architecture at

Harvard University, working part time in Carlo's stores. I cashed in several of my bonds to pay his tuition, and I bought back the Blue Note for Carlo. I invested heavily in North End real estate, turning over properties as I worked my way to owning several blocks of buildings along Boston's harbor front. I was as lucky as Carlo had been when he first came to America.

By the fall of 1980, the gold pieces I had bought in Rome in 1976 for $150 each were worth $800 each. My happiness quadrupled with my wealth. I had collected a bushel of coins in Boston, and had ten more bushels locked away in safety deposit boxes in Rome. Seizing the opportunity, I traded most of the gold for dollars. Still, I was careful with my money. On Atlantic Avenue we lived like normal people, which we were.

A few years into Mr. Ronald Reagan's presidency, I became an angel to Renato's theater. His grants had been cut back, or cut off, and the Teatro was haggling to keep its lights on. I ended up doing exactly what Virginia had intended to do with the money she had taken from Carlo. I bought Renato's theater, and the building next to it, so he could house a shop and rent out rehearsal space.

Meanwhile, in our household, Virginia's name remained unspoken. She became the ghost that lived with us. Both Renato and Carlo were tortured by what she had done. Alone every night, Renato said he tossed in his bed. Carlo would sometimes mumble about her in his sleep. "Was it my fault? I should have never trusted her with so much," he would say. I worried whether or not she had made it out of Jassy's body, and my house, before the explosion. Sometimes, at the Spediamo office, I had the spooky feeling she was watching me and whispering in my ear—but I wasn't sure. I had lost my vision.

Everything I did was successful—except I did not get pregnant. I did not understand why Umberto's seed didn't grow inside of me. As far as my vision was concerned, I didn't miss being involved in my brother's brain. I learned to use intuition instead—it was less complicated. Still, I knew Carlo was having a difficult time.

Smiling at his customers, each day he went through the motions of being a successful shopowner on Hanover Street. At six in the evening, after having counted the cash in the registers, he went home and continued sifting through everything that had happened to him when he was with Jassy. He didn't seem entirely alive. I didn't know what to do for him.

Then, one cold afternoon in December, Carlo ran into my Spediamo office. *"Gesù!* Alicia," he said. "Look at this!" His eyes were shining with the possibility I had seen in them twenty years earlier, when he was seventeen and had left Subiaco for America.

The white envelope, postmarked Basel, Switzerland, contained a slip of paper marked with a row of numbers. Carlo had recognized the numbers and the handwriting.

"It's Virginia," he shouted. "What a relief! In my weakness, so many nights I had wished she were with the devil." Carlo lifted and dropped his short arms. "She has given back the money." Money still excited my brother. "We must tell Renato!" he said.

He telephoned Renato at the Teatro and asked him to come over to Spediamo right away.

Renato took the news solemnly. "It's the message I've been waiting for," he said, loosening the collar of his shirt. "She's too insecure to be direct. Virginia wants me to bring her home." From Spediamo, he telephoned the Farm in Tennessee.

"She doesn't live here anymore," they said.

"Where is she then?" Renato's big eyes were impatient.

"Come here first and we'll give you directions."

His hand shook as he put down the receiver. Carlo and I reassured Renato. We told him Virginia must have moved to a nearby town. Neither of us dared to say what we were thinking: What if Virginia had started a family with another man?

I closed the shop early and walked with Carlo and Renato through the North End to our building on Atlantic Avenue. Umberto was at home tending the children.

"Will you take care of my theater while I'm gone?" Renato asked Umberto.

"Yes, my pleasure," Umberto answered, and I secretly planned on making love in the theater with my husband, at least once, while Renato was gone.

That night after the children were in bed, Renato washed his long brown hair and pulled it back into a neat tail, tucked a toothbrush, gloves, and an extra pair of socks into his jacket pocket. I shook his hand and gave him a bag filled with sandwiches. My husband assured Renato he would carefully manage the Teatro.

Carlo gave Renato keys to his van and a bearish embrace. "Say hello to Tennessee for me!" Carlo said, waving good-bye from the fifth-floor window. Then Carlo closed the curtains and slumped into the purple love seat. I sat next to him.

"Tell me," I said softly. "What are you thinking?"

"Renato has a chance to find her," he said. "I don't resent him that. But his going to get Virginia makes me realize I'll never find Jassy. It's impossible. She's gone and this dark feeling inside my heart is all I have."

"You have more," I assured him. But Carlo wouldn't accept my comfort.

Seven evenings later Renato returned alone. We didn't expect him to return without Virginia. We were in the front room.

"I've been driving for thirty-six hours," he said, wiping the dark circles under his eyes. "She wasn't in Tennessee. She was in New Mexico, living in a teepee." He sat in Carlo's purple armchair and rested his wide forehead in his palm. "She refused to come home. I even offered to marry her. I told her our children needed a mother. She held my hand and said she was sorry, that at one time my proposal would have meant the world to her, but no, we didn't need her here, she had her own work to do, and that the children were being raised well by Alicia." Renato lifted his head and stared at me, almost cruelly. "While I was driving, a light-bulb went on over my head. How did she know you were living here? Have you been writing to Virginia and not telling us?"

I shook my head no. It was clear Virginia had inherited my vision and had been spying on us in the same way I had spied on them from Italy. "She has special powers," I said.

Carlo laughed. "What do you mean?"

Renato went on to explain that Virginia didn't have a special power but had plenty of money. "More likely she has hired someone to spy on us. Her teepee has a fur floor—but no bathroom," he added. "And people come from all over America—especially California—to listen to her when she's in a trance. They pay her to look inside their brains. She said she can see inside people—but I wouldn't let her look into me." Renato brushed his arms. "She said something mysterious happened to her about a month after she left the North End. It happened while she was sleeping in Tennessee. Suddenly, she said, she felt as if she were more than one person." Renato imitated the way Virginia had told him the story. He shook his head. "Life is not theater, and theater should stay in the theater." He slapped the arms of his chair and didn't stop talking.

"American women are always chasing something new and

trying to lose whatever they have—whether it's weight, or sadness, or their old relationships. Someday when Virginia tires of being who she is now, we'll see her picture on the front of one of those newspapers in a story about people who visit spaceships. What is she good for? I do theater. Carlo does Hanover Street. Doesn't Virginia know her skill is making and taking care of babies? She was better off in Tennessee." He stomped out of the room.

Two weeks later, on Christmas morning, Bebe, Cher, Sera, and I unwrapped tiny boxes, which Renato handed to us from a plain manila envelope. I pulled open the marble-patterned tissue paper and lifted a long silver chain from which dangled a purple stone.

"The card is signed *From Virginia,*" Renato announced.

As quickly as Renato crumpled the card, I put the necklace back into the box and tucked it between the sofa cushions. I demanded that the children give me their boxes, and when the girls left the front room I explained to the others, "Your children won't have any privacy if they wear her jewelry. Virginia will know everything that goes on in their hearts—and yours. Is that what you want?"

"How can that be?" Carlo scratched his head, trying not to laugh.

"Her special powers," I said.

Carlo, Renato, and Umberto looked at their slippers, clamping their lips into straight lines. A familiar but almost forgotten feeling washed over me. It was the shame I had felt as a child when my cousins made fun of my long nose. I cupped my hand over the middle of my face.

Finally Umberto broke the silence. "Even if you're right," he concluded, smiling, "why do you assume Virginia would wish ill on us? Maybe she wants to guard us."

"You've become as impossible as Virginia was," Renato

said, clicking his tongue. "Why don't we forget this special-power business. Only through art can we see beyond the possibilities of our own lives."

Carlo, sitting next to me on the love seat, winked at the other men. "Women lose control up here, in the brain, when they are pregnant," Carlo said. "We've seen that before, haven't we, Renato?" He passed a knowing glance at Umberto. "You'll find out." My brother put his hand over mine.

"Aha! Now everything she says makes sense," Renato said, nodding happily. "Congratulations." He lifted his coffee cup. "Alicia and Umberto are going to have a baby! Hurrah! Another child for us to love!"

Umberto made a more formal announcement. "Our child will arrive in July," he said.

I was furious that my brother, Renato, and my husband would make light of my knowledge about the world beyond the real world and only accept my insistence of its existence by saying I was pregnant. Pregnancy gave me power. But the men preferred to say pregnancy was making me crazy. I was about to scold them, but Renato called Bebe, Cher, and Sera into the front room.

Since it was my body, I rushed ahead with the news. "Mama Alicia is going to have a baby," I said, rolling my hand over the top of my belly.

"Maybe she'll have two," Renato said. "It runs in the family."

"Like us!" Cher shouted.

"Or three," Sera said, holding up fingers.

"Triplets?"

"What about four?"

The young girls surrounded me with their collection of small soft arms. It was a happy moment, and I forgot about continuing an argument with the men. I might as well enjoy myself, I thought; the argument wasn't one I would win anyway.

The moment became even happier. The men joined in with the girls, and I received kisses, both smooth and scratchy.

Months passed. The money Virginia had put back into Carlo's Swiss bank account softened him up. But the birth of my son, Raffaello, put the spark back into my brother's green eyes.

"He's so beautiful," Carlo said, prying open Raffaello's tiny hand to wedge his own finger inside my son's palm. "His forehead is like our Papa's. I'm so grateful you found Umberto and followed me to America." Carlo nestled my son's head in the bend of his elbow.

Carlo had brought the girls to the hospital to introduce them to their brother. Bebe nudged her way to my shoulder. "Does he have a penis?" she asked. "Let me see it. Now."

"Oh, yuck," Sera said. "He'll have to do it standing."

On a hot Sunday afternoon in August, we held a christening party for Raffaello in the Teatro. The stage was set for *Six Characters*—Renato had finally taken on Pirandello. The Benevolents lent us three of their most beautiful, and legal, Madonnas to "give the room atmosphere."

After greeting our guests, Umberto read poetry in Italian, English, and Latin. He had a fine voice and commanded everyone's attention. I hoped Raffaello would have his father's confidence. Mrs. Musetta, the godmother, sang lullabies. Bebe helped actors pass around cucumber sandwiches and crab on crackers. Renato, Raffaello's godfather, dragged a dusty accordion up from the basement and played it while the twins danced. I sat in the spotlight, fanning myself. And

I hoped, if Virginia was spying on us, that she would celebrate with us.

As I nursed my son, I watched my brother handing out silver dollars to our guests. "Minds have to coin inside," he said. His head was held high, his posture was free of depression, and he seemed unbroken, ready to open the curtain on the next performance. That day, I was the one missing Jassy, and not only her but also Mama and Papa and the silent forgiveness of the dead which I carried inside me.

I thought about how Jassy had taught me all life deserved a party. But when I attended her baptism, giving her the last rites, I was concerned only with getting her soul through the veil it was trapped in, not with applause or celebration. I had forgotten to set out food and drink. There had been no music.

I noticed Carlo lingering behind the piano player, a thin woman, rumored to have been recently divorced. I didn't know her. She hadn't been involved with the Teatro for very long. It might have been her music, or red hair, that attracted my brother. For a brief moment I was jealous but repeated to myself what the old nun at the roadside shrine in Florence had said. She said if no one were ever jealous, too much life would be lived, too many circumstances made, and no one would understand that love required attachment and always threatens separation.

Carlo sank his weight into his broad feet, while the woman finished playing a Vivaldi sonata. Then he tapped her shoulder, offering her a glass of wine.

"Frascati," he said. "From a vineyard not far from where I was born."

The woman turned to take the glass. Her fingernails were painted a deep red, and she wore wire-rimmed glasses. I was as shocked as Carlo. The woman at the piano looked like Jassy. His chin dropped to his chest. Mine stayed raised so I could watch them. I felt the blade of a steel saw crack through my brother's breast. The curl of her full lips was the same as Jassy's and so was the straightness of her American nose. And her figure was so much like Jassy's that she would probably feel the same to kiss. The pain of missing Jassy, and all the pain Carlo had buried inside, was exposed to raw air and he hurt like a hole of bleeding flesh.

I cried out, screaming, wanting to drop my son and run to my brother, to shake him and tell him not to invite the new woman into his heart if he was holding Jassy there, too. Three was a crowd. But I did so much want him to reach out to her. Holding the past was no good.

Since I was the one to have screamed, our guest's eyes turned to me, sparing my anguished brother an audience. I apologized for my outburst. Raffaello clung to my breast. I prayed that Carlo was going to let the piano player in, that he would begin again, as if he had been reborn, and that he not compare her likeness to Jassy. In love we are always virgins.

The thin woman was brave. She spoke. "Thank you," she said to Carlo. "How did you know I was thirsty?"

I stopped holding my breath. Her voice was high and slow, not at all like Jassy's, and she had a British accent. At that moment, as sure as I ever knew anything about myself and my brother, I knew the spiral was set spinning for Carlo.

Raffaello began to cry. I put him over my shoulder and tapped his back until he burped. "Look at your uncle," I whispered to my son. "He understand we can never be destroyed because of the bits and pieces of us that continue to learn from hoping. We're all the same. What goes on between us is constantly reinvented—just like between you and me."

My son, impatient and still hungry, wanted my other breast. I gave it to him, and the party continued. I watched

Carlo and the new redhead. Though her voice was different, by the way she moved her elbows, I could tell she would stand up for freedom and be strong.

Umberto moved in next to me on the stage and read some lines from Dante about the working of divine grace—as seen by a lark—binding all the pages of the universe with love:

> "Quale allodetta che in aere si spazia
> Prima cantando, e poi tace contenta
> Dell'ultima dolcezza che la sazia,
> Tal mi sembiò l'imago della imprenta
> Dell'eterno piacere, al cui disio
> Ciascuna cosa qual ell'è diventa."

I sat there, sharing the spotlight with him, half listening and half letting my mind wander, like mothers' minds do wander when they nurse their infants. Love surpassed human thought, I said to myself. I wondered if my son, or his children, would ever see the angel without a hand, the angel I had shipped back to the Madonna in Florence, to the square where I had first been kissed. Raffaello was born because of that kiss. But I didn't continue the thought. It didn't matter. It was a deed done, which is what we do in our lives. Sometimes we can't look to either the past or the future for satisfaction or explanation. Again, I listened to my husband but I didn't hear his words.

I was thinking about the magnificent things I had touched in the tunnel under Harvard Square. The Benevolents had stolen the art believing it belonged to Italy, and I had shipped it there for them. But, according to Umberto, once in Italy, the golden things would be hidden in church basements. Most likely they would remain hidden until everyone forgot about them. But the initial impulse that had created the art would never be forgotten. That spirit of beauty and creation will never change. It belongs to everyone and can destroy as easily as it lets live. I had met that spirit inside myself—it is in everyone.

"*Bella,*" Umberto said to me, taking my hand.

Carlo lifted Raffaello into his arms and took my son over to the piano player, who had emptied her lap to hold him.

Renato was playing the piano and Bebe and the twins crowded onto the bench with him.

"Let's dance," Umberto said.

My legs were still clumsy. Why should they have changed in America? I wanted to please my husband. I surveyed the room, its theatrical set, the lovely statues, the people who had come to the baptism to celebrate a new life, and my family.

I breathed in their souls, I held them deep within my lungs, lifted my feet, and danced.